Condemned

Cursed by Blood Saga
Book Seven

Marianne Morea

Coventry Press Ltd.

Somers, New York

ISBN-13: 978-1-7325262-0-4

First Edition: Coventry Press Ltd. 2018
Cover Artist: Cover Couture

Printed in the USA

For my fans.
With love and thanks.

Only my blood speaks to you in my veins. And there is such confusion in my powers.

William Shakespeare
Merchant of Venice, Act 3, Scene 2

Chapter 1

Columbia University
New York, NY

"Jeez, Bels, and you rag on *me* about punctuality. Why are you so late? You and what's his name get tangled up in the tinsel again?"

Belinda Force shook her head at the goofy grin on Giles Newcomb's face "No, smart ass. And don't remind me about what's his name. He is officially toast. Plus, it's almost Easter, not Christmas. No tinsel, even if I wanted."

She peeled her jacket from her shoulders. "And I've already spent two hours on the phone long distance with Roxy talking about Neil, so don't ask."

"You do realize Rome is six hours ahead of us, so that makes it, what?" He glanced at his bare wrist.

"One a.m.," she replied with a quick exhale. "Again, don't remind me, and don't ask."

He chuckled. "Just saying, taking a long distance call in the middle of the night makes Roman Roxy a really good friend. Either that or your old roommate's a drama mama."

She rolled her eyes at him, tossing her jacket over the chair in front of her desk. "Is Adams around, or are we the only ones working nights—again?"

"He's here. He called looking for you about an hour ago."

"Giles!" Belinda shot him a dirty look and pivoted for the door. "Why didn't you say so the minute I got here?"

"Don't bother, Bels. He's not upstairs. He's across campus at the Art History and Archeology Department. Some big meeting tonight. He said for you to meet him there when you finally got in."

Belinda sank in a chair by the door. "I am so screwed. He's going to kick me off the team as lead researcher for sure, now."

"Probably," Giles teased. "Uneasy lies the head that wears the crown."

She dug a packet of M&Ms from her jacket pocket and threw a red one at him. "Again, don't be a smartass, G. I'm serious." He wasn't paying attention, so she threw another piece of candy at him. "What are you doing? You don't normally read anything with words unless you have to."

Giles's gaze scanned the newspaper on his desk. "They found another body." He glanced up. "Riverside Park."

"Wait. What?" She got up to skim the article over his shoulder. "That's only a few blocks from here." She plopped a handful of M&Ms in her mouth and chewed. "This city is going to hell in a handbag."

He nodded. "Designer. It's like the start of last year's bloodbath all over again. Same kind of M.O. If I didn't know better, I'd swear it was a vampire, not some weirdo serial killer the cops claimed."

"Vampires do not exist, G. They're folklore and fantasy. Literary creations taken from ancient mythologies that Hollywood loves to glamorize."

He snorted, sitting back in his desk chair. "Well, you're the expert on all things creepy, considering you're obsessed with the Lilith legends and all that nonsense." He picked up an envelope

Condemned

from the desk and bounced it in his hand. "Oh, yeah, and I forgot to tell you this came today."

"Is there anything else you forgot to tell me? Grave robbers dig up my grandmother? Aliens land on the quad?" She snatched the letter from his hand. "I swear, G, sometimes."

"What? I've got spring fever. I can't help it. Three more weeks, and the semester is dun-ta-dun-dunt."

She rolled her eyes. "Spring fever? More like sex on the brain. Surfing questionable sites on university servers is how you spend your workday. Don't make it how I spend mine."

"I'm serious, Bels. If girls want to check out glossy nudes to get their freak on, they should. Gender equality, babe."

Belinda snorted another laugh. "Will you *please* find your spring fling and hook up already? Spare me the excess hormones." She waved her hand in the air as if clearing a smell. "Seriously."

"Aww, you love the attention. Though you're way uptight these days. You're bordering on butt-clenched, and that's not like you. My guess is you need someone to help take the edge off. Especially since the boyfriend is *hasta las vista*, baby." He waggled his eyebrows. "I could do the honors, if you'd like. After all, we collaborate on about everything else around here."

She rolled her eyes again. "Nice try, bud. The odds of you getting into my pants are about the same as you getting into my research notes. *Zilch*." Belinda put her thumb and forefinger together, forming a big fat zero, and then carried the nondescript white envelope to her own desk across the cluttered room.

"C'mon, Bels, you know you're into me. I'm a tall, skinny millennial with zero muscle tone and pasty-white skin. The perfect academic boyfriend. Not like what's his name and his sexy telescopes. Admit it. You dig me." Giles winked.

Ignoring him, she sat in the chair in front of her desk. A frown tugged as she scanned the letter's postmark.

"What's wrong? It's not like you to pass up a chance to shoot holes in my portrait of male academic hotness."

Belinda wrinkled her nose. "Not wrong. Just strange."

"We dig up the long dead and buried, Bels. Everything about this place is strange. Including us. What's got you spooked?"

Still puzzled, she spared him a glance. "Not strange spooked. Strange confusing. This letter is postmarked Cairo, but there's no return address. Who would mail something to me anonymously from Egypt?"

"Your guess is better than mine. You're the one who spent last summer there working on your dissertation." He shrugged. "Which, I might add, you have yet to finish."

He swiveled in his chair to face her. "It's probably a solicitation for more free labor, though it's beyond me why anyone would willingly choose to spend their time off in a place where the temperature rivals the surface of the sun."

Belinda stuck her tongue out at him. "And that, my goofy friend, is why you aren't my type. You're a postgraduate student of archeology. You should be willing to give up a testicle to get anywhere near the Valley of the Kings." She paused. "And you're not pasty. You own a tanning bed and lots of other useless rich-boy toys, so don't go there."

"My name iz Elmer J. Fudd, millionaire. I own a mansion und a yacht." He grinned, mimicking the classic Bugs Bunny skit.

She laughed. "Ha, another shining example of why everyone thinks you're an overgrown child."

Giles got up from his chair to perch on the edge of her desk. He helped himself to her packet of M&Ms. "I may be an overgrown child, but spending an entire summer worshiping at

the feet of Akhenaton Ra and his modern-day minions won't help you keep your cushy lead research position. Not if you don't show Adams new pages soon."

He bobbed his head, chewing. "Rumor has it he's looking to fill positions with new blood, and your pretty, freckled face is old news, Red."

Belinda touched her hair involuntarily. At twenty-seven, she'd finally toned down the carrot red she'd lived with as a teenager, but the sting of two decades of ginger jokes still left her self-conscious.

She huffed, snatching back her candy. "And you'd be all too happy to steamroll right over me, right?"

Her phone rang, and Giles picked it up on speaker phone. "Either that or cut the brake lines on that sad bucket of bolts you're driv—" He stopped mind-snark, mouthing the word *shit*. "Hello... Shapiro Center, PhD Student Offices, how may I help you."

"You can help by giving *my* students *my* messages in a timely manner, Mr. Newcomb. Also, not everyone has a large trust fund to make up for subpar work."

Giles coughed, sending a spray of half-chewed M&Ms across Belinda's desk, and she slapped a hand over her mouth not to laugh out loud.

"Please tell Ms. Force to meet me in my office in the AHA department, ASAP. I need to speak with her. And, Newcomb—"

"Yes, Dr. Adams?"

"Stop sitting on Belinda's desk! You have your own to abuse."

Their professor hung up, and Belinda burst out laughing. "Way classy, G."

"I swear that guy gives me the creeps. It's like he knows."

She chuckled again. "And we know that he knows that we know. Give it a rest, Giles. What he knows is how *you* operate."

"Maybe you'd better get going."

"See?" She exhaled. "Didn't I tell you he wasn't a happy camper?" Staring at the empty doorway, Belinda raked a hand through her long hair.

Shoving her M&Ms into her pocket, she then searched through her folders for random notes and whatever chapters she had completed. Belinda blew her hair from her forehead and stuck the collected papers in a plain white binder.

She picked up the Cairo envelope as well, and then spared a glance for Giles. "Wish me luck."

Nothing to worry about, right? Hadn't she just discussed her progress with Adams? *That was January, babe. It's April.*

Belinda opened the heavy door to the Shapiro Center and rushed down the steps to the path. It was dark. Way darker than it should be this time of year. It was daylight savings time, for heaven's sake.

She glanced at the cloudless sky. No stars and no moon. Chalk another one up for light pollution. She ignored the creep factor tapping her on the shoulder and headed around the quad toward the Arts and Sciences Building.

Campus was empty. Then again, the undergrads who usually loitered around after dark were doubtless holed up in the library. They had two weeks left until finals.

What could Adams want with her this late in the semester if not to question the gaps in her dissertation? She hadn't been slacking. Everything was basically written except the conclusion.

Ugh. It was bad enough she was late, but that he had to track her down? Bad Bels. Very bad. Her boots clicked a staccato rhythm on the concrete, and the sound echoed in the empty silence.

Could this get any spookier?

According to the papers, yeah.

Don't go there.

Creeping herself out, she glanced over her shoulder as another set of footsteps fell in line with hers. She walked a little faster, quietly humming the 1812 Overture to drown out the inner alarms prickling the back of her neck. Just imagination run amok, right?

She glanced back, again, stiffening her jaw. "Whoever's scuffing their feet behind me, joke's over. Cut the crap!"

The muffled footsteps sped up, sending her heartbeat into her throat. She picked up her pace to almost a sprint.

Shoving her binder under her arm, she reached in her pocket for her car keys, sticking the longest one between her fingers and gripping the rest in her palm.

Years of karate had taught that fine-motor skills were the first to go in an adrenaline-soaked panic. Panting now, she held her keys tighter. With the way her hands shook, she'd never have the coordination to poke anyone's eyes, but she could certainly slash and run.

"Belinda—"

Someone called her name. It was soft, almost a whisper. Freaked out, she clenched her jaw tighter against the cold fear clutching her chest. Her head told her it was overactive imagination brought on by Giles and his rag newspaper. Her sympathetic nervous system warned otherwise.

You know better than that. Belindachka. Listen to your body.

Her grandmother's voice tickled from the back of her head. She pictured the old woman's face. Not the way she was before she died, ravaged with cancer. No, she thought about the pretty older redhead with the flashing eyes and quick laughter she remembered from childhood.

Bubbie?

I'm here, my darling girl. Just keep walking.

She squeezed the keys tighter in her hand, squashing the urge to run. Almost there. Just another hundred feet. Someone was there. Ignore it. Oh God! Behind her now. Closer…closing in.

A hand settled on her shoulder, and a scream ripped from her throat as she whirled on her heel, fist swinging.

"Ow! FUCK! What the hell, Belinda?"

Her eyes flew wide as she stared into a stunned, familiar face. Well, half a face, considering he covered his slashed nose with his hand.

"Ari?" She blinked. "What are you doing in New York, and why are you stalking me in the dark like some creeper?"

He pinched the bridge of his nose. "One, I'm in New York doing research for a few weeks, and two, I'm not stalking you. I was on my way to the Arts and Sciences Building to try and beg lab space. I saw you cross the quad, and thought I'd surprise you."

She exhaled a nervous chuckle. "First rule in New York, especially at night. Don't sneak up on people, thinking to surprise them. You could end up with a snout full of mace."

"Or car keys," he said, still squeezing his nose.

"Oh God. Are you bleeding? I gave you a pretty packed punch." She shook her head. "I'm sorry, Ari. That was all adrenaline. There've been murders in the paper lately, and the last two happened not far from here. I'm so sorry. I guess my overactive imagination got the better of me. I blame my research partner for putting dumb thoughts in my head."

"What dumb thoughts? That you don't want to be a statistic?"

She chuckled, embarrassed. "No. Vampires or some other breed of supernatural stalker."

He dropped his hand from his face. "Well, you studied the possibilities with us in Cairo last summer, so from that perspective, anything goes."

Condemned

Ari hadn't laughed at the notion, and she appreciated the tact. He tugged at his sleeve, checking his nose for blood.

"That's cool," she said, pointing to the tattoo on his wrist. "A Lilith sigil, right? Is it new? I don't remember you having a tat last summer."

She'd seen something similar in a book. She remembered it because it resembled three Templar crosses set perpendicular with a curved lowercase H like a devil's tail. Ari's tattoo was different, though, as it had Hecate snakes entwined.

He pulled his jacket sleeve down, covering the ink. "Yeah, I thought it was chill, considering my line of study.

"Ancient blood lore and mythology." She tapped the side of her head. "I remember. It is cool. Way cool."

Ari's gaze darted toward the trees on the quad's perimeter, and he seemed nervous suddenly.

"You okay?" she asked. "Don't tell me I freaked you out as well." She laughed.

Before he could answer, a woman walked from the shadows, a cigarette dangling from her fingers. Its red glow distinct in the gloom.

"A vampire could live in plain sight in this city of yours," she commented with a half-smirk. "Unless they were a smoker, of course." A grin took her perfectly lined lips, and she gestured with the cigarette. "Societal fringe, banished to the far corners to enjoy their vice."

Ari chuckled. "Blood, no problem. But, nicotine? Out, demon, out!"

The woman eyed Belinda. Her nostrils flared slightly before she shifted her gaze to Ari. "We should go."

"Oh my God!" Red-faced, Belinda shoved her keys back into her pocket. "You're Zahra Khalid!"

"Guilty." The woman inclined her head, giving Belinda a tolerant smile."

"Wow!" She giggled, not caring if she sounded more like a teenager than serious postgraduate student. "I took your seminar in Cairo with Ari last summer." She gestured to him with another giggle. "The one on Osiris and Set. This is unbelievable! What are the chances?"

Ugh. Fangirl much?

This woman was everything she wanted to be once she was done with her doctorate. Though, looking at the esteemed professor now, it was hard to believe Dr. Khalid was a day over twenty-five. Belinda mentally shook her head. The woman held more doctoral degrees than anyone in the field.

Belinda's nose tickled. Cinnamon and vanilla. The scent was almost mouthwatering, and it wasn't coming from a donut or an over-sweet latte. It was Zahra.

"This is going to sound strange from a perfect stranger, but you smell amazing. Is it perfume or a body scrub?"

"I think it's just sweat," Dr. Khalid chuckled lightly, "but thank you, anyway."

Oh my God, I didn't just go there. Ugh Just walk away now. A self-conscious giggle bubbled up, but she squelched it.

Zahra Khalid was elegance personified. The woman was exotically beautiful, and considering she had to be at least fifteen years older than Belinda, she must have won the genetic lottery when it came to bone structure.

High cheekbones kept the woman's smooth-as-silk skin taut and youthful. From her long ebony hair pulled into a sleek ponytail, to the pointed tip of designer Jimmy Choos, the woman could make Belinda's uniform of leggings and a concert tee seem runway chic.

"I'm glad you enjoyed my lecture." Zahra inclined her head again.

Practically bouncing on her toes, Belinda had to stifle the urge to squeal. "I did." She cleared her throat and tried to keep a serious student face.

"The way you covered the origins of their mythology and crushed accepted arguments over which legend came first, theirs or Lilith's— I was inspired. You spoke as though you witnessed the birth of their lore firsthand. To say the class was spellbinding is an understatement. Your lecture helped me get over the hump stalling my dissertation. After that, my fingers could barely keep up with my brain as I typed."

Ugh... Stop talking. Now.

Zahra seemed amused, rather than indulgent. "That's sweet of you to say."

Determined not to ramble any more, Belinda drew a quick breath. Her nose tickled again, wrinkling. The air still smelled like cinnamon and vanilla, but now there was an underlying sourness lacing the previously pleasing fragrance. Like something spoiled.

"So, you're working with Theo Adams." Zahra raised an eyebrow, and Belinda wasn't sure if she was adding a question to the matter-of-fact statement, or if she noticed the smell as well.

Belinda bobbed her head, lifting the folder in her hand with Dr. Adams's info scrawled across the top. "Most professors need a personal Rosetta Stone to decipher my margin notes, but you cracked my chicken scratch, crinkled and upside down."

"Well, I *can* read hieroglyphics, so..." Zahra's lips curled up, and she nodded. "I recognize you, now. You added quite an international flavor to my lecture."

The elegant woman's nostrils flared, and she lifted a perfectly manicured finger to rest over her lip beneath her nose.

Oh God. She thinks that stench is coming from me! Do I have stress-sweat stink? Am I rambling with rancid coffee breath? Belinda's stomach dropped and she took an involuntary step back.

Dark eyebrows arched even higher, and Zahra's gaze went from measured to sharp. Almond eyes narrowed, and her gaze moved over Belinda's face to the delicate cross at her throat and then lower to the scooped neck of her faded tee.

The woman's unnerving scrutiny triggered every leftover insecurity and lingering self-doubt she possessed. Belinda swallowed. Yeah, she had worn this tee-shirt to death, but it was clean, and yes, she'd showered this morning. Doctorate students were not fashion plates.

So, her red hair was usually in a messy bun held with a pencil and a random selection of odd-colored bobby pins. Faded, comfortable jeans hugged ample hips, and she wore standard-issue Converse sneakers on her feet. She looked no better or worse than any average postgrad student.

Irked, Belinda squared her shoulders. "Uhm, I'm not sure I understand what you mean by international flavor, but I hope it's not the number of questions I asked." She lifted her chin toward Ari. "Your teaching assistants didn't seem to mind."

Had she been the pushy, outspoken American? Was that what the professor meant? And why was she still staring at her as if sizing her up for a makeover? *Not all of us were born with exotic good looks, you know. Some of us suffered ginger hair and freckles and learned to rock them the hard way.*

Zahra's nostrils flared again, and she smirked even more as if she could smell Belinda's unease. "You added an element of surprise to an otherwise rote setting. I think we might have more in common than one would think. Perhaps something that merits further examination."

Not really an explanation, but okay. At least it wasn't a canned answer, but further examination? Zahra Khalid had written dozens of books on the subject they covered last summer. What else could anyone add, let alone a post grad student?

Zahra's lips curled again, and for a moment her gaze grew cold. She lifted a hand, plucking a stray hair from Belinda's shoulder. "Such a pretty color. Red hair is a rarity among my kind."

Okay, sure. Not many Middle East redheads. "Uhm, thanks, I guess."

The hair on Belinda's neck rose, and a prickle started in her stomach. This wasn't insecurity. This was the same creepy adrenaline spike she'd been getting on and off all year. The same baseless anxiety the campus shrink attributed to stress and an overactive imagination.

Like racing across campus thinking she was supernaturally stalked?
Yup.

Why would a quick conversation with an admired professor send her body into overdrive? And not in a good, *I kissed a girl and I liked it*, kind of way?

Great, not only wicked-stress-sweat stink, but now that stress had sent her off her nut. Maybe the shrink was right, and she needed to decompress.

They had been standing on the path along the empty quad far too long, and weird smell and groundless anxiety aside, she needed to get to Dr. Adams's office before the man totally wrote her off.

So, she asked a ton of questions and challenged other students and their theories. Nothing extraordinary in that. She was one of three hundred students in Zahra Khalid's lecture last year. Maybe the woman was into chicks, and this was her way of flirting.

Belinda swallowed and then forced a smile, glancing past her shoulder to the Arts and Sciences Building. "I appreciate you remembering me, Dr. Khalid, but I should get going. Dr. Adams is waiting, and I've already taken up too much of your time." She nodded to Ari. "It was great seeing you again. Call me if you want a tour guide while you're here."

Zahra's hand shot out to grip Belinda's arm as she tried to walk past. Not hard, but enough to startle.

"Fate has a funny way of throwing people together, Belinda. Like I said. Perhaps we'll see each other again, no?"

Belinda blinked. "You know my name?"

Dr. Zahra Khalid remembering her from a lecture was one thing, but remembering her name, when she barely bothered with most students, should have mind-boggled her into fangirl overload. Instead, the woman's touch sent her body into what-the-fuck, stop-touching-me mode.

Unease exploded into full-blown distress, and she wanted to jerk her arm free and run. She sucked in a quick breath and held it. The last thing she wanted was to cringe from a woman who could give her a kick-ass recommendation at some point.

"Okay, well. Thanks for taking the time to chat." Belinda tried once more, managing to slide her arm from Zahra's hold without cringing.

"Indeed. Very enlightening." The woman inclined her head and slipped away without another word.

Belinda squashed the urge for a full-body shiver. To think last summer, she was envious of the select students Dr. Khalid invited into her exclusive group. She sniffed. TAs and museum fellows. Disciples, following Zahra around Pied Piper style.

She moved at a fast clip, pushing her anxiety away. Her research position was precarious enough. She didn't need edgy

freak added to whatever list of complaints waited for her in Adams's office.

Dr. Adams's earlier trust fund comment was aimed at Giles's bottomless checkbook and perpetual-student mentality, but facts were facts. She didn't have a boatload of family money to fall back on. She needed to focus.

Focus and fight.

So, Zahra Khalid set her teeth on edge. Who knew? It's one thing to admire someone from afar. From three hundred students in one lecture hall, afar.

Truth was most of academia was a little off. Giles said it. They dealt in digging up things long buried, so in essence they were all members of the Awkward Academics Club.

Her fight-or-flight instincts were still winging around her stomach as she walked. It was one thing for someone set your teeth on edge, but quite another for a simple gesture to make your skin crawl.

Listen to your body, Belindachka. It will never lie.

Belinda exhaled.

Give it a rest, Bubbie. I'm in no mood.

She lifted her eyes to the sky, and mumbled an apology to her grandmother's memory, and squashed the remnants of yet another crazy leftover from the woman's nutty beliefs.

Her friends thought it creepy cool she heard her dead grandmother's voice at the back of her head. Still, Bubbie-the-Brilliant was nowhere to be found when it counted. Like on multiple-choice exams. If she had some special link to the wisdom of the ages, it should entitle her to buy a vowel or something, right?

During her life, Bubbie held a lot of irrational beliefs from the old country. Like the one where she claimed they were descended

from a *vĕdma*. A forsaken white witch whose bloodline gave them second sight. Nuts, right?

If she was a witch, then how come her ex-boyfriend still had his private parts? She'd wished that appendage to shrivel and fall off plenty of times since she caught him using his creepy voyeur telescope to look at more than just the stars.

Belinda tucked the amusing thought away, and rushed through the Arts and Sciences Building, catching the elevator before it closed. She pushed the button for the fourth floor and exhaled, still unable to shake the weirdness from her conversation.

See moya solnishka? Your blood knows. Your scientific mind might dismiss, but you won't forget.

Won't forget? She exhaled again, and for the first time in her life, she wasn't so sure her Bubbie was wrong.

The elevator dinged, and Belinda slipped out, walking the quick twenty feet to Adams's office. She hesitated outside the professor's door. Whatever he told her, she'd deal with. She'd invested every dime earned into her undergraduate degree and then her masters, and now, as a postgrad, she had more debt than she knew how to handle.

She'd earned the position of lead researcher through hard work and sacrifice. While Giles worked on his tan and his latest summer fling, she'd bartended and waited tables. Inner alarm bells or not, Zahra Khalid remembered her out of a class of three hundred. That meant something, right? No one was taking anything away from her today.

She knocked on Adams's door and waited.

"Come in," he called from the other side of the door.

Squaring her shoulders, she turned the knob.

"Ms. Force. Good. Have a seat." He gestured to one of the leather chairs not covered with dusty books and papers. "I read

16

over what you submitted so far for your dissertation. It's impressive. Better than any submitted in quite a while. Your work on the ancient blood sects of the Middle East, especially."

He dug through papers on his desk and then nodded. "Here it is." He held out an envelope like the one she had shoved in her binder.

"Over winter break, I submitted your name for consideration in a paid internship. I know the one you did last year wasn't paid, nor was it for credit. That you put in the time with no incentive other than the work itself, speaks volumes. Anyway, I got a response last week. I meant to talk to you about it then, but time got away from me. You were accepted. You start next week, if you want it."

Belinda exhaled the breath she'd been holding. She regarded the veiny, middle-aged man. If Giles thought pasty-white equated to academic hotness, then Theo Adams was its cover model. Still, right now, the man was a god.

"Dr. Adams, I don't know what to say. I thought you called me into your office to tell me I was out of the program." She opened the binder on her lap and held out a stack of research notes.

"I've begun working on my conclusion. There's a lot of material yet to tie together, but if you need to see my progress, I have it here. It's not typed, but I can do that, too."

Adams smiled at her. "I have no doubt about your progress, Ms. Force. I rarely say this to students, but you have a real aptitude for this field. A passion for history, as if you wish you lived it. You're a rare find, honey. A special talent." He jiggled the letter in his hand. "Aren't you interested to see where you're going? That is, provided you want the internship."

"Of course, I want the internship!" she blurted, sticking her notes in the binder again. "I don't even know how to begin to thank you." She paused, flashing a sheepish grin. "Where is it?"

He grinned. "On second thought, it'll be more fun for you to wait to find out on your own," he said, pulling the envelope back. "You should get your own letter of acceptance any day now. It'll have the information on where you need to go, whom to see, and the proper documentation you'll need, etcetera."

Excitement and nervous energy had her bouncing for real this time. She opened the binder and lifted the Cairo envelope from inside. "You mean a letter like this one?"

With a satisfied smile, he sat back in his chair and stuck his arms behind his head. "Exactly like that one. Congratulations, Ms. Force. Egypt awaits you."

"Wow. That was quite a buildup for a place I've already been."

Adams gave her an arched look as his hands slid from behind his head. He leaned forward at his desk. "Is there a problem, Ms. Force? I'm sure Giles Newcomb would go in a heartbeat if I offered."

She answered him quickly. "No...no problem, Dr. Adams. I'm stoked. Going back to Cairo is a good thing. I'm a little OCD, so I'm already making lists in my head."

"Good. In this instance, you can never be too prepared. Participating interns were handpicked by Zahra Khalid. She agrees with my opinion on your attention to detail and noted your passion for ancient traditions and lore last summer. You're quite the debater, Ms. Force. From what she told me, you gave her summer interns a run for their money, but I wouldn't assume you're going to Cairo."

He shook his head. "Assignments won't be finalized until after you've completed the in-person interview at the Museum of

Egyptian Antiquities. The posts are all over the Middle East, and that includes the newest digs in and around the Holy Land."

"But that's Israel," she said, surprised. "I guess I assumed this was funded by the Egyptian Antiquities Authority.

Adams waved his hand. "Academia supersedes politics in most cases, but lucky for us, Egypt and Israel are allying these days, so it's all good. Either way, you'll be working with five-thousand-year-old artifacts in a setting that dates to millennia before Christ."

She swallowed hard. "Holy shit," she murmured, and he laughed.

"Holy, indeed. I know you have a thing for the Knights Templar, so I put in a good word for you to concentrate on the era surrounding the Crusades. Their influence was all over the Middle East, so wherever you're posted, I'm sure you'll find plenty to fascinate."

"Dr. Adams…" She grinned, sitting back in her chair with an easy breath. "Wow. You rock!"

He met her smile with one of his own. "Thank you, Belinda."

She laughed to herself. Especially since Adams deigned to use her first name as if she were a colleague instead of a puerile student.

Zahra Khalid had messed with her earlier, and now she knew why. The thought of the woman still made her gut cringe, but this time Belinda dismissed it.

Weird or not.

Witch blood or not.

Right now, it was all good.

Chapter 2

Villa Corsicana
Rome, Italy

"Carlos, I can smell your agitation from here. Are you going to tell me what's bothering you, or are you simply going to pace?" Dominic De'Lessep pulled a cigar from his pocket and snipped the end, before putting it between his teeth. Lighting the tip, he puffed a few times until the end glowed red. "Your constant back and forth is interrupting my view, not to mention the tranquility of my cigar."

The younger vampire strode between two potted orange trees on the wide veranda. A billow of fragrant smoke blew his way and he halted his trek, leaning instead against the curved stone balustrade. "Better?" He smirked, crossing his arms at his chest.

Dominic winked, plucking a tiny piece of tobacco from his tongue, before taking another draw from his cigar. Carlos was preoccupied. He didn't need preternatural senses to see something worried the Spanish vampire. He'd tell him eventually. He always did.

"Do I really need a reason to visit? I thought you'd be glad for the company and news." Carlos flashed the elder a quick grin, but the man's unnerving gaze told him he wasn't buying it. "Okay, the truth is, I want you to come back to New York and take your place as Master Adjudicator again."

Condemned

The elder vampire didn't hesitate. "You already know my answer."

"Dominic—"

"A simple phone call would have saved you the transcontinental trip, though I do appreciate the gift." He picked up his brandy snifter and lifted the glass toward Carlos before taking a sip. "Not that I'm not happy to see you. On the contrary. I'm just sorry Trina couldn't make the journey."

"Dominic—" Carlos tried again.

The elder raised an eyebrow at his persistence. "I have no intention of leaving La Corsicana again. You and Trina are always welcome, as are the members of your family, but I have no desire to venture past the walls of my gardens."

"I knew I should have made Trina come." Carlos glanced at the man's lazy smoke rings floating toward the night sky. "You have a soft spot for damsels in distress, especially redheads. Maybe she would have had more luck convincing you."

Dominic snorted. "Doubtless, then again your mate is no longer in distress, and pretty as she is, I would've given her the same answer. No."

Carlos exhaled, sitting back in the wicker chair. "*¿Por qué siempre eres tan obsintado?*"

"I am not stubborn, *mon fils*." Dominic's lips curled up at Carlos's frustrated slip into his native Spanish. "I simply like my solitude."

Mon fils.

My son.

Two words as common to ordinary men as dirt. Yet the simple expression in Dominic's native French meant so much. The endearment was one he'd used for Carlos from the very beginning.

He wasn't the younger vampire's sire, but Carlos was the closest thing Dominic had to a son since waking to darkness.

Between the two, they spanned the Old World and the New. The spiritual and the profane. Lifetimes of coexisting with humanity's endless renaissance and reversal, yet like any parent and child, their thinking was generations apart.

"Anyway," Carlos continued, "Trina wanted to come, but she still struggles with her thirst. Being in close quarters with humans during the flight would have been hard."

Dominic met the younger vampire's eyes. "The lure of human blood is excruciating for most youngbloods. Not everyone born to darkness can resist, and with Trina's story, it's even less likely. She's strong, and she has you. That Trina clawed her way back from the abyss at all, is a testament to your love and her resilience."

The scent of lemons and pomegranates floated on the air, and a soft breeze from the direction of the famed Borghese Gardens teased Carlos's linen shirt.

"Since Sebastién met final death, Rémy has taken over as the Adjudicator General on the Vampire Council." He paused, "That is, until you return."

"Carlos, no." Smoke curled around Dominic's head as he stared at his son.

"You are relentless in your refusals and completely annoying, sometimes. You do realize you live like an old monk? Even your décor is a shrine to the twelfth century." Carlos swung an arm toward the great room, and its display of artifacts on the other side of the French doors.

"I know you were raised in a cloister, but back in the day, you were also a warrior. It's time for you to rejoin the world. It's been

too many centuries, Dominic. Come back to New York. The city is alive and waiting, and so are we."

"I'm nine hundred years old, Carlos. If I was a monk, I wouldn't be old, I'd be dust. Vampire life and its drama hold no interest for me."

"I know you served your time, but if ever a generation of youngbloods needed guidance in a lost century, it's this one. They need you. You're the Vampire Whisperer."

The elder smirked, raising an eyebrow. "I'm not even going to ask what that means."

Carlos grinned. "It means you have an easy talent for getting our kind to follow the law. Youngbloods don't even realize you're turning their heads. It's the reason I turn to you when there's trouble. You're calm, you're judicious, and you're fair. Even when the decision means delivering final death."

"Carlos, I would do anything for you, but don't ask me to return to New York. That city never sleeps because the nightmares are real, and I've fought too long and too hard for the little peace I have."

The night waned as the sky brightened across the dark canopy, Carlos got up to pace again. "I should have known debating you over duty to kind and culture, versus peace and quiet was an exercise in futility. Not that I blame you."

"I'm not the prodigal type, if you haven't figured that out." Dominic chuckled, relighting the end of his cigar. "When I abdicated my seat, I thought I made that clear."

"Yes, well. I could argue you left your post a tad too soon." The younger vampire held his thumb and forefinger close together. "Especially since Sebastién slaughtered an entire shadow house, human donors and vampires alike, *after* you left."

"And there you have it. So much for my being your Vampire Whisperer. I was sure Sebastién was ready to take my place, even more so after hearing he negotiated a truce with the Weres."

Carlos watched Dominic blow another lazy smoke ring toward the sky. "You weren't the only one who thought Sebastién had evolved. The fact he didn't flinch when his progeny was infected, convinced everyone he was ready and able.

"Sean Leighton and his Weres were the only reason we survived the plague. The Alpha of the Brethren and his wolves stopped the virus from becoming a supernatural pandemic." Carlos shrugged. "You know what happened then."

"Absolute power corrupts absolutely, *mon fils*. Still, Sebastién met his fate. New York will survive. You need to have patience and faith. Go home. Gather the wolves and other like-minded vampires. From there, plan your attack. Map the areas with the most dissent. You can divide and conquer before splinter factions organize. Experience shows there's always one agitator stirring the pot. Cut off the snake's head and the rest will follow."

With a quick inhale, Dominic put his brandy on the small glass table and got up from his chaise. "Problem solved. And I didn't have to leave my veranda."

Moving with singular fluidity, he headed to the balustrade overlooking a grove of fruit trees and the tall Italian cypresses beyond.

"For me, nothing equals the grounds here, especially this time of year. No other villa can compare, despite what the travel brochures claim." He exhaled, contented. "La Corsicana. I named the villa for Charmaine and the isle where I found her over a century ago."

Condemned

He turned to eye Carlos still in his chair. "I had hoped now you and Trina have settled, you'd visit more often, and not only when trouble is brewing."

"If I had known you'd channel your inner field general so easily, I might have come sooner."

"Despite living like a monk, I still know what to do in a fight." The elder vampire chuckled, before letting his gaze drift to the trees and shadow. "Sometimes you're too close to a problem to see the answer. Sometimes a different vantage point is all you need to see your way clear."

Clapping the younger vampire on the shoulder, Dominic led him back toward the wicker chairs, speaking in rapid French to the maid waiting inside the veranda doors as they passed.

Within moments, she brought a platter with an array of fragrant cheeses and two bottles of French Bordeaux.

"Still?" Carlos grinned, raising an eyebrow. "Does Charmaine know you're eating this contraband? You know it's going to make you ill."

Dominic picked up the cheese knife and grinned. "Sadly yes," he admitted, cutting a chunk of creamy brie, "but she pretends otherwise. As much as I appreciate the concern, at this point in my existence I find I can't do without the small reminders of home."

He plopped the cheese into his mouth, chewing before pouring two glasses of wine and handing one to Carlos. "My mother's kitchen is more on my mind now than ever before. Like you, I have a taste for memories."

A sad smile tugged at Carlos's mouth. "My housekeeper, Rosa, kept a bottle of Spanish rum on a silver tray in my bedroom, and another on the sideboard in my office for the same reasons. She was definitely *la pequeña jefa*."

"Was?" Dominic asked, putting the wine bottle on the table.

"She was collateral blood when Sebastién massacred that shadow house." He dragged in a deep breath and then drained his glass.

Dominic's grim face met Carlos's eyes, and the air chilled despite the night's warmth. "I'm sorry, *mon fils*. I didn't know. Now I understand the reason behind your visit. I would feel the same if it was my Charmaine who'd perished that way."

"Where is she, by the way?" Carlos cleared his voice, changing the subject. "I haven't seen her since I arrived."

"She takes to the outside world every night, often until daybreak. She slips through an old iron door at the edge of La Corsicana and into the Borghese Gardens." Dominic flashed an indulgent smile. "In that respect, she's more vampire than me."

"I know it's not our custom to turn humans unless there's no other choice, but she'd be yours in a heartbeat," Carlos prompted.

"Heartbeat." The elder vampire lifted his chin as he topped off his own glass. "That's rather the point."

"Aren't there exceptions to every rule? You've been alone far too long. If this year has taught me anything, it's to grab happiness with both hands when it's offered."

"For you, *mon fils*, yes...but not for me. I'm as happy as my limitations allow. Charmaine does not want the change. Probably because she knows I don't love her. Not in the way she wants or deserves."

Dominic paused with a shrug. "She's been my servant, my companion, and my friend, and yes, I've been selfish in that I give her enough of my blood to prolong her life and her youth, but it's not enough to take that life from her with nothing of substance to offer in return."

"You might not be in love with her, but she's a beautiful woman, and you're comfortable with her."

Condemned

The elder raised an eyebrow. "And how long do you think Trina would stay with you, if, after she gave up her human life, she found you didn't love her with every fiber of your being?"

"Not long," Carlos conceded.

"Love is not a trifle." His eyes dropped, and he exhaled. "I haven't loved anyone body and soul since— Well, not for a very, very long time." Dominic's lips curled in a half smile and he shrugged. "Besides, who needs the headache of youngblood appetites and their theatrics?"

"You said you're as happy as your limitations allow.'" Carlos cocked his head. "At your age, you're immune to almost everything that could deliver final death."

A shooting star changed the subject, and Dominic lifted his cigar, gesturing toward the sky. "Beautiful and fleeting, no?"

"I suppose."

"Like life. Human life." Dominic stubbed out the end of his cigar. "It's why I choose to live my existence the way I do. Alone, with few intimates."

"As one of those intimates, can I buy a vowel and try for New York again?" Carlos winked.

A scream echoed in the distance, jerking their attention toward the gardens. Dominic's hand dropped in slow motion, and he got to his feet. Glass and cigar ash crashed to the marble tiles as he shot from his chair, knocking the table in his haste.

"What is it?"

"Charmaine."

Dominic's nostrils flared. "It's her blood. Can't you smell it? Smell my trace?"

Fists clenched, he didn't wait. The elder vaulted the stone railing, landing without a sound on the ground below.

"Dominic! Wait!" Carlos followed, leaping over the edge as well. He landed on his heels as Dominic lifted his face to the breeze.

"Damn! She's not on villa grounds! Hurry!"

The two took off toward the wall separating La Corsicana from the Borghese Gardens. Preternatural speed blurred trees and buildings as they raced toward the concentrated scent of blood. They found her sprawled in the grass beneath a cypress tree, hidden by encroaching shadows.

"She's dead, Dominic." Carlos put his hand on his friend's shoulder.

"No!" He jerked his shoulder from his friend's grip. "I can turn her!"

"She's gone, Dominic. We're too late."

Anger coiled, tight and hot. The elder's fangs descended, and he wheeled on his heel with a hiss. His red gaze scanned the remaining gloom, and he circled Charmaine's body.

"Whoever did this, has a slow death waiting at my hands."

"Dominic," Carlos tried again, but the elder held out his hand for him to keep his distance. There was nothing calm or judicious about the elder vampire now.

"There's too much blood spilled for an undead, and the wound at her throat is too precise for a Were," Carlos reasoned. "There's no preternatural mark in the air, either. Charmaine carried your trace. Every vampire within a hundred-mile radius knew she belonged to our family, and Roman vampires, especially, know better than to cross into a master's territory. Even a passing rogue would recognize an elder's trace and look elsewhere for prey. A human took her life, Dominic. A stiletto was the means. Not undead thirst."

***

Condemned

The master vampire fell to his knees beside Charmain's lifeless form. He smoothed the hair from her face, the gesture smearing a line of cold blood across her pale cheek. His fangs retracted, and his chin dropped to his chest.

He fought the anguish screaming in his chest, instead dragging a ragged breath into his lungs. He sorted through the scents, analyzing and discarding one after the other until he exhaled, letting his shoulders drop.

Carlos was right. The scent was undeniably human. He inhaled again, letting the trace sear into his memory. Deathly calm, he lifted his chin. "We need to move her before someone stumbles on the scene and calls the police."

The sky had lightened to purple, which meant dawn was minutes away. "I can carry her," Carlos replied. "Why don't you go ahead to the palazzo? Gather whoever we need to help."

Dominic dragged in a breath. He touched Charmaine's cheek, and the tang of her cold blood assailed his nostrils again. He frowned at the dark pool drenching her hair and the ground beneath her shoulders. The same dark wetness that seeped through his pants to his knees.

"I need to cleanse the scene, first. Even without a body, the amount of blood spilled will arouse suspicion. I don't trust myself, Carlos. If the police show at the villa, I'm more likely to kill than to glamour anyone right now. There's much to do, and I need to keep my wits about me. This was no random act of violence. This was deliberate."

"What are you saying?" Carlos asked. "Charmaine had no enemies. She wasn't one of us, but she was well loved by everyone."

Dominic's mouth was a thin line as he slowly shook his head. "This was aimed at me, *mon fils*—" He glanced away, exhaling the

unfinished thought before his eyes found Carlos again. "I am nine hundred years old, and if multiple lifetimes have taught me anything, it's nothing is random. Not when it comes to the undead. Charmaine was murdered to remind me I am never alone."

"What are you talking about? You prefer solitude," Carlos questioned. "It's your defense mechanism. To be honest, when you found Charmaine, I thought...finally, someone."

"I chose to be alone because it was the only way to ensure no one I loved, died. But now—" He threw up a hand. "It seems the rules of the game have changed."

"What game?" Carlos asked, confused. "Dominic, you're talking in riddles."

"Charmaine is dead because she was important to me." Sadness squeezed his chest with a vise grip, and he closed his eyes again. "I can't bear her lying in her own blood another minute. Let's go."

Squatting to slip his arms beneath Charmaine's lifeless form, Carlos lifted her, cradling her inert form against his chest.

Curling his fingers into his palm, Dominic whispered words in an ancient tongue and, when he unfurled his fingers, flames sparked, scorching most of the pooled blood to ash.

"Three hundred years and you never thought to show me that trick?" Carlos whispered as they moved at light speed from the bloody scene to the hidden iron door that led to La Corsicana on the outskirts of the Borghese Gardens.

"There are many things I've yet to show you," Dominic replied.

The door creaked open and they climbed the stairs to the veranda. "Or tell me, it seems," Carlos muttered.

Condemned

Dominic's eyes swung to his son as they stepped onto the marble-tiled terrace. "I concealed things about myself, my past, for your protection, but like I said, the rules have changed."

He didn't say another word, simply gestured for Carlos to follow him to Charmaine's quarters. Dominic opened her bedroom door and waited as Carlos laid her body on her bed, placing her arms gently at her sides.

"The murderer's trace was human, but that human was a puppet. Once Charmaine is laid to rest, I need to find the puppet master and end this once and for all."

His words were more for himself than anyone else, and he turned on his heel to leave. Carlos followed until they got to the veranda again. Dawn streaked the sky with pink, painting the far landscape in spreading gold.

Dominic's shoulders bunched in anger and frustration, and he exhaled a harsh breath. "This is my fault. She died because of my inattention and complacence," he muttered, shaking his head. Finally, he turned. "I told myself Charmaine was safe because I never gave her the dark gift. I wasn't in love with her, so I convinced myself so much time had passed that maybe—"

He blew out a soft breath at the questions in Carlos's eyes. "I have secrets, *mon fils*. Ones I hoped would never become a burden to you, but now you need to know. Afterward, you must go back to New York. Immediately."

"Dominic, you're still talking in riddles. Are you telling me someone is killing the people you love on purpose?"

The elder nodded, knowing his face was deadpan. "Yes. That's exactly what's happening. Again."

"Again?" Carlos balked, indignant. "You mean this has happened before? You're an elder. Who could hold this kind of sway over you?"

Anger tightened Dominic's throat. "A vampire older and more vicious than any you've encountered, and she's tightening her net. It's why you need to go home. You need to keep your family safe."

"She? Who is this woman?" Carlos asked.

The elder turned his eyes from the horizon to consider his friend, his face like stone. "My maker."

Carlos's mouth dropped. "I've been with you three centuries. Why is it none of us has been touched until now?"

"Hell hath no fury like a woman scorned. That sums up the curse I've been living under for a millennium. I lulled myself into a false sense of security, believing we were safe for so long because she had met her final death somewhere along the way, or was satisfied I'd never found a soul mate. But now?"

He let go of the stone railing and turned on his heel. "Come. There's time enough for what needs to be done, but first we need rest. The dawn drags on us both, but you more so, my son. Death sleep calls."

"Do you honestly think I could go to my rest, now?"

Dominic flashed a soft smile. "Spoken like a true youngblood." The gentle grin faded until his lips pressed into a thin line. "Don't misinterpret my calm, *mon fils*. This is full stealth. When the time comes, I will find whoever is responsible, and when I do, I will rip their heart out with my teeth. To do that, I need my rest, and so do you."

Chapter 3

Dominic sat at a table, sipping wine. The warm night brought tourists and locals alike to experience the nightly ebb and flow of the city. His eyes scanned the vibrant piazza ahead. Blood pulsed everywhere he turned, but none of it interested him. He was there for one reason.

He'd been everywhere in the Eternal City in the two weeks since they'd buried Charmaine. Closing his eyes, he pictured the auburn-haired beauty. Her face while she waved to him as she descended the stairs to the garden that fateful night.

Was it only yesterday he'd spotted her on that bluff overlooking the Mediterranean, its water as dark as the night it reflected?

He'd watched her from afar, the wind blowing rich, burnished curls back from her shoulders. Just then, she turned haunted eyes to him, her soft peasant blouse and long skirt molding her curves in the rough breeze. He hadn't lusted for anyone in three centuries, afraid of what Sahira would do, but in that moment, he wanted the Corsican beauty in the same way men hunger for breath. It wasn't even the lure of her warmth or her blood. It was the sadness of loss in her eyes. Something he understood and shared.

Sahira.

His mouth twisted at the thought of the woman who'd condemned him to this cursed path a millennium ago. The same

woman whose name poisoned everything in his life, even as it poisoned the tender memories in his mind's eye, now.

"You're doing it again," Carlos said, tapping his unused fork on the table.

Dominic answered with a snort. "I can't help it. My memories are tainted."

"Not all of them. You have me and Trina and, for a hundred years, you had Charmaine. Stop wallowing. You know what to do. What I don't understand is why you waited this long to kill the bitch."

"Don't you think I tried that? She's my maker, Carlos. You know what happens to vampires who kill their sires. They have a choice. Either spend a century in a box lined with silver or have their fangs ripped out. She made that very clear the first time I attacked. Not everyone can fly under the radar for sire-slaughter like you. No one of consequence knew Robert turned you, and his human minions? They preferred your humanity to his vice and cruelty, so you, *mon fils*, got lucky when you ripped his head from his shoulders."

"I suppose." Carlos inhaled, letting his breath out quickly. "Who is she anyway? Is the bitch's name some sort of secret or are we doing this *à la* Harry Potter and calling her *She Who Must Not Be Named*?"

With a smirk, Dominic picked up his wineglass and swirled the fragrant claret. "I love those books."

"I know," Carlos replied, pushing his lips to one side. "At least it got you to crack a smile. Look, I understand the gravity of the situation, and I'm all-in as your wingman of death, but if you don't lighten up, I might have to stake you and take care of business myself."

Dominic burst out laughing. "You'd have to catch me first. Of all the vampiric gifts we share, you don't fly. Remember?"

Carlos grinned. "I don't, but Trina does."

"Really." Dominic's dark brows arched to his hairline. "When?"

"Yesterday. Rémy and Jenya took her to hunt the Rambles in Central Park, and of course, he had to show off, jumping to the top of the angel at the center of the Bethesda Fountain. Next thing, Trina launched herself from the pavement as well. She perched gargoyle-like on one of the bronze wings above him."

"Fantastic." Dominic's lips slid to a wide grin. "Did she suspect she had the talent?"

Shrugging, Carlos played with the paper napkin under his drink. "I don't think so. Apparently, she was just as stunned, took off from there with a whoop and flew toward the Belvedere Castle near the Turtle Pond. It was all Rémy could do to keep up with her."

"Poor Rémy." Dominic laughed softly. "God bless youngblood enthusiasm. Lingering human blood in their newly undead flesh fuels that impetuous behavior. No wonder she wore him out."

The expression on Carlos's face was wistful, and when he glanced up from shredding his napkin, his eyes were warm. "She's amazing, Dominic. You should see her as she is now. You're right. She's strong, and she's compassionate, even while battling her thirst. I'm going to charter a private jet and bring her to Rome as soon as this mess is over and done."

"You should go home, Carlos. I know you said you're in this with me, but there's no need. I can find this bastard on my own, and when I do, he'll give me what I need to find Sahira."

"That's her name, then. Sahira? Your maker."

Dominic inclined his head.

"You realize her name means witch in the language of the sands, right?"

He nodded again.

Carlos eyed him as Dominic played with the stem of his wineglass. "Is her name a product of someone's mordant sense of humor, or are there darker forces at work?"

"Considering mordant means *bitingly* scathing, it's apropos for an evil bitch vampire like Sahira. Unfortunately, darker forces apply more. Sahira means witch because that's what she is...or was, until she was turned. Which is why she's doubly dangerous."

"*Cristo Jesús.*"

"Exactly," Dominic said with an exhale. He regarded Carlos before gesturing toward the throng in the Piazza Navona. "I've got this. Go. Charter a flight home tonight. I promise I will not disappear into myself or anywhere else. I'll even promise to come to New York."

Carlos opened his mouth to reply, but Dominic shut him up. "To visit, *mon fils.* Not to rejoin the Council, *but* if things haven't improved by the time I arrive, I will meet with you, Rémy, and the Alpha of the Brethren of Weres to help plan your next move."

You might have to settle for the wolves' second in command. Sean Leighton might be otherwise occupied by that point." Carlos smirked. "His mate is about to give birth to their first child."

"*Ahh.*" Dominic shrugged. "Such is life. It always finds a way." He glanced at the table, a soft smile tugging at his mouth.

"What?"

"In all Sebastién's ravings on how we kept him prisoner, an exile, he spoke of the seer with such awe, it was almost sad."

"Seer?" Carlos asked. "You mean Sean's mate, Lily?"

Dominic bobbed his head. "Sebastién claimed she could walk between the living and the dead. He coveted her like no other. Not

as a lover, but as a possession. His madness believed her blood held the key to all things, including restoring the sun to the vampire race." He lifted his glass, cocking his head. "Without the long wait."

"Vampires can walk in the sun. *You* do." Carlos gestured across the table to Dominic. "We have to age into the gift."

"How is it we're not amazed and appalled at the same time when it comes to our race?" The elder winked. "And now your mate flies." He sighed, finishing the last of his wine. "The world turns with or without us, *mon fils*, which is why you need to go home."

"Dominic, I didn't spend the last two weeks scouring every seedy inch of this ancient city with you only to leave now that we're so close to finding this puppet."

He pushed his glass toward the center of the small table and then signaled for the waiter. "Go share this moment with Trina. Give her my love and tell her I'll see her soon. Either here or in that godforsaken city you call home."

"Don't get me wrong, I want to be there with my mate. Even give her the satisfaction of leaving me in the dust for once." Carlos grinned, but then eyed Dominic, hesitating. "If I leave now, I'm afraid you'll do something rash."

"I am nearly a millennium old, boy. What is it the kids say these days? Been there, done that?" He winked, reaching into his pocket for his wallet. "Go. These moments are milestones, and you need to share them. Besides, I'm leaving Rome as well. My gut is churning, and it's not the wine. Something is about to happen. I don't know what, but my fangs are tingling."

Carlos laughed. "You're horny. Either that, or you need to feed." The youngblood smirked as the elder paid the bill, leaving a

hefty tip for occupying the table for so long with a single bottle of wine. "But knowing you, it's probably both."

"Comedian." He pursed his lips in a side grin. "So, are you leaving for New York, or are you hell-bent on being my wingman of death?"

Shrugging, Carlos pushed his chair in after they both got up from the table. "Your inner revenge junkie doesn't need my help. I wanted to watch. I never saw a vampire rip a heart out with his teeth before."

"Funny. Ghoulish, but funny."

Carlos paused as they headed toward the edge of the tourists crowding the *gelato* stand at the end of the piazza. "Unless, you want me to stay. With your fangs tingling, you might need me for a different kind of wingman tonight."

"Youngblood, I may live like a monk, but my appetites do not. I have no problem procuring what I need, regardless of which taste *tingles* my fangs. You forget who taught you everything you know about seduction."

Carlos laughed out loud and gripped the older vampire's shoulder. "Old Monk, you're okay in my book."

Dominic smirked, sliding his eyes toward his son. "That's Sir Monk, to you."

***

The hair on Dominic's neck rose. He'd said goodbye to Carlos at Neptune's Fountain on the north end of the Piazza Navona. He grabbed a cab for the airport, and Dominic dissolved into the shadows along the narrow streets to follow the tingle in his fangs. La Corsicana was half a city away, but light years from his mind.

The sea of humanity ebbed as the moon rose toward midnight. The crowds thinned the farther he walked from the tourist throng, making the sounds and scents of the city easier to decipher.

Condemned

Charmaine's killer wasn't some random mark Sahira glamoured. He was a plant. Someone sent specifically. Dominic didn't tell Carlos, but after the youngblood went to his rest that night, he went back to the bloody scene.

By then, Rome's police had come and gone. Yellow crime tape cordoned off the site with a beefed-up police presence canvasing the area for witnesses. Being a vampire came with its own set of perks, preternatural speed being one. Dominic blurred past the police line, getting what he wanted.

He sat in his bedroom afterward with the blackout curtains drawn tight. The villa was quiet. He broke the news of Charmaine to the staff as gently as possible before dismissing them for the time being.

Dominic wasn't worried about loose tongues. Those who called La Corsicana home were fiercely loyal. They knew him for what he was and accepted the surreal reality.

His few employees weren't afraid, but neither were they sycophants looking for a rush or a fast pass to immortality. They were people Dominic had saved, either from death or a life worse than that. Moreover, they loved Charmaine. Her quiet, ethereal nature had been peace incarnate. For them and the horrors some had endured, her serenity was a godsend.

He left them to grieve in their own way and saw to Charmaine's remains himself. Wrapping her body in the finest linen as they did when he was still human, he lit candles at her head and feet, offering prayers for the repose of her soul.

Then, in the quiet darkness of his room, he did the unthinkable for a vampire. He drank Charmaine's dead blood. Not from her throat, but from what hadn't turned to ash on the ground where she died. The act wasn't some morbid, macabre act. He wanted the last trace memories hidden within the cold copper.

Marianne Morea

The moment Charmaine's congealed blood touched his tongue, he gagged. Black blood rose in his throat, but he forced it down. Squeezing his eyes closed, he focused instead on the residual impressions the foul fluid brought.

He saw her there. Her smiling face, auburn curls dipping to her waist as hazel eyes flashed with humor and concern for him and everyone in their household. He saw her moving wraithlike through the gardens she loved. The trees dappled in moonlight and shadow as she took in the cool air.

Terror flooded his mind, tightening his throat. Human hands shot from the darkness, grabbing at him from behind. Dominic's hands rose, clawing at invisible fingers. He coughed, finally, dragging in a jagged breath.

Visceral memories from Charmaine's blood grabbed hold, and he felt each one, as if happening to him. Gooseflesh skittered across his preternatural skin. The sensation was so alien, he didn't recognize it at first. Human fear. It had been almost a millennium since the emotion bloomed in his quiet chest.

"No one can save you now, blood whore," the attacker's voice taunted from behind, and the feel of his hot breath sent rage coursing through Dominic's body.

His fangs pierced his gums, and her scream reverberated in his mind. He steeled his mind, separating himself from the visceral sensations until he merely watched like a witness to a crime.

Using all her strength, Charmaine threw the assailant off. Years of taking drops of Dominic's blood made her strong, even as panic flooded her veins. She bolted, taking seconds to race for the safety of the estate's iron gate.

Her heart hammered, and its feel still pummeled his brain. Dominic's fingers dug into his temples and he hissed.

Condemned

Terror squeezed her throat as her attacker closed the distance. Stronger, faster, he caught Charmaine beneath the cypress and slit her throat, ending her life like snuffing a candle.

That was two weeks ago, and now he waited. Dominic blinked back the images burned onto his eyes, focusing instead on the shadows creeping along the narrow streets of a sleeping Rome. Every sense heightened, and his eyes attuned to every silhouette.

He drifted through the darkened alleys on autopilot, letting the trace from Charmaine's dead blood guide him. His fangs tingled, and a knowing shiver climbed his spine.

Sahira's puppet was here, and he would die tonight.

The vampire smirked to himself, but the sideways grin was mirthless. Killing Charmaine was one part of the fervor-driven mission. Rubbing Dominic's face in it was next. So predictable.

"Come out, come out, wherever you are," he murmured, scanning the street ahead.

A neon sign for Lavazza espresso glowed in the window of a café at the next corner. The ambient light sent a dull-yellow swath across the sidewalk, the illumination fading as it reached the street.

The sign flickered and then went out as two women emerged from the café door. Dominic waited, listening to their muffled goodbyes and quick double-cheeked kiss before one left in a cab and the other started toward him.

She was oblivious to him as he watched. Clouds had rolled in earlier, obscuring the moon, but as if God himself commanded, they parted as she stepped off the curb, and his breath caught in his throat.

"Beauty," he murmured.

A riot of auburn curls framed a heart-shaped face, and soft hair kissed creamy shoulders. It fell in waves over bare skin

highlighted by an off-the-shoulder spring sweater, and when she glanced toward the sky, he saw her eyes were amber.

Carlos said it. He had a weakness for pretty redheads, and this one was gorgeous, with just enough curves to make his mouth water and his fangs tingle.

You're horny. Either that or you haven't fed in a while...

Dominic smirked to himself at Carlos's words.

...Knowing you, it's probably both.

Dominic watched the woman turn the corner into a darkened street. Rome was safe. At least, that's what the travel brochures liked to claim. Average humans had no idea what prowled the ancient streets in the small hours of the night. It wasn't just muggers hunting for a quick hit.

He followed, keeping his distance. No matter how tempted, he had other business to attend to, but he could play the Good Samaritan for now and watch her safely to her door.

Her footsteps echoed in the silence, the tap-tap of her boots bouncing off buildings on either side. He hung back, but her senses were keen, and she glanced over her shoulder as if she knew someone followed.

She picked up her pace, heading for the fluorescent light under the façade canopy of a typical three-star side-street hotel. Two blocks. That's all she had to walk before he got back to the task at hand. Once inside, the pretty woman was no longer his concern.

"Belinda..." a voice called from the shadows. "The mistress waits for you, and so do I."

Startled, she stopped short on the sidewalk and glanced across her shoulder. "Is someone there?"

The voice laughed, and she took a step toward the darkened alley to peer into the gloom. "Who's there? Show yourself!"

"Come see..."

As if mesmerized, she took another step, but before she could move into the darkness, Dominic knocked her back to the pavement.

She fell with an expletive, pivoting on her heel to break her fall with both palms. "Ow! Shit!"

"Didn't your mother tell you not to play in the dark?" His mouth pressed in a harsh line, but at the stunned expression on her face, he softened.

"No." She slapped his hand away and got up on her own, dusting herself off. "She told me not to talk to strangers, especially pushy shovey ones!"

Taken aback, he almost laughed at the fire in her pretty amber eyes. "I'm sorry, but you were about to step into that alley, and someone was there, stalking. Someone you wouldn't want to tangle with. Dangers live in the shadows, and they do much more than whisper."

"Wait, you heard that?"

Dominic nodded.

Belinda raked a sore palm through her hair. "So, I'm not crazy. I thought I was hearing things." She hesitated, sparing a glance for the dark alley before glancing back to Dominic. "But he knew my name."

He dipped his head, taking in every inch of the pretty redhead standing there confused, but defiant. "I heard. Belinda. It's a beautiful name for a beautiful girl who almost got into a situation she might not have been able to get herself out of."

She exhaled. "I've never been the dumb girl before, but I guess there's a first time for everything," she mumbled, giving him a sheepish smile. "I'm usually pretty smart."

He bent to pick up her purse and handed it to her, itching to touch the satin of her skin. "Then do me a favor, smart girl," he

said. "Go back to your hotel and lock the door behind you. Pull the shades and don't answer the door for anyone, at least not until morning."

"Wait," she said as he took a step toward the alley. "Where are you going? I don't even know your name."

He considered her, fighting every urge to take her and kiss her then and there. Another place, in another time. Maybe.

"It's better that way, beautiful." Dominic took off after the voice, knowing exactly who it belonged to.

***

"C'mon, c'mon…"

Belinda fidgeted with her room key, turning it over and over in her hand the longer the elevator took to get to her floor.

The car dinged, and she skirted through the sliding door. "Goddamned ancient piece of crap." She hurried down the hall and stood fumbling with the old-fashioned lock and key to her room, cursing again. "Jesus!"

Finally, the door opened, and she slammed it shut behind her, slumping against the painted wood. She dragged in a quick breath and locked the dead bolt.

"Some fucking night." She moved toward the bed but then turned, standing in front of the dresser mirror instead. She raked a hand through her hair and frowned at her reflection.

"What the hell is wrong with you, girl? You aren't drunk enough to be that stupid! You could've said yes when Roxy offered you a ride back. *Noooo*, you had to play all big and bad because you're from New York. You're an academic, Bels. You live and breathe books. Classroom. Lab. Dig site. That's your world. You are not a badass."

She dropped her hand and exhaled. "How the hell did that creeper from the shadows know my name?" Belinda closed her eyes and turned her head in self-disgust, trying to collect her thoughts.

"If it wasn't for that other guy—" She shivered not wanting to think about what-ifs, and guilt slashed at her a little for lumping him in with that creep.

She pushed her hair from her forehead and pursed her lips. He came out of nowhere like Batman, handsome in an old-world sort of way. With his broad shoulders and brushed-back wavy hair. Like an old-fashioned movie star. A soft grin tugged, and she shook her head, forcing her mouth into a grim line.

"No romanticizing." She glared at her reflection and then at her raw palms. "The man tackled me like a human football."

Yeah, well. What else could he do? You were halfway to becoming a statistic.

Her entire body shivered at the thought, and she rubbed her arms, slumping to the edge of her bed. "I shouldn't have had that last glass of wine."

She closed her eyes and tried to piece the puzzle together. How would someone know her name? Other than Roxy, she knew no one in Rome. Visiting her college roommate was just a stopover on her way to her internship. Roxy had invited her to dinner, and they were together all night. They ate and then hung around for drinks and music afterward.

Belinda's eyes flew open. "The dude at the bar."

Her gaze dropped in the mirror to the necklace at her throat. There it was in 14K gold. The nameplate her bubbie had given her for her twelfth birthday.

She reached to touch the polished gold. "Ugh, and I thought I had outgrown the age where I had to be wary of putting my name

on things like backpacks and lunch bags, but I guess not." She exhaled. "Not in this world."

The guy at the bar had commented on her necklace. He'd also left the bar slightly ahead of them, but even if he turned out to be that creeper in the alley, how did he know where to find her? She wasn't followed. She would have seen him or at least heard his footsteps. She hoped.

Anger slashed at her chest at feeling both vulnerable and used. Her fingers curled, squeezing the small brass key ring still in her palm. She looked at her fingers and the old-fashioned skeleton key poking out between her thumb and forefinger.

There it was. The little embossed tag attached to the ring she'd had in her back pocket the whole night. The Hotel Templar.

She snorted to herself. "Leave it to me to pick the one hotel in all of Rome to have a distinctive key instead of one of those plastic card thingies."

All because the hotel had the word Templar in its name. She exhaled hard. Not only did she go home late alone, a huge no-no, but she telegraphed her details to the stalker at the bar.

She threw an annoyed hand in the air. "You fail, Bels. A big, fat F for Self-Defense 101. So much for all those karate classes."

She lifted her face to the ceiling and exhaled. "Thank God for Good Samaritans." Closing her eyes, she issued a silent thank you to the universe for sending a real knight in shining armor to her rescue. An unbelievably good-looking knight.

Chapter 4

Dominic chased through shadow and light, wheeling down alley after alley with knowing laughter taunting him the whole way. There was no doubt the man in the shadows was Sahira's human puppet.

He skirted the main roads so he could focus, but part of his mind wandered back to the pretty redhead. How did the puppet know Belinda's name? Was the man clairvoyant? Did Sahira's blood give him such a gift, or did he guess Belinda sparked his desire from observation alone?

Too many questions whirled through Dominic's mind, but only one goal mattered. Find the culprit behind Charmaine's death and rip his heart out.

He dismissed the questions for now, refocusing his attention as he approached the Coliseum. It was well after midnight, and the shadows were long and ominous. Dominic followed the trace, the dull thrum that had lived in his veins since he'd tasted Charmaine's dead blood.

"You're close, human. You like to play at being a vampire, hiding in the shadows. How about I show you how it's done in plain sight?"

Laughter drifted on the air again. "Sahira taught me well. What do you think of my little game of cat and mouse?"

The human was too cocky for words, and it would be his end. Dominic climbed the hill into the Palatine across from the

Coliseum and scanned the ancient site. He found Sahira's minion lounging among the ruins like one of the arrogant cats that used to inhabit the place.

The man leaned casually against a ruin wall, his foot resting on ancient rubble. He toyed with the handle of a stiletto. Dominic inhaled, catching Charmaine's scent on the sharp steel, and venom clenched his gut.

"Not bad, vampire...but not good." He smirked, pushing himself from the wall to stand with his arms crossed, almost goading Dominic to attack.

"It took you twice as long to find me as I thought. Sahira will be so amused when she hears. She gave you more credit. Then again, she doesn't see you the way the rest of us do. Old and weak. You don't hunt, and you don't kill. You barely feed when it's spread for you on a plate like that redhead. You're such a sorry excuse for a member of the undead, I can't understand Sahira's obsession."

Dominic's eyes narrowed. Not because he took the human's bait, but because it was time for him to die. "What is your name, mortal?"

"Why? Going to run home to mommy and complain?" the man scoffed.

Dominic didn't blink.

"I'm Malik. Not that it's any of your business," he spat.

Dominic smirked at the man's overconfidence. "Sahira's blood is strong, Malik. I should know. It runs through my veins. It has kept you young, but you overestimate its power in your weak form."

Before Malik could open his mouth to argue, Dominic was on him. He gripped the man's throat, lifting him off the ground. Malik's face reddened and his eyes bulged as he gasped for breath.

Condemned

Dominic tightened his grip until blood ran in trickles from the man's sockets, his eyeballs near bursting.

With a snap, Dominic cracked the man's neck, but just enough for him to slump to the ground, convulsing. Ragged gurgles issued from his throat as Malik tried to breathe. Dominic knelt on the man's gut, making it even more difficult. "No quarter shown, so no quarter given."

Malik flailed, the fear in his face palpable, but Dominic lifted his hand, plunging his fingers through the man's ribs into his chest cavity.

"Still want to play cat and mouse?" he growled, before ripping open the bones to expose his beating heart.

The organ beat with a sluggish pulse, and what should have been a healthy red was streaked with vampire black.

With a hiss, Dominic bared his fangs. He leaned forward and grabbed the polluted organ with his teeth. The man's blood coated his tongue with Sahira's essence, and foul memories of the woman and her evil clutched at Dominic's chest. With a snarl, he tore the heart from Malik's chest and spit it out beside his body.

"That was for Charmaine," he said, watching the man's eyes widen for a split second before growing dim. As the last of the light left, Dominic fisted Malik's hair and twisted his neck like a bottle cap, severing his head from his body. "And that is for the poor girl you nearly tortured tonight."

Dominic tossed Malik's head over the ruin wall and then stood, wiping the man's blood from his mouth onto his sleeve.

The puppet's blood told him everything he needed to know. Sahira expected him soon. Well, who was he to keep her waiting?

***

Dominic walked through La Corsicana's sumptuous entrance only to hear the television playing in the great room. After his human encounter in the Palatine, he tensed for a moment. Not that a would-be assailant would stop to watch TV, and average immortals would never come into his territory, let alone his home unannounced, for fear of repercussions.

Still, Sahira wasn't an average immortal.

Angling his head, he inhaled, listening. *Carlos*. Clearly, the youngblood had missed his flight. Either that or he'd changed his mind and decided to hang around to watch him rip out a human heart out with his teeth.

Too late.

Wiping a hand over the dried blood on his shirt, he pursed his lips and turned toward the muffled voices, courtesy of CNN's live satellite feed.

"Miss your flight?" he asked, crossing his arms before leaning on the doorjamb to the great room's double-doored entrance.

"Not exactly," Carlos replied, muting the television.

Dominic closed the doors behind him, giving a chin pop toward the suitcase by the door. "I figured you'd be enjoying your complimentary beverage service halfway to New York by now."

"Charter flights don't have complimentary beverages. They're strictly BYOB. The airline couldn't find a sober pilot on such short notice. Apparently, one glass of wine with dinner disqualifies you from flying, so I scrapped the whole idea and booked a commercial flight instead. My plane takes off at one tomorrow afternoon." He motioned to Dominic's bloody clothes. "Seems you had an interesting night."

Dominic smiled to himself, pouring a brandy at the bar.

"That's human blood on your shirt," Carlos stated matter-of-factly. "Does it belong to who I think, or should I be worried you went rogue?"

The elder's satisfied smirk widened. "It was a rewarding night, *mon fils. Very* rewarding."

"Details, Old Monk. I tracked you as far as the redhead you stalked off the Villa del Artiste, but considering how your fangs tingled earlier, I didn't want to intrude. I'm not into being a voyeur."

"Carlos."

The younger vampire grinned. "Well, like I said. You have a weakness for—"

"Red hair." Dominic cut him short. "I know. You don't have to keep reminding me."

"So, did you kill the puppet bastard?"

Dominic nodded, sipping his drink.

"Good, so what now? Did you get what you needed from his mind?"

"Not quite. Hence the mess." Dominic lifted a hand to the front of his shirt. "His blood told me enough. I'm going back to the beginning, much like you did when you faced your ghosts in Spain, but first, come." He put his snifter down on the bar. "There's something I want to show you."

Determination took Dominic's stride as he moved quickly, not waiting for Carlos to fall in behind him. He headed down a curved staircase off the villa's main level.

From there he slipped through a nondescript servants' door and down even farther to the kitchens and staff quarters. It was too early for anyone to be up and about, so Dominic moved without pause toward a locked elevator secured behind a faux wall.

"Please tell me you're not working for the government." Carlos arched a brow at the high-tech biometric panel beside the elevator bank.

"No." Dominic pressed his hand to the glass screen, and the lift door slid open without a sound. "After you."

"Wow, so you're Batman, then? Are we going to war with Poison Ivy?" Carlos chuckled, stepping into the car's dark interior.

Dominic appreciated the attempt at levity. "On second thought, maybe you should forget your flight and send for your wife to come here. That city is making you stupid."

"C'mon, old man. You have to have heard of the Caped Crusader. Justice League? The Avengers? DC and Marvel comics?" Carlos laughed at Dominic's uninterested blink. "And don't give me your, I'm too cultured for pop culture look, Mr. First-in-line-for-all-things-Star Wars."

"I'm still not as bad as you, youngblood."

"Hey." Carlos shrugged. "I'm married to a millennial. It rubs off." He winked at his friend.

Dominic rolled his eyes, holding his hand to yet another biometric panel on the inside wall. "Boy, I am the *original* millennial, and don't you forget it."

"Next to love, humor is the best antidote to anger and hate. You taught me that." Carlos smiled, clapping his hand on Dominic's shoulder.

"I'm trying, my friend. Believe me. The need for revenge is clawing at my insides, but I know better than to let that singular emotion cloud everything in my life." Despite the success of tonight's kill, Dominic swallowed the bitterness rising in his chest at the thought of Sahira.

Carlos angled his head. "Good. Charmaine wouldn't want you to be rash. She'd want you to rip the witch's head off and shit down her neck but plan it first."

Dominic laughed at that, but grinned even wider when the elevator dropped, and Carlos's eyes flew open, and his hand went to his stomach.

"Whoa! Jesus, Dominic! Vampires do suffer vertigo from time to time," the younger vampire ground out. "Especially those of us who can't fly."

Dominic tsked. "You really *are* a complete youngblood sometimes. This lift was designed by the same engineers who did the private elevators for your vampire club in New York."

The elevator slowed to a seamless halt, and Dominic's mouth curved in a pleased smile. "I always liked the name chosen for your underground club. *The Red Veil.* Very apropos, and the perfect way to house a vampire sanctuary and council headquarters."

The doors slid open, and Carlos stepped out of the lift, his eyes widening in amazement. The room ahead housed Dominic's private collection of medieval weaponry and artifacts.

"Wow, and I thought your nerdy attachment to all things medieval ended upstairs. No wonder you were so angry when I messed with that altar cloth all those years ago. These make the artifacts upstairs seem like toys."

Broadswords and axes hung on the walls, along with sumptuous tapestries embroidered with gold thread. Glass cases lined the four walls, each holding priceless hand-scribed manuscripts and ancient tomes. On the far wall hung the room's centerpiece. Two lances crossed behind an ornate shield, and painted on the center was the coat of arms of the Knights Templar.

"You mean this altar cloth?" Dominic pointed to the silk runner embroidered with a red Templar cross at its center and miniatures of the same lining the borders.

The cloth was spread over a dais and resting on top was a magnificent sword and scabbard, complete with an embedded cross in the black-enameled grip. A knight's head graced the pommel with three-point cross guard finials, each holding a sapphire as big as your eye.

"*In hoc signo vinces,*" Carlos whispered before slowly turning to gape at his mentor. "Is this just a collector's item, or was it yours personally?"

Dominic moved past Carlos to pick up the sword. The grip molded to his hand as if he'd wielded it yesterday, instead of nearly a thousand years ago.

The overhead lights glinted on the flat edge of the sword as he pivoted the blade. "With this sign, you will conquer," he murmured, translating the Latin engraving.

"Why didn't you tell me?" Carlos asked. "It's not like I would've fallen prey to gossip. You fought to protect Christians in the Holy Land. Back in the day, your decision was born of the same moral compass I had when I fought to protect Spanish Jews from the last vestiges of the Inquisition."

Dominic returned the blade to the dais. "It wasn't gossip I feared you'd fall prey to, Carlos. It was Sahira—and you're wrong."

His eyes turned to the one empty case in his collection. "I didn't choose to fight in the Crusades. It was fight or die." He walked to the table with the unoccupied box, putting his hands on either side of the glass. "Ironic, considering my time in the Holy Land is where my human life ended and this one began."

He stroked the top of the lined lead with his thumbs. "I saw hate and loss bleed the sands of the Holy Land red. I swore I would never take another life, for any reason. To kill in God's name was not why God put me on this earth. Even when I was turned, I trusted it was for a divine reason. I held onto that belief in my deepest despair. I solaced my soul by making it my mission amid the darkness and the thirst to keep the light alive within me and to teach others to do the same."

His head dipped to his chest as his fingers curled over the lead sides of the case. "No more. I've turned the other cheek for too long. I once swore an oath to protect and defend, and now it's time to send the evil that's plagued me for a millennium back to the hell that spawned her."

Drawing a sharp breath, he lifted his head. "I will finally put an end to Sahira the way I should have from the first. Like you did with your maker."

"Wait a minute. Robert tricked me into killing the first woman I loved. Did Sahira do the same?" Carlos asked.

Dominic's lips pinched "No. She let me find what was left of my betrothed…Céleste. Sahira's message was delivered loud and clear. If she couldn't have me, no one would.

"I hunted her then," he continued. "I tried to kill her for what she did to Céleste, to me, but that was before I knew the extent of her crazy." He smirked, gesturing to a short, curved blade encrusted with jewels. "I left my mark on her, though. Every time she sees her reflection, she sees my handiwork, and no amount of vampire blood will fade the scar because I cut her with a spelled blade." Carlos drew a curved line from his temple, down his cheek to the corner of his mouth.

"Christ." Carlos raked a hand through his hair. "We are really a fucked-up race."

"That Bedouin sorceress was evil before she was turned, making her grip even more venomous. So, yes. I guess I am at war with your Poison Ivy." He gave Carlos a close-lipped smile. "I was deceived and left for dead by one of my own. Sahira and her harem of followers found me. I was entranced, at first. Her scent was beguiling. Cinnamon and the sweetest vanilla. I became her latest plaything, but when I refused her dark gift, it was—" He shrugged. "Game over."

"Is that box for her heart when you cut it out of her chest?"

"No." Dominic lifted two fingers to his lips before pressing them to the glass. "It's for the one artifact I covet more than any other. The cross Céleste gave me before I left for the Holy Land."

He glanced across his shoulder. "It was taken from me the night I was turned, and I've been searching for it for nine hundred years. I will find it someday, and when I do, it will rest here along with my heart."

Carlos raised an eyebrow. "I hope you're speaking metaphorically because, if not, I'm going to have to find a vampire whisperer to talk *you* down from the ledge."

Dominic chuckled softly. "Metaphorically yes, but then again, you never know." He gave Carlos a tired wink before dragging in a quick breath. "Come." He pushed past Carlos, heading for the elevator.

"Wait. Where are you going? I have a thousand questions for you." Carlos spared a glance for the artifacts before eyeing Dominic waiting in the lift. Dominic held his hand to the biometric sensor. "When this is over, I will tell you whatever you want to know. Right now, it's time to pack."

"Pack," he repeated, scooting into the elevator as the doors slid closed. "Road trip, Mad Max style. Me and you."

Dominic shook his head as the elevator rose. "No. By pack, I mean me. You are getting on your flight to New York."

"When I faced my ghosts, I had a starting point. What are you planning to do? Roam the desert, hoping to stumble over your psychopath?" Carlos asked.

"I won't have to. Sahira will find me."

"How? Does she expect you to retaliate for Charmaine?"

Dominic's gaze hardened. "She threw down the gauntlet, forcing my hand, but she'll still come. I have what she wants."

"You mean you *are* what she wants."

His lips pressed tight. "That, too, but it's not what I meant. When I scarred her face, she swore she would use that knife to take her final revenge. She knows it's here at La Corsicana. She knows while it rests in this vault, she will never have it. So, I'm taking it with me. The blade alone will bring her out of the shadows."

"I'm starting to think you're crazier than she. I think I'd better go with you."

The elder ignored his frustrated expression. "No, *mon fils*. I have to do this alone. I didn't stand in your way when you faced your past, so please don't stand in mine. I have to face Sahira and end this one way or the other. If I meet my final death, then so be it. I've lived too many lifetimes, most of them in the shadows, alone. So, it's fitting."

He gripped Carlos's shoulder. "Charmaine, you, Trina, the rest of your family in New York, you have been the light that chased those shadows into retreat. You have brought me joy. Now it's time for me to take back whatever life I have left and finally live it."

"I understand," Carlos acquiesced as the elevator slid open to a handful of anxious eyes as the staff readied for the morning.

"Good," Dominic replied. "I leave for Jerusalem tomorrow, after you leave for New York."

Chapter 5

The cab pulled to the curb at Leonardo da Vinci Airport, and Belinda peeled her vice grip from the taxi's *holy shit* handle. "Is this Terminal Five?" She held up five fingers, peering out the passenger window.

The cabbie bobbed his head. "*Si, signorina. Cinque.* Terrrminal five," he replied, rolling his Rs in heavily accented English.

He got out of the car and went to get her bag from the trunk while she fished in her pocket for the flat-rate fee. "Death Race, Italian style," she mumbled. "What's the average tip for not dying in a car wreck?"

With an exhale, she opened the door and stepped into the narrow strip of pavement between the taxi and the curb. The cabbie already had her roller bag out and ready.

She paid him, and he nodded, touching the brim of his cap. "*Buon viaggio,*" he muttered, climbing back into his taxi and pulling away from the curb like a madman.

"Jesus. Where do these people get their driver's licenses? Box tops?"

The airport wasn't much better. Controlled chaos with a third-world feel. She'd been all over the planet on various digs, but this was the first time she wasn't part of a bigger group.

Squaring her shoulders, she gripped her roller bag and backpack and headed for the terminal's revolving doors. If she was

Marianne Morea

lucky, her bag would make the cut for overhead storage, and she wouldn't have to check it through.

Years of preparing for digs had taught her to pack light. Taking only things you could easily rinse in a basin and hang dry. Party clothes were simply unnecessary. Not that she owned any.

As usual, the Italian military was ever present, but there wasn't a single uniform belonging to the airline in sight. "So much for customer service." She hoped once she made it through security and got to her gate, it would be better. All hands on deck to get them boarded and on their way.

"Egypt Air...Egypt Air..." she mumbled, staring at the departure board on the wall behind check-in. "*Shit*, they changed the gate."

Cell phone in hand, she scanned the terminal left and right, trying to figure out which way to go. Her cell buzzed, and she glanced at the alert on her screen. "Now? I'm just getting this now? Goddamned slow-ass international Internet! You've got to be kidding me!"

She squinted past the milling crowd and spotted the one airport employee in a sea of travelers. Rushing toward her, she realized the long serpentine line ahead was the one for security.

"Excuse me!" she said, breathless, as she hurried forward.

"Can I help you, *signorina*?" the Italian TSA officer asked.

Belinda nodded, trying not to seem as panicked as she felt. "Yes, I'm a little turned around. I have to catch my flight to Cairo, but my gate was just changed, and now my plane is boarding early." She held up the alert to show the woman.

"Documents," the TSA officer said, holding out her hand.

Belinda handed the woman her boarding pass and passport, hoping for a save.

Condemned

You should've left earlier, Bels, instead of rolling over to finish your X-rated dream about last night's save.

Shut up.

Handsome hero from the shadows. He certainly looked like a young Gary Cooper. Dreamy eyes and that slight accent. Oooh la la.

Ugh. I'm trying to do something here.

Yeah, you tried to do something earlier, too. I'm surprised you can still move your fingers, dirty girl.

Shut. Up.

The woman glanced at the flight number and then at her watch. Her gaze narrowed as she looked up from Belinda's passport. "What is the reason for your travel to Egypt today?"

"A postgraduate internship. I start day after tomorrow." Belinda slid her eyes toward the very long security line.

"An internship. Human rights? Politics?"

Belinda quickly shook her head. "No. Archeology. I'm an ar-ar-archeologist," she stuttered. "Or I will be, once I finish."

The TSA agent's eyebrows rose slightly, and she scrutinized Belinda's papers again. Finally, she folded the boarding pass into Belinda's passport and motioned for her to follow.

"Come. My sister works for the Italian Antiquities Commission, so I know a little about how this goes. I'll get you through security, but you are cutting this very close, Ms. Force." She gestured for Belinda's roller bag. "I'll have to check your bag through, though."

"Of course." Belinda wasn't about to argue. She handed the TSA agent her bag without issue, praying it made it to Egypt on time or she'd be borrowing a toothbrush from someone come morning.

She took her documents from the woman's hand and bobbed her head. "Thank you so much." She was going to make her flight, after all.

***

Belinda walked at a fast clip down the wide terminal gateway. Her stomach growled, and she reached into the wax-coated bag for a piece of bready pastry she bought on the fly. She hadn't eaten since that plate of pasta before—

She shook her head willing herself not to remember the gorgeous nutcase that rocked her world for about five minutes.

But—

No buts. You don't have time for buts.

Nutcase or not, he had an amazing butt...

Ignoring her own head, she plopped the flakey goodness into her mouth and chewed, dodging passengers and staff alike as she hurried to her gate.

"Imbarco definitive per volo 9721 sul Cairo."

She slowed, cocking her head to try and understand the muffled announcement. Damn. She didn't catch it all, but it was definitely something about Cairo.

"You just had to have that pastry, didn't you?" Picking up her pace, she crimped the wax-paper bag and sprinted. She pulled her backpack around to fish for her cell phone.

"C'mon, c'mon," she muttered, shoving her hand deeper into the canvas bag's mess. Running now, she found her phone at the very bottom. She pulled the device free and scanned her notifications.

Bam!

Condemned

Belinda's breath left her chest in an audible *whoompf*. She jerked backward, arms flying as she collided with a solid wall. Or what she thought was a solid wall.

Her phone skidded to the floor along with her backpack and food as she landed flat on her back, her head bouncing off the industrial floor with a smack.

***

Dominic dropped his shoulder bag and blurred to her side. He knelt, sliding an arm under her head. "Belinda?" She was the last person he'd expected to run into. Literally.

Her eyes fluttered open for a moment. "You," she murmured, but that was it. She'd gotten her bell rung good.

People crowded around, pushing in to see what happened. Airport security rushed forward, and Dominic tightened his arm under her shoulders, rattling off what happened rapid fire.

"*Chiamate un'ambulanza!*" one of the officers shouted before turning to Dominic. "Are you traveling together?" He gestured to Belinda.

Dominic nodded yes, not sure why.

"The airport medic is on his way. He should be here momentarily," the man informed him in stilted English.

Dominic didn't move from Belinda's side. Instead, he picked up her smashed cell phone. The screen was shattered, but her boarding information was still visible.

"Her bag was already checked through," he said, reading the flight information from the digital boarding pass. "Flight 9721 to Cairo."

The security agent's walkie-talkie chirped, and he answered the static-filled call before addressing Dominic again. "That flight

has already moved away from the gate. We won't be able to get your luggage."

"No matter. I'll have my people call the airport in Cairo." Dominic dug for his phone in his pocket and scrolled through his contacts. Holding the phone to his ear, he spoke quickly in French before hitting end.

"I have a private car coming. I'm taking my friend to my physician in Rome. If you could assist us to the terminal entrance, I would be most grateful." He didn't wait for the man to reply. He pulled his sunglasses from his eyes and stared at him until the security agent dipped his head in agreement. A little glamour went a long way.

Belinda's eyes opened and she blinked, moving her focus from security to the man who held her where she fell. "I'm okay, people. Seriously." She struggled to sit up. "I have to get to my flight." She winced, still arguing as Dominic scooped her into his arms.

Her scent told him she was fine, just knocked for six. He'd take her back to La Corsicana, and if she needed a doctor, he'd get her what was required, then.

"You missed your flight, love. You got your bell rung pretty badly, so for now, just enjoy the ride." Dominic put a tiny bit of glamour into his voice and carried her back toward security, accompanied by the agents.

She sighed in her mild stupor, pressing her cheek against his chest. Her eyes flickered open as they got to the entrance of the airport where his car was already waiting. Security left them the moment they saw everything was in order.

Belinda focused on him, her eyes clear and scrutinizing.

"You took quite a tumble," he said, meeting her gaze.

"You knocked me down, *again*. Can't help yourself, can you?"

Condemned

He grinned, tightening his hold on her against his chest. "When it comes to you, it seems not." Dominic signaled to his driver.

"Wait, I can't leave the airport. I have a flight to rebook," she said, sparing a glance for the chauffeur standing beside the now-open rear passenger door.

"You can reschedule your flight, but right now I think you need to rest. If it's any consolation, I missed my plane as well." He shrugged. "We collided, Belinda. It seems the fates want us to spend time together, so much so, they threw us to together again. Literally."

He let her down gently, careful to keep his hand on her elbow in case she got dizzy. "You banged your head pretty hard. I feel responsible, so the least I can do is make sure you're safe."

"I checked out of my hotel this morning." She raised a hand to her head as if trying to think. "The Templar is the nicest three-star in Rome, so it's usually booked solid." She chewed her lip.

"C'mon. We can figure it out as we go. My driver will take us anywhere you want. I just want to make sure you're okay."

***

She glanced at him still holding her backpack, and she had to bite the side of her tongue. The man was impeccably dressed, from his thick brushed-back hair, to his dark eyes and chiseled features. Her worn-out field pack seemed completely out of place on his shoulder, though he'd look good in anything. For a moment, she pictured him dressed Indiana Jones style, complete with whip, and the mental image was so good, she licked her lips.

There was something about him that was almost hypnotic, and the way his mouth moved as he spoke and smiled made her want to reach up and touch him.

"How can I go anywhere with you? I don't even know your name," she said candidly.

A gorgeous smile spread across his lips, and he held her gaze so intently, she didn't know if she should look away or not. Her mouth was dry, and her head a little fuzzy, but that was from the collision, right?

"My name is Dominic De'Lessep, and my car has been idling in the no-standing lane far too long. I think we'd better get going."

He winked, and she couldn't help but smirk. Handsome and intelligent. Quick, even.

Dominic De'Lessep. It figured. Mr. Gorgeous International Superman would have an equally gorgeous international name.

"Okay, Dominic De'Lessep. You've knocked me down twice, but you've also saved me twice." She angled her head and gave him a teasing smile. "You sure it's fate that wants us to spend time together?"

He laughed out loud. "I'm hedging my bets."

The man wasn't giant tall, six feet one, maybe two…but next to her barely five-foot nothing, he might as well be a Viking. A mysterious, old-Hollywood dark-haired Viking.

"I'm Belinda, but you know that from last night." She cleared her throat, ignoring the erotic images of what she let him get to *know* in her head after he left. "Belinda Force. It's nice to officially meet you."

She held out her hand, even though his was still on her elbow, and the feel of his fingers on her skin made last night's dreams seem almost real.

Yeah, Bels. You wish.

Shut. Up.

"Well, Belinda Force. Your mother certainly named you well. Beautiful and strong." He held his hand out toward the car.

With only a moment's hesitation, she pulled her arm from his protective hold and climbed into the back seat.

Dominic followed and in seconds, they were zooming back toward Rome. What was it about Roman drivers and breaking the sound barrier?

The car was like something out of James Bond, and she ran her fingers over the intense control panel on the passenger door, careful not to press anything.

"Is one of these an ejection seat?" she joked, sliding her eyes to him. "You know, in case you get bored with tackling me."

He grinned. "Considering your wit is intact, we can safely assume you're no worse for the wear, post tackle. What do you say to us spending the evening together? It's after seven, and I'd like to make up for you missing your flight by taking you to dinner."

She glanced down at the leggings and tank top she had donned for the flight and then at Dominic's GQ clothes and shook her head. "I never say no to food, but with my clothes currently on their way to Cairo, I'm not dressed for anything other than a burger and fries."

"If it means anything, I think you look beautiful. But I understand. We can always go back to my place. I can order in food or whip up something if you'd like. I have a very specialized diet, but pasta is always an option."

She eyed him. "Your place."

He nodded. "No strings. Just conversation. For instance, what's in Cairo that would make a pretty woman run like she's being chased by the devil?"

"Pyramids?"

He smirked, leaning back to stretch his arm over the back of the leather seat. "I meant that would interest you so much."

Marianne Morea

Dominic's fingers were scarcely an inch from her bare shoulder. One sharp curve, and she'd be in his arms.

Back-seat bingo, anyone?

He inhaled, and she felt her cheeks flush with the way he took her in completely, as if he knew her thoughts. The man was super classy and elegantly striking. There was no way he was the back-seat type.

One can still dream.

You sure did, and now you've got him in the flesh.

Stop. He's a perfect stranger.

Perfect indeed.

"Are you all right, love?" he asked. "You're a little flushed."

"Fine," she croaked, clearing her throat. "All good."

She fidgeted under his gaze, ignoring the fuzzy feeling spreading in her head and the sudden heat racing under her skin. "My wit might be intact, but maybe I'm not as okay as we thought."

He lifted a hand, gently dismissing her embarrassment. "Don't worry. I can call a doctor anytime, but for now, we're here. This is my place."

Outside the window, two enormous iron gates opened to a cypress-lined drive. Flowers bloomed in abundant color as the car wound its way up the curved drive. At the top was a stately palazzo. Stuccoed and columned and every bit like it belonged to the Renaissance.

"This is your place?" The question was a murmur. "I expected a city flat, not a villa straight out of the fifteenth century. Who lived here? A Pope?"

He laughed as the car pulled toward the front portico. "No, a Cardinal."

Condemned

Opening the rear passenger door, Dominic climbed out first, holding his hand for her. She took his hand, trying to keep her mouth from dropping as she gaped at the expanse.

"Unfortunately, the original owner lost his red Cardinal's hat for selling indulgences. It's quite a story," Dominic said as they walked toward the front door.

"Heavenly fast passes." She snorted, still in awe. "To half the Holy Roman Empire, no doubt."

They passed through the ornate door into a magnificent atrium. This time she couldn't help it, her mouth dropped. It was like stepping into a church. Arched buttresses painted with colorful frescos trimmed in gold leaf covered the ceilings, and the furnishings would make a museum curator cry.

"Your place is amazing. I don't know where to look first."

Dominic stood with her in the wide hall. "I love history. In fact, you could say I embody it every day of my life, so I surround myself with what I love."

"I know what you mean. Sometimes I wish I had a time machine, just so I could see things as they were. History isn't always pretty. In fact, the eras I love most were brutal and raw, but isn't that the essence of birth and growth?"

Dominic looked at her, nodding. "You sound like an academic."

She rolled her eyes. "God. Does it show?"

"All over you." He chuckled. "What's your field of study? If I had to guess, I'd say archeology."

She touched a finger to her nose. "Ding. Ding. Then again, you had a heads-up knowing I was headed to Cairo, so not much of a guess, Sherlock."

His hand went to his heart. "Ouch."

Belinda stifled a yawn "I'm sorry. It's not the company. I didn't get much sleep last night, and I feel like I was run over by a truck." At the expression on Dominic's face, she burst out laughing.

"Touché." He moved toward a set of double doors, motioning for her to follow. "We can relax in here. I need to let my staff know what happened. Are you hungry? Like I said, pasta is always a staple in Roman kitchens."

"Thanks, I am a little hungry," she admitted with a small shrug.

He pointed to the double doorway. "Go ahead in. There's an open bottle of merlot on the bar. Help yourself."

"Thanks, but considering our collision, maybe it's not a good idea for me to drink. I'll take a bottle of water or something soft, though."

He nodded. "Of course. Make yourself comfortable."

Chapter 6

Belinda stepped through the double doors and froze. "Oh my *God*," she murmured.

If she hadn't known where to look first in the atrium, this place could stop her heart. Shields with ancient crests she actually recognized lined one wall. And the tapestries! This room was an antiquities scholar's wet dream.

She turned to scan the rest of the room, and this time she nearly lost her breath. Hanging on the wall above the fireplace was a Templar cross. Not a banner. A real cross. It was at the center of two lances, and she hurried to get a closer peek.

"Holy shit!"

Right in front of her was the sentinel piece used to lead the warrior monks into battle during the Crusades. Glancing around, she grabbed a hard-backed leather chair from a corner desk and dragged it to the hearth. She had to know if the piece was a reproduction or the real deal.

A real sentinel cross would have the crest of the military order's founder hidden somewhere on the cross points. Not many people knew to look. Only those who'd spent their lives researching that time in history would know that obscure fact.

Them, and serious collectors, and based on what she saw in this room so far, Dominic was a serious collector. He said he embodied history every day, and he wasn't kidding.

She climbed onto the chair and stood on tiptoe, craning to see if the mark was under the base of the three-point cross. Her hand shook as she reached under the flat edge of the gold base. As her fingertips grazed the underside's surface, her stomach flip-flopped. The mark was there.

If this piece was real, that meant it was nearly a thousand years old. If it was a reproduction, then it was the best she'd ever seen. Real, it should be in a museum where she could test it and stare at it whenever she liked. Not in a private villa.

She climbed down from the chair and stood gawking at the other artifacts in the room. Dominic was definitely a rarity. Old-Hollywood good looks, intelligence, chivalry, and, of course, bravery. Those qualities were a thing of the past. Men like that didn't exist anymore, at least not in her world. Exhibit A, Giles Newcomb. He would have slept with her and then stepped on her face to get this internship.

On the surface, Dominic was everything she'd read about and romanticized her whole life. Knights and their valor that filled her dreams as a little girl.

Maybe you need to dig a little deeper, dream girl. After all, digging is your specialty.

This time, she didn't tell her muse to shut up.

This time, she agreed.

Dominic returned with a tray laden with crusty bread, butter, a serving dish of linguini with fragrant tomato and basil, and a pitcher of what looked to be fresh-squeezed lemonade, one plate, and two glasses.

He put the food on the coffee table and set out the plate along with a napkin, fork, and spoon. "You know," he said, holding up the spoon. "No self-respecting Italian eats pasta with just a fork. The beauty is in the twirl."

Condemned

Grinning, he put the spoon on the napkin next to the fork and waved a hand over the presentation. *Bon* appétit, chéri."

"Aren't you eating," she asked, sliding onto the couch to help herself to the food.

"No, but I will have a glass of wine, if you don't mind."

Belinda lifted one shoulder and let it drop. "Not at all. It's your house, and under normal circumstances, I'd join you."

She picked up the fork and stabbed the linguini, picking up a few strands to try and twirl in the spoon. The pasta curled easily around the tines, forming a perfectly compact ball the right size to plop into her mouth. She closed her eyes, chewing.

Swallowing, she wiped her mouth on a napkin. "This is so good. Whoever made the sauce has real talent."

Dominic grinned. "I'll tell my cook. She doesn't get to prepare meals very often. She was delighted to do so for you tonight."

"Well, this is the real deal," she said, spearing a few more strands and twirling them while trying not to splatter sauce on her clothes. "Speaking of the real deal, are these artifacts authentic?"

"Yes. Every one of them, including the cross above the mantel." He smirked, gesturing to the chair she'd dragged to the fireplace. "I see you've been snooping."

"Yeah, sorry about that. Again, I couldn't resist."

He shook his head. "Don't be sorry. I'll show you my entire collection if you want but eat up. I've taken the liberty of having a guest room made up for you. It's just at the top of the stairs to the left. If you're okay with staying, that is. I don't want you scrambling to find a room at this time of night. I also placed a call to my travel agent. I had to rebook my own plans, so I did the same for you. Same flight, same time, but first class."

Belinda put her fork down and wiped her mouth again. "I don't know what to say, Dominic. That's a very kind offer, thank you."

"It's not generous or kind, Belinda. It's selfish. I know you have to leave tomorrow. I have to travel as well. We both have things to do. Important things. Until then, I want to spend time with you. It's that simple. As much time as possible. So much so, I nearly went back to your hotel last night, but it wouldn't have been appropriate. No matter how much I desired it."

"You said not to open the door for anyone."

"True, and for good reason."

"I would have opened the door for you," she replied softly. "Truth is I would have opened more than that if you'd asked."

Dominic was out of his seat and beside her in a heartbeat. His hand cupped her cheek. "Don't say things you don't mean, *chéri*. I did what any decent man would do. You are not beholden to me."

Belinda's hand came up to cover his. Her stomach prickled, but this time with butterflies instead of alarm.

"I always mean what I say, and say what I mean, Dominic. I don't like games. I never have."

He caressed her face with his thumb, angling his head so his lips hovered close to hers. "Boys play games, Belinda, and I am no boy. Love is a man's domain."

Dominic kissed her, and her breath caught in her throat. His kiss was gentle as it brushed her mouth. Soft, but lingering with so much promise.

***

With her eyes closed, she let her hand slide from his, but didn't push him away. Her lips parted, and her sweet breath fanned his

nostrils. Belinda shivered, and he inhaled her luscious scent, savoring the perfume on his tongue.

He hadn't glamoured her into compliance, and the knowledge she wanted him unsolicited made his fangs tingle.

Encouraged, he kissed her again. This time, his tongue swept hers for a quick taste before feathering a sensuous line from her mouth to the tender skin beneath her jaw.

Belinda lifted her chin, and he continued, kissing his way toward the steady pulse quickening beneath her flesh. Her pulse thrummed with life. Hot, desire-laced blood waiting for razor tips to slide painlessly into a thick, blue vein.

It would be so easy.

Appalled at how quickly his thoughts turned predator after one kill, he squelched the urge and concentrated instead on the woman in his arms. Her curves, her scent, and the way his cock throbbed from holding her this close.

Her arousal filled his senses, and he lifted his face from her throat. It was natural and definitely reciprocated. Dilated pupils were dark in liquid-amber depths. Her lips were wet, and her breath eager. Her need was a gut punch straight to his groin, and his jaw tightened. He'd never wanted a woman, redheaded or not, so much in his life.

He slid his fingers into her thick red curls and wrapped his hand over the back of her neck. "Tell me to stop, Belinda," he whispered. "Tell me before I can no longer stop myself."

She drew her tongue over his bottom lip in reply. "I don't want you to stop."

Dominic held his breath for a moment. Vampires didn't need air, but the indecision warring in his chest forced the rote human response.

Belinda had no clue what she asked. Not that he'd ever do her harm. No matter what her body invited or how much her scent enticed, she was out of her league.

"Kiss me, Dominic. Pretend I'm a damsel in distress and you a knight sworn," she murmured with a smile. "Look around. It shouldn't be too hard to imagine."

His fingers tightened in her hair. "Easier than you think, *chéri*." His mouth crushed hers, and she fisted his shirt at his back as his mouth captured every part of her.

She moaned, opening to him without reservation. Her taste was almost elemental on his tongue. Conjuring the essence of wind and rain, fire and dark earth.

He slid his arm around her back and pulled her close. His hand dropped from the nape of her neck to caress the curve of her waist. Fingers trailed across her ribs over her thin tank top, traveling higher to cup the weight of her full breast.

"Don't stop," she murmured.

Finding her nipple, he rolled the hardening nub between his thumb and forefinger. Belinda sucked in a breath, her head falling back to expose the slender line of her throat.

Every sense fired in that moment, and he dipped his face to the scooped edge of her tank top, his fingers on the thrum of her pulse at her throat while his lips kissed the swell of her high breasts.

"What do you want, Belinda? Tell me." Her pulse was so loud and inviting in his ears, he could barely think.

"I want to know you, Dominic. All of you. Who you are. What you want."

His tongue trailed over soft flesh to her throat and circled the tender spot over her pulse. His breath came in short, ragged pants. "Are you sure, Belinda? I'm not who you think I am."

She lifted a hand and ran her fingers through his thick hair, forcing him to look up. "I trust my intuition, Dominic. I listen to my body. Right now, it's buzzing. In a good way."

He straightened, but before he could say a word, she put a finger over his lips. "There is nothing about you that sets my inner alarms blaring, and believe me, they blare. Loudly."

Belinda's eyes locked with his, and she shrugged. "So, no more talk. Just kiss me, and whatever happens, happens. I'm open." She hooked her fingers into the hem of her tank top and pulled it over her head, letting it fall to the floor beside the couch.

"Even if it's for one reckless night." She unclasped her bra, dropping it to the floor as well. "Guys like you don't happen to nerdy girls like me, so if the fates want us to spend time together"—she lay back on the arm of the couch, pulling one foot back to let her knees fall open— "who says that time has to be all talk?"

Dominic climbed between her legs and with a soft growl, buried his face in her breasts. He gave himself over to the elemental feel of her and breathed her in again.

Her body hummed beneath him, and her scent was saturated with anticipation. The hard bar of his member strained against his pants, the pull of her pulse and the scent of her wet sex pushing him to the edge.

He slipped his hand beneath her waistband, and Belinda gasped as he followed a line of heat to its peak between her legs. Lifting her hips, she let her head drop back.

Dominic stroked between her moist folds, and he curled his fingers into her sex. She was so ripe. One push and she'd climax. His lips curled against her throat as he circled her G-spot, using his preternatural speed like a personal vibrator. She sucked in a

breath, her whole body tensing as her climax exploded. Release saturated her blood, pushing him over the precipice.

One taste. That's all.

His fangs descended and, with a groan, he slid them painlessly into the blue vein throbbing at her throat. Her blood filled his mouth, but the moment the coppery taste hit his tongue, he could hardly breathe.

Stunned, he pulled back and licked his lips. Untapped magic assaulted his senses. Dominic's mind whirled, a warning for him to stop, but he had to know for sure. Belinda's scent was intoxicating from the first moment, but he should have sensed the underlying lure.

Belinda's blood. Witch's blood.

The one compulsion he'd yet to break from Sahira's cruelty. Sahira's sorceress blood had left its mark. His Achilles heel, almost impossible to resist.

He sank his teeth once more, and her taste filled him, flooding his senses. Belinda's blood was ethereal light and warmth. Magic incarnate. Heady in a way he'd never known possible. It was different from Sahira's. Hers held nothing but cold darkness. It willed death, not life. Demanding the very last heartbeat.

There was no blood connection between the two women. Of that, he was sure. He groaned with the visceral flavor, pulling at Belinda's vein while searching the hot, coppery liquid for both explanation and redemption.

Withdrawing, he willed his addiction to subside. He hadn't succumbed in nine hundred years, and he wasn't about to now. With a quick tongue swipe, he sealed the wounds on her neck, healing them instantly.

He pulled his palm from between her legs and knelt to kiss her mouth. "Belinda?" he whispered, rousing her from her stupor.

She blinked, pushing her damp hair from her face to stare at the man kneeling between her legs. "What happened?"

"You really don't remember?" He bent to pick up her tank top and bra, handing them to her as she sat up.

"My body feels boneless, and my panties are soaked. *That* part I remember. The rest is kind of fuzzy." She pulled her tank top over her head, not bothering with the bra. She hesitated, letting her eyes dip to his still-thick crotch.

"You're fully dressed, so I'm guessing I did, but you didn't?" she asked with a sheepish shrug.

He smirked, answering with a shrug as well. "I was happy to oblige."

"I don't know why the rest is so fuzzy, but"—she hooked both forefingers into his waistband above his zipper— "I'd like to oblige you right back, if you're up for it."

She waggled her eyebrows, and Dominic laughed. "Oh, I'm *up* for it all right."

In one fluid move, he flipped her onto her back on the couch, kissing her as his palm traveled the length of her Lycra-covered leg. "You're beautiful, Belinda."

Her fingers trailed the buttons of his shirt. "I showed you mine, so you show me yours." She tugged one button.

Dominic's body vibrated with her infused blood as he straightened. Taking hold of his shirt, he tore it wide, sending buttons everywhere before shrugging out of the soft linen.

He reached for her, brushing his hand the length of her inner thigh to the juncture of her legs. "I want to look at you, Belinda. I've tasted your breasts and your mouth. Now, I want to see all of you. Taste all of you." His voice was thick.

She skimmed her hands under her waistband and tried to wiggle her leggings from her hips. High color stained her cheeks. "Ugh, there's just no sexy way to do this lying down."

Sliding off the couch, she teased playful circles over her hips before dipping beneath the clingy fabric. Facing him, she shimmied her yoga pants to her feet and then kicked them to the side.

Standing braless in just her underwear and tank top, she lifted her shirt over her head once more and dropped it to the floor.

"Hey." She shrugged, giving a quick turn. "Nothing's sexier than field boots and lacey underwear. If my luggage wasn't halfway to Cairo you could've had the super sexiness of cotton granny panties, too."

Dominic laughed out loud as his eyes traveled her full length. "*Chéri*, you'd be sexy in a potato sack," he whispered, closing the distance between them.

Holding her bare waist, he dipped his mouth to her breast and flicked his tongue over one nipple.

"Not until you're as naked as me." Belinda stepped back, shaking her head. "C'mon, Gary Cooper. Strip." Grinning, she circled her hand impatiently.

"Gary Cooper?"

"Long argument with myself. Don't ask. Just strip."

Dominic unbuttoned the top of his black jeans and pushed them over his hips to strong, muscled thighs. He watched Belinda lick her lips as his corded length jutted from its dark nest. "I never wear underwear," he said kicking off his loafers before dropping his pants to his ankles and kicking them to the side.

"Very *Euro*-chic," she teased.

With a single move, he swept her into his arms and laid her on the soft leather couch. He sucked and teased her breasts while one hand slid her panties from her body.

"My boots. I have to unlace my boots," she said, tearing her mouth from his.

"Leave them," he growled. "Very *Ameri*-combat sexy."

She laughed out loud, and the sound vibrated like electric satin against his skin. It was her blood in his veins, of course, but the hyper-sensation made his cock jerk.

He skimmed over her belly to the pretty ginger fig leaf between her legs, and she shivered under his touch. "True red." He circled her nub with his thumb. "Now that's a turn-on."

With feather light strokes, his fingertips circled and grazed her sensitive skin until her slick wetness pooled in his palm again. She lifted her hips, arching into his hand. He kissed her mouth, his tongue teasing her as he spread her soft folds again.

With a single stroke, he delved two fingers into her slick cleft, pushing deep and hard. She panted as he devoured her lips. She reached for his cock, matching him stroke for stroke as he worked her slit.

Hips raised, she pushed her knees wider, and he picked up his pace, curling deeper and harder, over and over.

Her climax came fierce and fast, and as her body rocked with aftershocks, he broke their kiss. Dark eyes met hers as he pulled his hand from her and fisted his shaft.

Squeezing his cock, he pressed his thick head to her lips. A shiny wet pearl glistened at its bulging end, and Belinda licked it clean. Opening her mouth, she swirled her tongue under its ridged edge.

Dominic's breathe hitched sharp and fast, as she worked him with her hand and mouth. A low growl left his throat as she

sucked his member in balls deep before scraping her teeth along his corded length.

He whispered in soft French, easing himself from her mouth. His fingers caressed from her cheek to her breasts. He slid lower between her thighs and pushed her knees wide. "You're so wet, *ma fleur*," he said, dipping his face to her red fluff.

Her sex was flushed and swollen with blood as he spread her folds. He dragged his tongue across her soaked satin, his fangs begging for a taste. Flicking her hard nub with the end of his tongue, he nipped the stiff bud but didn't draw blood.

She gasped, bucking her hips higher. He delved his tongue, faster, deeper until she edged toward another climax. He pulled his mouth from her and got to his knees, his cock swollen with need. He entered her with a single thrust.

He rode her hard and fast. His mind whirled with the scent of her climax and the tight feel of her channel as she squeezed his cock, coming again. She met him thrust for thrust, his balls tightening as he pounded faster, harder until his cock head bulged, ready to blow.

Belinda lifted her arms above her head. Her back arched as her neck stretched to one side, exposing her throat.

"*Mon Dieu, aide-moi.*" Dominic's growled prayer for strength was muffled in Belinda's abundant hair, his fangs lengthening as the lure of her blood swelled along with his cock.

He snarled, fighting the draw. He wouldn't take from her again. Not until she knew and understood. Straining, he threw his head back, willing his fangs to retract as he exploded inside her with a cry.

Too late.

With a scream, Belinda raked her nails down his chest, her eyes wide as the cool flesh healed almost instantly. Adrenaline-

soaked strength shoved him from between her legs as another scream ripped through the room. His fangs had withdrawn, but she already saw.

"Belinda, please. Let me explain."

Shaking her head, she scrambled off the couch, grabbing her clothes as her academic brain tried to make sense of what she saw.

"Belinda, it's not what you think! Please." He moved slowly, reaching for his pants.

"No? Then what is it? I should've known this was too good to be true." Near hyperventilation, her chest heaved as she backed away. "You probably have corpses rotting in closets. Or maybe you just bury the bodies on your property. Hell, you've probably got a freaky cult following!"

Dominic's heart squeezed. Eyes that reflected such want only moments before, now looked at him in fear.

"I'm out of here! And don't you dare try and stop me!" Her eyes flew to the closest weapon she could reach, and she yanked an Ottoman scimitar from its display. Holding it in front of her, she backed toward the door, naked.

"Belinda, please. I know you're afraid, but I would never hurt you. Let me explain!"

Cringing against the door, Belinda shook her head. "Stay away! I swear I'll cut you and your protruding parts!"

If this wasn't so serious, it would be comical watching this petite redhead going ghetto-fierce with an ancient blade twice her size.

"That blade you're holding is ninth century Ottoman Empire. I thought you'd like to know before you use it to dispatch me."

She blinked.

"Actually, you look a little like *Jeanne d'Arc*, standing your ground. Except for the naked part, of course. The Maid of Orléans

preferred armor when she fought for France." Dominic shrugged. "I could tell you things about her no history book could share."

Belinda snorted, tightening her grip on the curved blade. "Are you telling me you knew Joan of Arc personally? What next? That all these artifacts are yours? Not just a personal collection, but *yours*?"

"Yes. To all of the above." He gestured to the scimitar. "Except that blade. I wasn't yet born when that was forged."

"Oh yeah?" She snorted again. "Okay, I'll buy a vowel. For shits and giggles, when were you born?"

Straight-faced, his eyes held such severity. "In the year of our Lord, 1097. I was twenty-two years old when I was turned to what you see before you now." He spread his hand wide. "Everything here, including this villa, I acquired over my long existence. They have been my lifeline—until now."

His eyes found hers, and he watched them widen as his surreal reality dawned. The scimitar dropped from her hand with a clatter, and Belinda crumpled along with it.

Out cold.

Chapter 7

The fasten-seat-belt sign dinged off, and Dominic reached for his tablet and his wireless earbuds. The flight from Rome to Jerusalem wasn't long. Three-and-a-half hours tops, but as per usual, the plane sat on the tarmac at Leonardo da Vinci-Fiumicino airport for nearly as long.

They finally took off, reaching their cruising altitude without a hitch. First class was more than comfortable, but he couldn't relax. Not after what happened with Belinda.

The entire night had not gone the way he hoped. Still, Belinda left a mark on him as indelible as the one she now wore from his bite. Her humor and bold inquisitiveness surprised him as much as the decisive way she took control and let go with him. Belinda was a force in her own right.

Her strength and presence astounded him. Even in fear, her intellect was unflappable. He probed her thoughts as he carried her unconscious to the guest quarters. Even then, her mind clicked on all cylinders, searching for plausible explanations.

Exhaling, he decided against a downloaded movie and put on his headphones, queuing up iTunes instead.

"Can I get you anything else?" the flight attendant asked, "Another cognac, perhaps?"

Dominic glanced at the dark-haired woman as she leaned over to take what was left of his complimentary drink. There was a definite scent of possibility about her. A gentle probe found more

than willingness in the flight attendant's mind, but nothing she offered sparked much interest. Not after last night.

Belinda was an enigma. She was a complete stranger, yet she captivated, him mind and body. She preoccupied him, and not because he didn't get a chance to explain. It was more. The attraction was visceral.

Of course, it's visceral. She's a witch. Her blood is your kryptonite.

Carlos's voice niggled from the back of his head with yet another pop reference.

Superman, my friend, whom you are not when it comes to witch blood, remember?

Belinda doesn't know she's a witch. I'd bet my fangs on it.

Does it matter? You need to be careful.

The flight attendant waited for a reply, so he pulled a single earbud loose. "I'm good, thanks."

"You sure?"

"Positive." He stuffed the bud back into his ear, punctuating his noninterest. She turned away disappointed.

Was his pent-up desire an invisible, sexual magnet, humans could sense? Seduction was the undead's stock in trade, yet he'd lived without it for centuries. He'd kept himself sequestered for so long his sexuality had waned to nil. An asexual vampire. The thought was laughable.

Charmaine was mostly the reason why. As the decades passed, the pull of his sexual connection to her had faded, growing less and less with every drop of his blood taken. His noninterest somehow bled through and caused her noninterest.

Arousal awakened again last year when they traveled to Spain to help Carlos with Trina. Carlos's passion for Trina was so thick it hung in the air like heavy perfume. The effect ignited passion and

possibilities, but he held it at bay, burying his longing instead, and telling Carlos, Charmaine was off-limits because of their creed.

Dominic turned up his playlist. Shubert always brought solace when unwanted memories invaded. Especially the composer's swan song. Burying his feelings seemed proper last year. Charmaine was a constant in his life, and he refused to use her comfortable availability for purely physical release.

The concerto swelled, and he reclined his seat, resting his head. He closed his eyes and let the rich melody fill his mind. Shubert's music was potent. Full and vivid.

Like Belinda.

A soft smirk tugged at the image of her with that scimitar. Fiery-red hair with a temperament to match. Confident and quick thinking. Like Céleste, but not.

Still, she had that certain something that reminded him of the Gallic beauty he'd lost nearly a thousand years before. A frown tugged, warring with the music calming his mind.

Céleste wasn't lost. She was slaughtered.

Memories knocked at the back door, unbidden. Images he kept at bay for the guilt and pain that slashed even now.

He pictured her so clearly. Céleste's face. Her laugh. The sadness in her eyes the day she folded her silver cross into his palm. Ironic now, considering silver was anathema to his kind.

She had snuck away to see him one last time, pinching a cloak from the Mother Superior to meet him, knowing the abbess's robes would scare the devil himself into keeping his distance, even on the Marseilles docks.

The abbey of Mont Majeure in Marseilles wasn't a refuge. It was a prison. With a harpy holding the keys to freedom. Céleste had been condemned to that cold place. Her sin?

Him.

Sahira had ripped Céleste's gift from his throat, ravishing his body and his blood the night the cunt punished him for defiance. The smell of burning flesh when the silver scorched her thieving hand filled his memory.

The pain only fueled her desire for vengeance, and later her plans when the witch read his mind and heart.

He banished the dark image, but the memories of the last months of his human life beckoned. From the sunlit countryside with its swaying wheat, to the monastery where he'd spend his youth, to the rolling meadow where Céleste won his young heart. He sighed, resigned to let the memories take him.

***

Lyon, France
December, 1118

"Dominic, you are playing with fire, boy, and I don't mean the one in that grate! Your future is at stake. Young passion burns hot, but it doesn't last. And not with a girl sworn to another." Frère Michel stood watching Dominic poke at meager fire in the small stone hearth.

Dominic ignored the man's concern. "I'll go for more kindling after vespers. The wind is colder than a witch's tit tonight, and your old bones won't survive if the fires aren't banked."

"*Mon fils, écoute-moi, s'il te plait!* Heed me. If not for your own soul, then for Céleste's sake. Talk has reached my ears, and it's only a matter of time before it reaches her father. Èmile Colbert has many enemies, and they won't hesitate to use Céleste's sins to make an example of him before the bishop."

Dominic straightened, wiping his hands on his rough breeches. "The bishop?" He snorted, returning the poker to the

hook on the stone lintel. "Everyone knows His Excellency has a concubine and a houseful of brats to his name. What Céleste and I share wouldn't be a sin if you would agree to marry us." He turned, spreading his hands in a gesture of *fait accompli*. "I love her, Michel. How can that be a sin before God?"

"Simple. Céleste is promised to Georges Delacroix. Her father signed the marriage contract in front of the king. You, my son, are noble of mind, but you have nothing. No name, no fortune. Her father would never agree."

Dominic's smile faded as he sat on the edge of the room's rough cot. "She's already given herself to me, Michel."

"*Dieux*." The priest's invocation was a mere whisper. "You took her outside the bonds of marriage! Foolish, foolish boy! What if she's with child?"

The fire crackled in the hearth, its embers flickering in the twilight glow through the paned glass. Evening called, and the small stone room seemed suddenly smaller.

Dominic glanced up, his eyes following the priest's agitated back and forth. Michel stopped mid-pace and turned as if with a thought, but his expression fell at the look on the young man's face.

"Please God, no." Eyes tight, he moved to where Dominic sat. "How long?"

"I don't know. Long enough for the child to quicken, I think."

The monk smoothed a hand over the shaved circle at the top of his head. "Why didn't you tell me sooner? You were brought here as a child, Dominic. We raised you, not as a lay cleric, but as a free man. Educated you so you might elevate your position. You were taught to read and to cypher, to strategize and to fight. Our hope was that you serve almighty God in whatever way He saw fit. Not throw your life away on a country whore."

"Michel, Céleste is no whore. You've known us both since we were children. Give us your blessing. I know we'll be happy together."

The monk shook his head. "I wish I had the power to grant your wish, my son, but Céleste lay with a man not her intended. She must carry the stain, and you?" He exhaled, throwing a hand up. "You will be lucky not to be shunned or even excommunicated for seduction and vice."

Dominic stalked from the cot to the window, his boot steps tapping in staccato defiance. "You make us sound dirty. Céleste and I are bound in the eyes of God himself. Through love. Through a shared bond in the child we created."

"Spoken like a wheedling child. You are young, Dominic. You have nothing, while Céleste is used to having the best. Dresses, jewels, a fine home, and stables. Passion's snare has caught you both. Had there not been a child, perhaps. But, now?" He exhaled.

"Céleste is strong-willed and far too outspoken for her sex." The priest paced again. "I blame her mother for letting her have her head. She's a fickle child of Eve and will suffer as Eve did." He stopped and turned for the small writing desk across from the rough cot. "Frère Hermann must be made aware. Perhaps he can mitigate the situation with her father and dissuade Colbert from killing you outright."

Michel reached for parchment and a quill, dipping the feather's sharp end in the ink pot. "Though I don't see what Frère Hermann could say to spare Céleste. She's Colbert's daughter, and therefore his property."

With a single swipe, Dominic cleared the desk. The pewter pot clattered to the floor, its contents spreading in a black stain across the cold stone floor.

"That letter will be Céleste's death warrant." The young man's voice shook with both anger and fear. "Colbert would rather strangle her with his bare hands than let her dishonor his name."

Frère Michel shot to his feet, letting the simple cane chair bang to the floor. "You should have considered that before you seduced the silly girl! A woman's body is a devil's cup! One taste and you're damned to hell. Céleste Colbert sealed her fate the day she followed in Jezebel's footsteps. Frère Hermann can only do so much. I will suggest she live out her days with *Les Soueurs du Sacré-Coeur* and her bastard child be left to the fates. The rest is up to God."

Dominic picked the old man up by his robe and threw him onto the narrow cot. "Hypocrites! Frère Hermann married Pierre Dumont and his whore in the chapel at Saint Simeon not six months ago! The woman was a common prostitute!" He threw a hand in the air before lowering it to point at the cowering priest. "You know he fornicated with her, and yet he still received benediction. Tell me, Michel. How much did his 'blessing' add to monastery coffers?"

"Dominic! Stop this madness! Your actions are the root of this evil. Pray for your soul's salvation and stop browbeating me!"

Dominic scoffed, pacing. "You worry for the good of my soul, but what good is my soul without my heart? For pity's sake, the woman I love is carrying my child!" Dominic's voice broke as he stood over the old monk. With a strangled prayer, he sank to his knees, took the man's brown robe in his hand, and kissed it. "As you say you love me, Michel, I beg you. Marry us. On my knees, please!"

"I can't, my son."

Dominic raised sad eyes. "Then you leave us no choice." He got up from the floor, leaving the monk on the cot.

"Where are you going?"

"If you won't marry us, I'll find someone else who will."

***

Dominic raced down the night stairs and across the corridor to the side exit off the kitchens. He kept to the shadows, praying Michel would give him enough of a head start before he sounded the alarm and all hell broke loose.

If Michel refused to help, there was only one other person to whom they could turn. Dominic crept across the outer keep toward the stables and quickly saddled one of the horses. He grabbed a sack and a few food items from the kitchen, tying them to the horn above the saddle's pommel.

Where they headed was a day's ride over dry roads, but with the way the weather had turned, it could be longer. He shivered. The wind didn't bode well. Taking three woolen blankets from the horse trunk at the back of the stable, he threw them over the saddle.

He led the horse out of the abbey keep, choosing the path through the woods. Past the tree line, he mounted up, and as he crested the first rise, glanced back to see the windows were still dark in Frère Hermann's room. He issues a whispered thank you to Michel and kicked the horse's flank, disappearing into the darkened forest.

"What are you doing here?" Céleste whispered, eyes wide as Dominic climbed through her window. She swung her legs over the end of her feather bed, hurrying to help him inside. "My father will skin you alive if he catches you."

"We're leaving. Frère Michel knows about you, and Frère Hermann will be here at first light to speak with your father. I

won't see you thrown into a nunnery. We have to go now if we're to have any chance at being together."

Céleste swallowed hard but nodded. "Let me gather my things," she said, turning for her dress trunk.

"*Mon Coeur*, no," he said, reaching for her arm. "Quickly, get dressed. We haven't time for anything else, and the journey is long."

She blinked at him. "One dress? Nothing more? Dominic, how will we live? Where are we to go?"

He pulled her to him and kissed her quickly. "Marseilles. A friend lives in a villa near the coast. He can help me find a commission in the new guard. The Templars."

"The Templar Knights? My father will squash any commission that crossed the lord commander's desk with the name Favreau."

"I can read and write, and I'm good with a sword. The man who trained me fought in the first Crusade."

She sat on the end of her bed, her hands twisting in her lap. "He's a monk, Dominic. Loyal to God, first."

"No. Leandres Garneau is a warrior first. He trained me, my love. He'll help us. I know it."

The full moon rose as they rode, and silver light dappled through the trees like a divine blessing. Dominic galloped, not sparing the horse until their town receded far enough into the void to feel safe. He finally slowed their pace to a soft canter, sliding his arms tighter around Céleste's waist as she slept against his chest.

The hooves monotonous *clip clop* and the warmth of their bodies wrapped in one of the thick blankets lulled him into a lazy haze. He rode holding loose reins, letting the animal have his head for the last half of the night's journey. They'd stop at an inn or make camp anywhere he could find shelter.

Céleste stirred, lifting her head from his chest. Green eyes blinked in the moonlight, finally waking.

"How long before we get to Marseilles?" she asked with a yawn.

"Tomorrow, love. We'll stop soon and rest."

She went back to sleep, and he stretched his neck, trying not to wake her. About an hour later, he spotted a ruined cottage half-hidden in an overgrown clearing. Part of the roof and one side wall were nothing but scorched stone, but the rest seemed sturdy enough to keep out the wind and the threatening rain.

Dominic steered the horse toward the structure, stopping near the rotted front portico. "Céleste. Wake up, *ma fleur*," he said, feathering kisses along her cheek to her ear.

She blinked like she did earlier. "What's this?" she said, as Dominic slid from the saddle first.

"A haven for tonight, love. Tomorrow we'll arrive in Marseille and our life will begin," he said, tying the beast to a broken post.

She slipped from the horse without waiting for him and threw her arms around his neck. "Our life has already begun, and he's kicking in my belly." She held his hand to her stomach and giggled.

Scooping her up in his arms, he carried her into the cottage.

"If I'm capable of running away with my lover, don't you think I'm capable of walking on my own?"

He leaned in and took her mouth, kissing her until she shut up. "It's a husband's prerogative to carry his bride over the threshold."

"But you're not my husband," she whispered with a wicked grin, nipping his lip.

"Yet..." He nodded, letting her down inside the ruined room. His fingers trailed from the flush in her cheeks to the swell of her

breasts peeking from the low scoop of her gown. "Other things are a husband's prerogative, too."

"You don't say," she murmured, slipping a hand behind his head and urging his mouth toward her soft flesh.

***

They got a late start, falling asleep entwined on a horse blanket Dominic tossed on a pile of old hay. The day wore on as they closed in on the last part of the journey.

They ate while they rode, and now the city of Marseille was a hope-filled silhouette in the distance. Anticipation coursed through his veins at being so close.

Leandres Garneau had trained him in the art of war since he was old enough to hold a sword. He had saved Frère Hermann's life during the first Crusade, and the two had been sworn brothers since. Garneau left the order after all he witnessed, and though he was no longer soldier or priest, neither Michel nor Hermann would risk betraying his trust, regardless of how much money Èmile Colbert dangled. It would take a direct order from the bishop or the king.

Last he heard, Garneau was living in a ruin of a villa off the southern port, in a place called Les Fleur de la Vie. He and Céleste would seek him there, first.

The cobbled streets and crowds hawking their wares in the market made passage on horseback almost impossible. Dominic dismounted, but held tight to the reins as he guided them toward the southern port.

It neared sunset as he led their horse through the grimy streets lining the dock, grateful for the salt breeze that wafted the rank air away from their destination.

"Are you sure Garneau lives here?" Céleste asked, raising a gloved finger to her nose.

"Off the port. I haven't been here in a while, *chéri*, so let me think." Dominic squinted toward the hills behind the brigand taverns and inns, nodding absently as the landscape jogged his memory.

With a youthful yell, he swooped onto the saddle behind her. "There! I knew I'd find it." He gave her cheek a fierce kiss, kicking the horse into a gallop.

They trotted through the crumbling back garden walls and the overgrown orchard. Bees buzzed wildly in the rotted fruit fermenting on the ground, and the sweetly sour scent wafted to their noses. The villa's once abundant vines now hung untended and twined in choked knots along the path toward the house.

He halted the horse and dismounted across from the crumbling veranda, holding his arms out for Céleste to do the same.

"Garneau!" he called over his shoulder. "Where are you, you broken-down wreck of a soldier?"

Céleste slapped his shoulder, teasing. "*Ssh*! Don't insult the man before he's agreed to help us."

Garneau moved with a clipped gait through the back portico doors, his face nothing like the picture of pleasant surprise Dominic had expected.

"What's with the sour expression? Not happy to see me, or has something happened to make you even more dour than your usual curmudgeon self?" Dominic went to greet the man, opening his arms for an embrace only to have Garneau hold him at arm's distance.

"Listen to me, boy, because we only have moments. Thank God you remembered the orchard entrance and not the main road.

Condemned

Colbert is here. He arrived about an hour ago and is chomping at the bit for your blood. I told him I hadn't seen hide nor hair of you in two years, but he insisted on waiting until nightfall."

Garneau glanced past Dominic's shoulder to Céleste. "There's nothing either of us can do for your love, my friend. I'm sorry. You don't have the rights of a husband in this matter, not even the rights of a contracted betrothed. She is to go to Mont Majeure this evening and stay there until the child is born. After that—" He lifted one shoulder and let it drop.

"No!" Dominic shook him off. "She's carrying my child, Leandres! I have to stand and fight."

"You'll stand and die, if you don't listen to me. I managed to get a message to an old friend who served with me when we took Jerusalem. He's got a ship bound for the Holy Land. Go with him. I'll send you with papers under a new name. Dominic Favreau will now be Dominic De'Lessep. It was my mother's maiden name. As of today, you are my nephew, a legacy granted immediate entry into the Order of the Templar Knights."

Dominic's mouth dropped. "Have you finally taken one too many blows to that thick skull? No! I am not leaving my unborn child to the base caprices of a man who hates me."

Garneau grabbed Dominic by both shoulders and held him firm. "I will take your child and raise him as my own until your tour is done. When it's safe, you can return and claim him, and if Céleste is still unwed and hasn't been made to take the veil, then you can finally marry." His eyes were severe. "You have no choice, Dominic. If she was legally your intended, we could fight this. Force a marriage. But she's promised to another and has brought disgrace on her family. My only wish is that her father would've showed more compassion in the convent he chose. Mont Majeure is a nightmare with a fiend for an abbess."

"Sounding better and better, Leandres." He frowned, turning to see Céleste's pale face.

"Can't we run? If we left now, went back through the orchard the way we came, we could get on a ship and find a priest or someone to give us their blessing." She ran to Dominic, her eyes wide with fear for the first time. "Please!" She glanced between both men, pleading. "Don't make me go to that awful place!"

"Whore!" Her father's voice bellowed from inside the ruined villa. "Disgrace made flesh! Show yourself!"

Garneau pulled Dominic free of Céleste's clutching fingers. "Go! Remember where you went whenever you shirked your lessons? Dominic, please, before he separates your head from your shoulders!"

"I'm a man, Leandres." Dominic lifted his chin. "If I'm to die, let me do so as God intended. Standing on my own two feet, not cowering like a child."

Leandres eyed the boy, finally tossing him a spare blade. "I hope you remember everything I taught you."

"I do, but it won't come to that."

"Céleste!" her father bellowed again, and heavy footfalls grew loud as her father and his men rounded the edge of the inner courtyard only steps away.

She reached for Dominic, but he'd already moved to guard her flank with Garneau mirroring him on the opposite side. His hand curled around the hilt of his borrowed sword.

"Do not draw first blood, Dominic. Remember what I taught you. Feel out your opponent. Talk to him. Get him off balance. Draw him in but keep your sword hand flexed and ready."

Céleste's eyes slid to Garneau. "My father has no honor. He'll kill Dominic the first chance he gets and if not, he'll hunt him like a beast. I know Dominic will try something rash," she whispered.

"Seigneur, if he survives, make sure he gets on that boat." She nodded, more for herself than anyone else. Her gaze pleaded with the old knight, and her eyes filled with unshed tears. "Swear you'll take our child. On your honor, swear it now!" She gripped his arm, digging her fingers into his solid flesh.

"The boy's ship leaves with the moon's tide. Rest assured, I will make sure he's aboard," he whispered back. "It will be years before he can return but have no doubt he'll move heaven and earth to keep his oath, and I vow to raise your child like my own flesh and blood."

She squeezed his arm again, and then squared her shoulders to face her fate as Colbert and his men rounded the outer courtyard.

"Hello, Father," she said taking a step away from the protection of Garneau's arm, putting herself purposely between Dominic and her father's wrath. "What a disagreeable surprise."

Colbert's lip curled in anger. He snarled, backhanding Céleste with a ham-like fist. A rush of blood dripped from her nose and lip.

Dominic rushed forward, but Garneau held his arm. The old knight silently telling him to wait.

"Slut, your filthy actions and disrespect have disgraced me once too often. I blame your mother for indulging you."

"You leave my mother alone! This was my decision!"

He yanked her arm, causing Céleste to cry out. "Your shrew's tongue is just as quick as hers. Well, she's been made to pay. I had her tongue cut out and nailed to the door of the manor for raising such an ungrateful brat."

With a cry, Céleste jerked her arm free of her father. She ran to Dominic and buried her face in his chest, sobbing.

"Get away from my intended, you cur!" Georges Delacroix pushed his way past Colbert's men and stood in front of them all.

Marianne Morea

"You may have ruined the little bitch, Favreau, but the prize for her pretty cunt is too rich to resist. Even carrying your brat, I'm claiming what's mine. Doesn't it comfort you to know I'll be the one to raise your bastard? Maybe I can teach him to lick my boots."

The men laughed, but Colbert's eyes were cold as they darted to Dominic. Garneau glanced between them and put his arm on Dominic's wrist as the young man reached for his blade.

"He's baiting you, boy. Don't fall for his trap."

Delacroix snorted. "Why would I bait an apprentice monk? Or are you a eunuch now that Colbert has got you by the balls?" He turned nodding with his hands spread. "I'll take Colbert's ruined goods and the extra gold he threw in to sweeten the pot, and then my men can take her one at a time—or two at a time, I don't give a fuck. What good is having a whore for a wife if not to keep your men happy?"

Dominic drew his sword, the blade sweeping down toward Delacroix's turned head. The man ducked just as the razor edge whooshed past his skull. Shock spread across his face as his hand jerked to the side of his head.

"You cunty monk! You took my ear!" he snarled drawing his sword, but Dominic pivoted striking again only to sever his other ear.

Delacroix's fury bubbled over, and he licked his lips, tasting his own blood. Dominic circled the man, watching his steps, but also the nuanced twitches in his arms as he held his sword.

"I'm no monk, Delacroix. I'm trained to be a warrior. Now, do we discuss this like men, or do I continue to take you piece by piece?"

The man screeched, charging with his sword. Dominic sidestepped him, giving Delacroix's ass a swift kick and sending him to the ground.

Condemned

"Emotions will get the better of you every time, Delacroix. Stay calm, and you might stand a chance against me," Dominic taunted.

Colbert moved to draw his sword, but Garneau's fingers curled over his own grip. "Colbert! This is not your quarrel. This is my home and my property, and while you're on my land, this will be a fair fight. I'll slice you from your balls to your throat if you interfere."

"Fine," he snorted. "But if Favreau tries to speak to my slut of a daughter, I'll nail his tongue to my door as well, after I cut off his head and stick it on a pike."

Delacroix got to his feet while the two argued. Eyes narrowed, he circled behind Céleste and grabbed her around the throat from behind. A garbled scream jerked Dominic's attention, and he pivoted on his heel. Delacroix backed with Céleste toward the crumbling stairs.

"Follow me and she dies! It's time I sampled what she's been giving away for free while I was made to wait."

Blood from Delacroix's severed ear dripped over Céleste's shoulder as the man stepped on broken rock and pieces of the façade. Dominic gripped his sword, waiting. He pulled his arm back, cocked and ready.

Delacroix got to the first broken stair, taking his eyes off Dominic for a split. Dominic sprang. Throwing his sword javelin style, he split Delacroix's skull like a sliced melon.

The man's sword clattered to the ground, and he fell backward, nearly taking Céleste with him.

Colbert's mouth dropped before mashing to a thin line.

"Draw your sword and you'll have both of us to contend with, Colbert, and I taught Dominic everything he knows." Leandres Garneau glanced at the pitiless man. "All this over a boy and the

Marianne Morea

girl he loves. This didn't have to end this way. Needless hate and needless blood. It still doesn't, but I don't expect compassion or thought from a man who cuts out his wife's tongue simply for loving her daughter too much."

Céleste scrambled to her feet and wiped a hand across her bloodied face before spitting on the ground at her father's boots. He raised his hand again, but Garneau drew his sword and took a step forward.

"Your lover is a murderer. He slaughtered Georges Delacroix. My men will all swear to it."

"Georges was a pig about to rape me! Don't you even care?" She stood, shoulders squared, staring at her father.

"Whores can't be raped." He sniffed.

Céleste's lip curled. "You should really thank Dominic, Papa. Now you won't have to pay Georges my dowry."

The man shot her a look.

"Let me marry Dominic, please Papa. Georges is dead, and we don't want your money. Neither I nor my child will ever darken your doorstep. Just let me go." Her eyes pleaded with the man, but he was unmoved.

He jerked his head to his men. "Take her. The abbess at Mont Majeure is waiting."

She screamed as they dragged her away, and Garneau had to hold Dominic's arm. "No! You'll only make it worse for her."

"I'll come for you, Céleste! I swear it on our child and to Almighty God. I will come for you! Wait for me!"

Leandres stood with Dominic in the deafening silence. "You have to get on that boat tonight. Èmile Colbert is not one to let things lie." He glanced at the bloody mess on the stairs to the veranda. "I'll call in help from the docks to clean up this mess, but come the tide, you cannot be here."

Condemned

"You'll remember your promise?" Dominic asked, keeping his eyes on the empty space where Céleste was last.

Garneau clapped him on his shoulder. "Yes. Your child will be safe and happy with me until you return."

Dominic's sad, angry gaze found his old mentor. "And if I die?"

Leandres stopped to blink at the boy. "Then, your child will be happy with me for a lifetime. Now, let's go. There are papers to put in order for the new Dominic De'Lessep."

***

The gulls cawed, diving for their food as Dominic swabbed the deck. He'd been at sea for a month and only now gotten his sea legs enough to earn his keep. He wasn't afraid of hard work. In fact, he welcomed the mind-numbing chores aboard the Fleur dis Lis. They kept his mind from wondering about Céleste and their baby. If she lived or died. If she had found peace.

After leaving the port of Marseilles, the ship's route took them east, rounding the Italian peninsula on its way to the open expanse of the Mediterranean Sea. They carried precious metals smelted into bars, iron, wines, oil, and wax, all intended for the port of Akko. In return, the East provided spices, perfumes, and exotic silks for the trip back.

The seas were calm while sheltered by the Italian land mass, and Dominic was fine until they rounded Corsica and the ship hit open water. Then he took to his bunk, green for weeks.

"*Sadiqaa*, drink this. It will calm your belly and let you sleep," a softly accented voice said.

Dominic squeezed tighter into a ball. "Go away. This is punishment for my sins. Let me suffer in peace and pray for death to be swift."

Marianne Morea

"Allah does not punish men with stomach upset. He's far too great a God to think that small. Now, drink. Please."

Dominic lifted his lids to find two of the darkest eyes he'd ever seen staring back at him. They were set in a face the color of the sweetest caramel.

A hot drink steamed from a blue-and-gold ceramic cup painted so ornately it was as dizzying as it was beautiful. The man held the brim close enough for Dominic to smell.

"What is it?" he asked, wrinkling his nose at the spicy scent.

"Ginger and honey. The ginger will quell your upset, and the honey is for soothing your raw throat."

Sniffing again, Dominic took a sip from the cup the kind man held, expecting it to come right back up. Almost immediately, he felt better.

"Thank you." Dominic exhaled, slumping back against his bunk.

The gentle stranger placed the cup on the railed bedside table. "You are most welcome, *Sadiqaa*." He stepped back, touching his hand to his chest and then his forehead in a strange bow.

Intrigued, Dominic moved to sit up, amazed he didn't have to dive for the chamber pot. "*Sadiqaa*. Is that Arabic?"

The man inclined his head. "It literally translates to, 'my friend.' I did not know your name, and as you weren't getting better on your own, it was time for me to help."

"Thank you again—" Dominic paused, giving him a weak smile. "I don't know your name, either."

The man grinned, showing two gold teeth. "I am Salim Saar. I am on my way home from trade negotiations in Genoa. And you are?"

"Dominic... Dominic De'Lessep." He'd hesitated, remembering Leandres had changed his Favreau surname on his papers. "I'm to take my post in Akko."

The man angled his head, studying Dominic's face. "I see. You are a Templar Knight, then?"

Dominic dipped his head, not sure if he should have admitted as much.

Salim moved to the brazier for a curved metal teapot and topped off the ceramic cup on the narrow table. "You are rather young for such an august post, no?" He turned, cocking his head once more. "By my guess, you can't have seen more than twenty or so summers."

Dominic didn't reply, and the man sighed, resignedly. "May Allah grant you wisdom beyond your years, so you see the ones you war against as men and pray for peace."

The man left, issuing another strange bow, and Dominic sipped the tincture he made, wondering about the kind stranger.

Weeks flew, and Dominic's new friend taught him phrases and meanings in his mother tongue. *Alsalam ealaykum*, peace be upon you, and *'in sha'allah*, God willing.

Salim was foreign to him in every way, from his speech, to the flowing garments he wore, to the manner in which he prayed every day. Yet this unlikely friend slowly became a comfort. Especially in his wise words and gentle nature.

He found him one evening on deck, sitting cross-legged with a candle burning at the center of a circle of strange cards. They were fanned around the squat wax pillar, each with a colorful picture unlike any playing card he'd seen.

"Card game?" he asked, coming to his friend's side.

Hunched, Salim stared at the smoke as it rose, the flame protected from the wind by stacks of barrels along the ship's rails.

The man held one finger to his lips. He mumbled something and then sat back, glancing up from where he sat. "Capnomancy," he replied as if the word's meaning was obvious.

"Capnomancy. Is that the name of the card game?"

Salim patted the deck beside him and then leaned in to gather the cards into a pile. "No. In all your studies have you never heard of *Ilm al-Falak*? The study of the heavens? Or what some of your ilk call sorcery."

Dominic angled his head and then scooted back. His eyes darted from the candle to the cards and then to his friend, aghast. "Witchcraft?" he whispered.

Salim laughed. "You Christians find the devil in everything you don't understand." He beckoned him closer again. "Capnomancy is the art of divining God's will be revealed in the smoke. The cards simply help us understand the messages. Some are warnings. Other times they speak of blessings bestowed."

Curious, Dominic inched closer.

"*Almaerifat al'iihia*," he said. "In my mother tongue, it means divine knowing. For many years, the Saracens conscripted a certain group of Turkish slaves into their armies. They were the *Maluk*. Independent, warrior-like, with a gift for healing and divination."

"Are you telling me you were once a Saracen slave?" He gawked at the man, stunned.

"I was lucky." Salim gestured to the cards in his hand. "I saw opportunity in the smoke and used my skills to manifest my destiny."

"But it's a sin," Dominic hissed, glancing to see if anyone heard.

"Only in your world, infidel. In mine?" He shrugged. "It's *haram*...unlawful, but not a sin." Salim flashed a gold-toothed

smirk, gesturing to the cards. "Would you like to see what the cards hold in store?"

Dominic licked his lips, fascinated. He nodded, but quickly glanced over his shoulder again. He watched, rapt, as the man shuffled the cards and spread them in another circle around the candle, except this time they were facedown.

"Pick five cards and turn them over, facing me," he said.

Dominic did as instructed, watching Salim with each card thrown. The man's gaze narrowed, his lips pulled down in a frown, and by the time he drew the last card, Salim's face had paled.

"What do you see?" Apprehension bloomed in Dominic's chest as his friend studied both the cards smoke.

Finally, Salim turned his gaze to him. His eyes were haunted, and doubt edged their dark depths.

"For God's sake! What did you see?"

The man hesitated. "Perhaps this wasn't a good idea. You're a Christian and don't believe in omens and prophecy."

Dominic felt the blood run from his face. "Tell me."

"In all my years, no one has pulled these five cards at once. There's always an element of warning or some harbinger of bad luck, but not like this." He shook his head, resting a finger over his lips. "Betrayal is coming. Betrayal and sadness."

Snorting, Dominic relaxed a bit. "You sure these cards tell the future? I've already suffered a lifetime of both."

"The Devil." He tapped the center card. "This is the greatest warning card in the deck. It means negativity and ensnarement, but when paired with the Death card and the Tower—" He tapped again. "Something is coming. A transformation."

Dominic sat back with a smirk and shrugged. "Transformation." He nodded. "Good. I welcome a change. Maybe

Marianne Morea

I'll make my fortune and manifest my destiny like you and go home to claim my love and our child."

He clapped the old Saracen on the shoulder and moved to get up, but Salim clutched his arm, his eyes pleading.

"This in no omen of good tidings, *Sadiqaa*. Something dark is coming. It lurks, waiting, and once it has you, it will never let you go." He tightened his grip. "Trust your faith and remember my words."

"What's going on here, De'Lessep?" Jaquan Fouquet's footsteps stopped in front of Dominic's ring of cards. The Templar Marshal's eyes scanned the setup, and he scowled. "Knights Templar is a holy order, De'Lessep, and you are under my command. Leandres Garneau vouched for you when you were given your commission. I doubt he would have done so if he knew you dabbled in the dark arts."

Salim let go of Dominic's arm and gathered his cards. "The knight was only observing, sir."

With a guttural dismissal, Fouquet turned on his heel and strode away, clipping Salim's shoulder in the process. Dominic squatted beside his friend to help gather his things.

Salim looked across his shoulder. "Betrayal is coming." He glanced in Fouquet's direction before turning back to Dominic. "Coming from one of your own. Too many crave the power of coin and glory it can buy. Be vigilant."

***

Jerusalem
Temple Mount
Summer 1119

"Who asked your opinion, knave? Tend to my horse and don't question my orders!"

Dominic lifted his gaze from scanning the map the Grand Master gave him in their strategy meeting. Jaquan Fouquet stormed past, shooting him a dirty look before disappearing into his tent.

It had been three months since the Fleur de Lis made port at Akko, and Fouquet was on the poor boy every day since. Dominic bobbed his head to the terrified page, offering him a sympathetic smile, but, too terrified of the Templar Marshal, the boy glanced away, afraid to even acknowledge the gesture.

"De'Lessep!" the Grand Master's field page called, beckoning him from the tactical tent.

He folded the map and got to his feet, walking at a fast clip to find out what troubled the man. Lifting the tent flap, his gaze met four sets of questioning eyes. The Grand Master signaled him to the table.

Fouquet stormed in after him, not waiting to be called. He marched to the table and leaned two hands on the side of the large-scale map.

The Grand Master gestured to Dominic, and the knight cleared his throat. "Saladin is a master at hit-and-run. His cavalry is swift, and his horsemen skilled with their bows. I've studied the maps and believe the best way for us to engage would be to ambush his forces before he can stake a foothold and employ his fire catapults."

Dominic pointed to a set of jagged mountains outside the city. "The foothills are our best bet. Akko is protected on one side by water. Our forces have a stronghold to the north, but we're vulnerable in the south." He tapped the southern portion of the map just slightly north of Jerusalem. "Saladin wants the Holy City.

Marianne Morea

It's his sole objective. My guess is, he'll use the desert and then cut through a passage here."

Fouquet snorted. "Your guess? What, have you been practicing the divination your Saracen friend taught you on the voyage over?"

"Unlike most of our army, I'm educated. I can read and can work the sums. I've scoured the reports on Saladin's methods and done the calculations on the strain this siege would put on our supplies. He's cut off the supply lines north of us, and any provisions that try to get through from the south are raided. We have limited food and water as it is. A strategic ambush is the only way this standoff will work. Otherwise, we risk losing our troops to famine instead of the blade."

The Grand Master sat back in his chair, glancing between the two. "Do you have an alternative suggestion, Fouquet?"

The man turned to their commander but didn't reply. He simply stormed out.

"Don't take Fouquet's gruffness as a personal affront, De'Lessep. He's not used to peasants who are more educated and have better sense than his own blue blood. He may be a noble, but he doesn't have half the knowledge you've accrued in the short time you've been here, and the fact you can speak the language a bit has been invaluable." The Grand Master nodded. "Fouquet will get over it."

"And if he doesn't?" Dominic asked.

The man didn't respond. "Tell the quartermaster what you need and then get the men ready. We march at dawn."

Dominic turned for the tent flap but then glanced back. "Are you leading the siege?"

Condemned

The man considered him. "I haven't decided yet. Perhaps it would be best to let you and Fouquet handle this together. My orders are as stands. We use the mountains."

***

The sun was at its zenith. Sand rippled in serpentine waves along the heavy dunes as the air shimmered, hovering over the sweltering landscape. Dominic rode ahead of their front line, scanning the horizon.

Dressed in loose robes and a traditional headdress, he drew the nomad-style scarf across his face. His clothes were a gift from Salim before they'd parted at the dock. Of course, Fouquet scoffed. Still, in this heat, their armor was tantamount to wearing a body-shaped oven, and he needed the freedom of movement to scout ahead of the others if necessary.

"We take the desert. I'm ranking officer, and we cross the sand. You may have the Grand Master beguiled with your words and sums, but experience shows it better to cut the head off a snake before it has a chance to strike. We'll meet Saladin head-on and crush him before his men can vanish into the crags." Fouquet eyed Dominic, his intense gaze almost daring him to argue.

"If we use the mountains, Saladin won't have time to find those crags. We have our orders. Moreover, we don't have enough water to support a change in plan." Dominic stared at the man, unbelieving. Could he really be stupid enough to risk the heat and the distance with so few provisions?

The Templar Marshal's eyes narrowed. "Are you refusing orders, De'Lessep?"

"Your orders are a death sentence. Saladin's forces know the open sands. They're prepared for the heat, the blistering sun with

Marianne Morea

no relief. They move like the wind in the open. Their horses aren't encumbered, and neither are their men."

A grin spread across Fouquet's face. "Sentries!"

Two sergeants-at-arms rode forward. Fouquet lifted a hand toward Dominic. "Arrest this man for desertion."

Even more perplexed, they blinked, exchanging a confused glance.

"But, sir, De'Lessep is right beside you. He hasn't deserted." The man earned a backhand, nearly knocking him off his horse.

Fouquet took Dominic's reins and gave the horse a shove. "Take him and tie him to the nearest scrub, or do you wish to join him for not following orders as well?"

The men exchanged two more glances, sparing one for Dominic.

"There's no reason for this, Fouquet. Mark my words. You hunt Saladin out in the open and you will not survive the sands," Dominic tried once more before sliding from his horse.

"Lie low. We'll come back for you when it's done," one sergeant whispered.

Dominic pulled his saddlebag from his horse, daring Fouquet to argue. Regardless of what Fouquet thought, he was a knight. His tunic and sword went where he went.

He turned on his heel and strode toward the sparse scrub at the foot of a small set of dunes.

Fouquet watched, giving orders for his men to march. He stood still as they fell into formation, riding toward the wider expanse.

De'Lessep was fifty yards away, and Fouquet squinted before kicking his horse to follow. He rode up beside Dominic, unable to resist one last dig.

Condemned

"You may be dressed like a Saracen, but they'll slaughter you on sight, you stupid boy. Still, after I scatter your remains, I can go back to Marseilles and tell Èmile Colbert you are food for the buzzards."

Dominic wheeled around, and Fouquet laughed.

"Did you really think no one would know you, Favreau?" He snorted. "Leandres Garneau's reach isn't as long as he thinks." He laughed again, rearing his horse. "Not compared to Colbert's money."

Fouquet pointed his horse toward their legion, but then wheeled the reins, charging. He drew a short blade and threw it, aiming for Dominic's chest.

Dominic twisted to deflect the shot, but the blade hit home below his shoulder, above his heart. His hand shot to the hilt, and he staggered forward before falling to his knees.

"Have fun dying. I hear jackals eat you alive if they smell fresh blood."

Dominic watched the man ride off before pulling the blade from his shoulder, the man's laughter fading with the sound of his horse's hooves.

Salim's words rang in his head. Betrayal at the hand of one of your own. He squinted toward the scrub, wondering if this was where he'd meet the darkness that waited and wouldn't let go.

***

Night fell, and so did the blistering temperatures. Hours after Fouquet left him for dead, Dominic's eyesight dimmed. The wound bled and bled, making him think the blade had been poisoned.

Warmth eluded him, despite heat from the day radiating from the sand beneath him. The full moon rose and hung sentinel-like in

the dark sky. All day, he'd kept vigil. Watching for any sign of the Templar legion. Not a sign of life emerged from the horizon except vultures circling in the distance.

If Saladin was victorious, at least the men would have a decent burial and not be left for carrion. In that respect, the Saracens showed more respect to nonbelievers than their Christian counterparts.

He sniffed, shivering. Fever parched his skin and his throat. And the wound festered. Colbert had gotten his wish. He would die where he lay and never see Céleste or his child.

Reaching for his saddlebag, he winced, but still dug for his tunic. Slipping the thick linen over his head, he hunched for extra warmth. He would die as he lived. A Templar Knight. Unafraid. Even so, he chuckled at the specter his bones would make. A dead man boded ill, but one dressed in nomad's robes cloaked with the mark of the fiercest warriors in all Christendom?

Sleep beckoned, despite his chattering teeth and papery flesh. Weakness invaded every muscle. Fingers clutched the hilt of his sword, even as he rested on his empty saddlebag. He needed to stay alert.

The bladder of water given him by the quartermaster was nearly gone. He'd have to sell his soul to the devil for more. As the thought crossed, he squinted at the dark horizon.

Fever and the moonlight played tricks on his eyes, and he leaned up, concentrating on the shadows crossing the sands. They were no shadows. It was a caravan.

Hope infused his fever-ravaged body, and he struggled to his knees, taking ragged breaths.

Camels bobbed with an ungainly telltale stride, closing the distance. He tried to call out, but barely croaked. Mustering every

ounce of strength, he lifted his arm, letting a painful shriek rip from his throat.

Dizziness took him, and he fell forward. His last conscious thought was of the sand in his mouth.

***

Consciousness dragged, thick and jumbled. Dreams hazed behind his lids, but he couldn't wake. Voices muffled in and out as he fought the murk trapping his mind, only to have the fog pull him deeper.

Images formed in the thick haze, fragmented and frightening, making his psyche rebel. Wherever he was, he wasn't alone. That much he knew, even from his obscured senses. Nothing about the voices was familiar.

Pain, worse than Fouquet's blade, flooded his body and his fogged brain. Flesh revolted as every nerve burned with agony only to quiver afterward with pleasure as intense as a skilled whore's mouth.

His lids fluttered open. Dark, haunting eyes hovered close in his fevered haze. "Help me," he rasped, lifting his hand only to watch his skin curl to nothing but bones and sinew.

Gritting his teeth, he squeezed his eyes shut. His mind rebelled. None of this was real. These were nothing more than visions from a fevered brain. No other explanation fit. The scent of fresh blood filled his nose, and he gagged.

"You're suffering now, but soon you'll wake to mouthwatering bliss," a feminine voice whispered, nipping his ear. Punishing fingers gripped his member. He groaned half in pleasure, half in pain. "Do you like to play in the dark, Templar?"

A cruel laugh punched through his haze, but he gasped at the feel of delicate hands sliding over his hard length. He groaned again, unable to stop his body from its own wicked will.

Laughter echoed through his consciousness, as razor pain pierced his cock, jolting his lower belly. His eyes flew open, and through the blur he saw a long ebony cascade spread across his thighs while a woman worked his member, her mouth smeared in blood.

Fear gripped his throat. The woman lifted her head from between his legs and dark, haunting eyes found his as he sank into blackness.

***

"Thirsty." His eyes opened, and he grimaced at the sharp taste in his mouth, like the scent of hot iron from a blacksmith's forge.

Wetness, sweet and fresh registered on his parched tongue, and his hand shot up, gripping the slender wrist holding a dripping cloth above his lips.

"Allah be praised. You live."

Dominic jerked his head toward a voice on the opposite side of the bedroll where an older woman lifted her hands in thanks. Her eyes weren't frightened like the servant girl tending him. She was calculating and very pleased.

He released the poor girl's wrist, self-reproach scorching his feverish cheeks. *"Aghfir li,"* he rasped.

His apology was barely audible, but the woman's face softened, and she nodded, sparing him a shy smile.

"You speak our tongue," the other woman commented, impressed. "Though, there's no need for forgiveness. The mistress has taken a personal interest in your survival." She sniffed. "Consider yourself lucky."

Condemned

The older woman's clothing was vibrant azure against her smooth, coffee-colored skin. Long, thin braids adorned with intricate beads flowed from her uncovered head, and from her manner it wasn't hard to see she was their mistress's right hand.

"Luck hasn't been my lot in this life," he replied, as the shy woman lifted a cup filled with the same sweet mixture from the rag.

"Perhaps you'll be gifted a new life. The desert holds many secrets, and the realm of man is not always privy to them. Perhaps you'll be one of the fortunate." Her eyes glinted, and from where Dominic lay, he knew there was something behind her meaning he missed.

Dismissing the gut feeling, he drank deep gulps from the cup, finally stopping for breath. "What is this drink?" he asked, feeling his weakness and malaise ebb.

"Honeyed wine, with a special ingredient to help your transition," the older woman answered, not giving the shy girl a chance.

"You mean healing?"

She didn't answer. Instead, she snapped her fingers, and the servant filled his cup again before turning to leave. The shy girl gave them both a small bow before scurrying through the tent to an adjoining chamber.

"Where am I?" he asked, struggling to sit up. "Who is your mistress? I'd like to give her my thanks for taking me into her care."

"Where we are, is of no consequence. The sands shift, and we move with them. As to my mistress—" A slow smile took her mouth, her eyes glinting as before. "You'll find out soon enough. She has a penchant for men such as you."

Marianne Morea

His eyes followed her gaze to his tunic and sword. Both had been cleaned, and his blade and enameled hilt polished until it shone.

"Too bad you don't have your armor. The mistress prefers warriors who don't fear spilling blood." She smirked, but then turned toward the tent flap as four other women entered carrying steaming bowls.

"Wash and dress him well. The mistress expects to receive the Templar when she rises." She turned on her heel to leave.

"Wait!" Dominic called after her.

She stopped and glanced back with a raised brow as the women set up their work.

"What is your mistress's name?"

The servants froze in their preparations, but their matron's face took on an almost reverent air. "The mistress is called Sahira."

***

Dominic sank lower in the canvas tub, letting the hot, fragrant water soak into his muscles. The maids had left clean clothing for him on his cot after they prepared his bath. His skin glowed with oils they'd massaged into his aching body.

Much to his surprise, his wound had closed. The scar was reddened and swollen, but not the gaping fester he envisioned. Obviously, this harem had healing talents unequaled anywhere.

He dressed quickly. The servants left the guest tent with a giggle, and furtive eyes glanced back as he followed them to an intricate runner linking two tents across the sand.

The carpeted path led to a large tent aglow with torches. Music played, soft and inviting, as he walked toward the wide canvas entry.

Condemned

Inside was another world. He had no idea where they were in this barren expanse or how far he'd traveled with this harem of women, but right now his mouth watered with a hunger he hadn't felt since before he left for Marseilles with Céleste.

The lavish interior dripped with decadence. Swaths of jewel-colored silk draped the tent walls, with soft, squat pillows set around low tables laden with exotic food and drink.

Women gathered in small clusters, some with their faces veiled, others not. They stood or lounged on small couches, but all conversation came to an end as he entered the dwelling.

"Welcome." The matron smiled, gesturing him toward a low chaise at the head of the room. "We've been expecting you."

He greeted her with a nod. "Thank you—" he hesitated, with a small chuckle. "I'm sorry. I don't remember your name."

She inclined her head. "I am Fatima. The mistress's *gouvernante*," she said in stilted French, appearing pleased at the surprise on his face. "I manage the mistress's harem."

Dominic took a seat on a long chaise, and a servant brought him a cup of wine. "I didn't know women could have a harem. I was led to believe a harem was the domain of man's pleasure."

Fatima arched a brow. "A harem, by definition, is a sacred inviolable place for women. Protected. Inaccessible to men." She spread her hand toward him. "Except by invitation."

She turned for a jeweled carafe to refill his glass. "Like most things in this world, men have corrupted the sanctity of the harem, making it a playground for their personal vice." She straightened, licking a drop of wine from her thumb. "Women have appetites, Sir Knight, even if men refuse to acknowledge so."

Fatima inclined her head before moving toward the others, and he took in the entirety of it all. A caravan of women nomads, living and thriving in the heart of a hostile desert. The notion was

almost unthinkable, but the proof was irrefutable before his eyes. He drained his cup, and a servant was at the ready to replenish his wine before he even thought to ask.

The vintage was sweet and heady, different from the earlier brew, yet like the other, it infused his body with strength instead of drunken fuzz. He ate, savoring the music and the harem dancers as much as the food.

The melody stopped abruptly, and the women bowed their heads, keeping their eyes lowered. Fatima did the same, so he rose from his seat, not knowing what to expect.

He kept his eyes on the entrance, and a hush fell as his host and rescuer stepped through the canvas threshold. The woman held herself like a desert queen.

Exotically beautiful, with ebony hair that hung in a silken mass to her waist, she scanned the room before her gaze found him. His eyes widened. Sahira's almond eyes were as black as the night sky and just as intense. The same eyes he saw in his fevered dreams.

Sheathed in sheer golden silk, every inch of the woman's body was a feast veiled in translucent mystery. Dominic's gaze climbed from her ringed toes over her long limbs to ample hips and the dark patch between her legs, to her full, rounded breasts and puckered nipples.

Sahira approached, and for a moment he wasn't sure if he should bow or kiss her hand or what the proper protocol was when greeting a nomadic queen. His eyes met hers, and he lifted a hand to his heart and inclined his head.

"Your gratitude is appreciated, Templar. Please, sit." She gestured to the long chaise. "You are my guest, and I wish to know you better."

She settled herself on the tufted end of the same lounge, tucking one leg under as she angled her body to face him. Reclining on one elbow, the relaxed position arched her breasts even higher beneath her sheer costume.

She signaled the musicians, music filled the tent once more, and the harem dancers took center floor.

"So, you are well?" she asked, as her delicate fingers toyed absently with the edge of the translucent fabric.

"Surprisingly so," he replied, trying to keep his eyes on her face. "I don't know what your healers did, but I'm better now than I was before I left France."

Plucking an apricot from the table, she brought the small, succulent fruit to her lips and let a knowing smile spread across its smooth skin. She didn't bite the plump fruit. Instead, she peeled the skin in narrow strips with her teeth.

Sahira's dark almond eyes mesmerized him, and when she licked the side of the peeled apricot, trapping its juice with the tip of her tongue, he nearly gasped.

The wine had finally taken effect. His head clouded, and his limbs felt heavy, but his vision was clear, and all he saw was Sahira.

"I was afraid you might not have the strength to survive the night, but now I see I chose well. You're strong and worthy," she breathed. "A warrior with a noble soul." She cocked her head, considering him. "Yes, a rarity among your kind. So appealing with your virtue and decency."

Somewhere at the back of his mind, Salim's words appealed for him to remember his faith…to guard himself. He never saw his shipboard friend again, and now he dismissed the man's portent.

Sahira's lips smirked on one side, and her eyes danced with amusement as if she heard his thoughts. Getting up from her seat,

she waved her hand once and cleared the floor. Without a word, she walked toward the center of the tent and turned.

A sultry rhythm began, and Sahira's hips twisted in a slow, seductive spiral. She coiled her arms over her head, letting the erotic music take her. Dominic's eyes followed every move as her curves teased the eyes to the hypnotic beat. He rose to his feet as the tempo swelled. Pulsing faster, the woman's body would arouse the devil himself as her belly undulated with the beat.

Sahira's arms beckoned for him. He licked his lips but didn't join her. She danced closer. So close, she wound her arms around his neck.

Losing all sense, he pulled her against him, crushing his mouth to hers. Her lips slid into a slow grin against his when he finally broke their kiss.

"Come," she said, as he stepped back dazed. "I want to taste you, Templar. I want to show you the pleasures of my world." The main tent fell silent as she led him back through the threshold.

Fatima waited on the opposite side of their camp, outside another large tent. Sahira's quarters. Where no one dared enter without leave.

The matron bowed her head. "Everything is in readiness, milady."

Sahira barely acknowledged the woman. She moved through the tent flap and then turned, unfastening the shoulder clip to her costume so the diaphanous silk floated to her waist, baring full breasts.

Cupping the heavy flesh in both hands, she walked backward to a large feather bed strewn with pillows and silks.

"Suckle me, Templar," she said arching her back. "I want your mouth on me until it's time for mine to take you to places you've never been."

Dominic's lips parted. Templars were supposed to be celibate, but only the most devout sacrificed to that degree. As it was, Céleste's memory had kept him too long without a woman. Months of denial took its toll, and his cock thickened at the overt sensual display.

Glad for the loose linen pants and matching tunic that hid the bulge at his crotch, he stared at the beautiful woman who'd saved his life and haunted his dreams. His nightmares were just that. Dreams brought on by fever. He had nothing to fear from this woman except perhaps sore balls from want of her.

Sahira unclipped the jeweled belt at her waist, tossing it to the floor along with the short blade and holster attached. She stood tall, letting his eyes drink in every curve as sheer scarves puddled at her feet.

Dominic yanked his tunic over his head, not caring if the tent flap was open or closed. Bare-chested, he knelt at her feet and buried his face between her legs. The silver cross at his neck swung forward, and she hissed as the metal grazed her inner thigh. She yanked the crucifix from his throat and flung it across the room.

He blinked, staring at the angry imprint seared into her palm. With a snarl, Sahira fisted his hair and ground her wet sex into his mouth. All questions left his mind at the intoxicating taste of her slick folds. His cock jerked at her heady flavor, and he loosened the drawstring on his pants as he savored her sweet slit. Wrapping a hand around his shaft, he rolled his palm over his head, his tongue delving deep into her dark wetness.

With a low growl, she shoved him from her. "There," she ordered pointing to the bed.

In a daze, Dominic stepped the rest of the way out of his pants. Sahira licked her lips, following the length of his body, from his

dark eyes and scruff-chiseled jaw, to his sword-hardened shoulders and rippled planes of his flat stomach. Her eyes slipped lower, stopping at his thick, corded member.

She climbed onto the bed, her movements predatory and determined. Crawling toward him, she cupped his balls in one hand and his shaft in the other. Lowering her head, she licked the vein-ridged underside of his cock, circling his engorged head with the tip of her tongue.

Taking him deep, she let her teeth graze his hard length, drawing blood. He hissed, but Sahira moaned, sucking him deeper. She licked his cock clean, releasing him with an audible pop.

"You taste like salt and the sun," she purred with a knowing smile.

Dominic blinked. The woman's teeth were red with blood, and two sharp canines jutted from her gums. He scrambled back from her, jumping from the bed. This was no coincidence. This was his nightmare come true.

Sahira laughed at him. "Do you really think you can run from me?" She angled her head, a mock question in her eyes. "Where would you go, Templar? No one here will help you, Dominic De'Lessep. They all belong to me, as do you."

"What are you?" He recoiled as anger and fear spiraled in his breast. She'd never asked his name, and he hadn't told her.

"I am power, my brave knight. Goddess and whore. Salvation and ruin. I am life and death. All things men desire, but also fear—and I choose you."

"Choose me? For what?"

"I've decided you will be my newest plaything. You're mine, until I decide otherwise. My blood healed you, so now you belong to me." She blurred with unnatural speed, knocking him to the

bed. With strength untold, she locked his hands over his head, her legs pinning him to the mattress.

"Let's play a little game, shall we? Let's see how long your honor lasts once you taste me as I've tasted you." Biting her bottom lip, she drew blood, letting it coat her tongue as she kissed his mouth.

Light-headed, he groaned at the forbidden coppery tang. Instead of revulsion, his mind spun with the flavor and his blood raced. His body betrayed him as if he had no control.

His cock swelled to near painful as she teased his swollen head, pressing it to her tight slit. He gasped, ripping his mouth from hers. Sahira grinned, impaling her sex on his rigid length.

"Don't fight me, Templar. I own you," she said, rolling her hips as he bucked higher. "Your body, your mind—"

His cock-head swelled, and his balls tightened, a gasp ripping from his lungs as his climax crashed.

Sahira reared up, nostrils flaring. Dominic's body went rigid as if held by an unyielding force. "Even your beautiful soul. Mine!" With a snarl, Sahira plunged her fangs into his throat.

A cry strangled choked in his throat as she took long pulls from his veins. Sahira's beautiful face had distorted beyond recognition. A graven image in the flesh of a demon from hell.

His mind rebelled at the horrid sight, even as his body hardened again, still inside her. One word rang through his ravaged mind. Succubus.

She lifted her hips, releasing his throat as she plunged her sex onto him again. Her nails scored his chest and arms as she milked his cock. Crimson rivulets dripped from Dominic's throat to silk sheets already wet with his blood. She moaned, leaning down to lick the trickle before plunging her teeth again, drawing deep gulps.

Marianne Morea

His heartbeat skittered, until it slowed, sluggish and weak. His hands fell to his sides, and his body went slack beneath her. The hold she had on him dissolved, and his heavy body seemed light, almost floaty.

Sahira pulled her fangs from his throat. His lids fluttered, and his eyes rolled back. "No!" she snarled, still straddling his hips. "I did not save you just for you to die now!"

Gripping his shoulders, she shook him so violently his head snapped back and forth, his teeth rattling.

"No!" Eyes blazing, she yelled for Fatima before grabbing hold of Dominic's face. Squeezing his cheeks, she forced his lips open. "You will not die!"

Fangs tore at her own wrist. She held the wound to his open lips and fisted her hand, forcing the blood to pool from the gash, filling his mouth. "Drink! Damn you!"

Dominic's mind reeled, despite his body's pallid stillness. Sahira's thick blood trickled down his throat, scoring his gullet. He cried silent screams, sickened by the surreal reality, yet he craved more.

His eyes flew open, and his hand shot up, grabbing Sahira's forearm. His mouth fastened on her wrist. He gulped the hot red poison, choking down thick mouthfuls.

Sahira gritted her teeth, her fangs cutting into her bottom lip. "Fatima!" she called again, slipping her wrist from his mouth as he slumped back.

Cradling her arm, she climbed from Dominic's lap. Lifting her wrist to her mouth, she sealed the wound with a swipe of her tongue.

The matron came through the tent's entrance, breathless. She stood at Sahira's side, staring at the bloody mess but didn't dare question.

Condemned

***

Dominic's face contorted. His breathing shallow. Icy-hot spikes scorched his belly, spreading to his chest. Panting, he cried out as flames licked at his innards before fanning the inferno to his arms and legs.

"What have you done to me?" His body writhed, curling into a tight ball.

"Your human body is dying, Templar," Fatima answered, bringing cool water and a cloth to the table beside the bed.

Pain scored every nerve, and his back arched in agony. "Why did you save me just to kill me now?" The question ground out through clenched teeth.

Sahira moved so quickly her image blurred to his side, and he flinched when she lifted a hand to his cheek. "I haven't killed you, Dominic. I've given you new life. Once your fragile human flame is finally extinguished, you will wake to a world you never dreamed existed."

"Dreamed? This is a nightmare, and you are a demon from hell!"

She laughed. "Such a temper. We will have such fun together you and me. The world will be at your fingertips, and you will be at my feet."

He sucked a jagged breath through his clenched teeth at the cold burn razing his body. "At your feet? I am no one's slave, Sahira."

Fatima gasped at his use of the mistress's name, but Sahira raised a quieting hand.

"I've given you the gift of knowing, Dominic. I've opened minds to you to do with as you wish. No thought, no rush of

emotion will be hidden from you. A simple probe, and you will know everything you need to lord over enemies and prey alike.

"Did you think I found you by accident? Or that saving you was a whim or a random act of kindness?" She laughed. "We found your legion in the desert. Dead. Not from the heat of battle, but from the heat of the day. They died from exposure where they fell. All but one. The Saracens didn't unsheathe a single sword. Feckless command did the work for them, leading your men into the teeth of the desert sun.

"The one that survived—" She snorted. "He soon learned the true meaning of fear, but not before I probed his arrogant mind." She tapped the side of her head. "Imagine my delight when I found you in his thoughts. Strong, handsome, with a soul so delicious it made my mouth water. I made up my mind then and there to have you."

"No!" he cried out, despite the pain.

She lifted the wet cloth from the basin and wiped the blood from his face. "You have no choice, Dominic. I am your maker. You are bound to me. Eventually, you will learn to accept. You may even learn to love me," she said, sparing a glinting smile for Fatima.

She slipped a hand behind the older woman's head, and as if ordered, Fatima bared her throat and Sahira slipped the tips of her fangs into the throbbing vein beneath her jaw.

Licking her lips, she sealed the small wound and then pressed a kiss to the woman's temple. Releasing her, she turned to Dominic with a red grin. "Of course, Fatima will be yours for the taking as well. Any way you like."

"I'd rather face the hell that awaits me than live like a demon here on earth! I am bound to no one, Sahira, let alone your black

soul. My heart belongs to one woman, and now you've made me unfit for her." He spat, letting the weak spray hit Sahira in the face.

"Unfit?" She wiped the same bloodstained cloth across her mouth and cheek, licking her lips in mock delight.

She lifted a hand and fisted his hair, yanking it mercilessly. Closing her eyes, Dominic felt her in his mind. He twisted his head to shrug her off, but she was too strong. Sahira forced images forth, reading them from his mind like so many pages in a book.

Throwing her hand off, she scoffed, tossing the wet rag to the basin as if what she saw in his mind was just as worthless. "Your love is a worthless human. I've made you a prince, and you will rule the desert at my side."

Dominic gritted his teeth and rose from the bloody bed. Preternatural speed already taking root, he grabbed for Sahira's dagger still on the floor and whirled with it, aiming for her heart. Fatima screamed, and Sahira blurred from his reach. She laughed at the attempt, but Dominic pivoted again, his battle skills sharpened by his newfound strength. The curved blade sliced Sahira's face from her brow to her lip, the wound crossing her cheek in a bloody crescent.

Laughing at his pitiful attempt, she scraped her finger across her cheek and licked the blood clean. "You were already a predator, Dominic. You killed in the name of God. Now you'll kill in my name, for pleasure."

He opened his mouth to argue, but worse agony ripped through his body. He crumpled to the floor, muscles convulsing beneath his skin. Blood dripped from his nose and ears, and his sight dimmed.

"Never raise your hand against me, Dominic. I am your maker, and you will suffer every strike. I own you now. Blood will be your life, as I am your life. If you choose to leave, I will destroy

everything and everyone you love. Without pity and with such pain and fear as you could never imagine." She stepped over him and took a gold embroidered robe from Fatima's hand. "Sleep. Your new life begins when you next rise with the moon."

Shadows clouded his brain, and he watched Céleste's face melt into nothing as he succumbed to blessed blackness.

***

Dominic woke as the sun set, his eyes darting to every corner of the tent. Fatima slept in a chair beside the bed, Sahira's trace in her blood making his mouth water.

His eyes burned, but not with pain. He saw and sensed everything, and the onslaught was overwhelming. He dragged in a breath and cocked his head, listening as beetles scratched deep in the sand beneath the tent. Desert mice scurried for shelter out in the expanse, and he sniffed, knowing a lizard hunted close behind.

Voices talked at once in a cacophony of sound. He recoiled, squeezing his eyes closed before realizing it was a deluge of thought from the camp women as Sahira had predicted. Newfound instinct helped him filter the onslaught to a soft hum as he listened for Sahira's thoughts alone.

"You won't hear the mistress, Templar. Her mind is closed to you and every one of your kind," Fatima said with a yawn.

Her breath and the rush of blood through the relaxed beat of her pulse made his mouth water even more. Fangs slid from his gums, and he winced at the alien feel and corresponding pain, but nearly groaned at the taste of his own blood in the process.

"God help me." He dropped his head to his hands, grateful his fangs retracted almost as quickly as they appeared.

"God cannot help you now, boy. Only Sahira can do that. You have much to learn of your new existence," the matron murmured.

Condemned

Dominic lifted his head, his gaze flicking to hers as she sat in her chair. "Why can't I hear her? I can hear you and everyone else in this camp."

"Her witch blood. It's both blessing and curse. Now that you've fed from her, it will be your Achilles' heel. You will crave its taste, and if you cross another with magic in their veins, you will want their blood like no other, but Sahira will be the only one to truly satisfy your thirst."

His hand moved to his throat, and she laughed. "You feel it even now."

"We'll see about that." He got up from the side of the bed and strode toward the tent flap, pulling it wide only to hiss as the last of the day's rays scalded his hand.

Fatima laughed. "The sun is no longer your friend, Templar. Its heat killed your friends, but they died of dehydration. You will char to a blackened hull. The sun means death for your kind. You will have to live centuries of lifetimes before you can withstand even the weakest sunlight.

"Sahira is old enough to walk in the sun at its zenith, but she chooses not to as it saps her strength. Milady was a powerful sorceress before she woke to darkness, and the sun weakens her powers too much."

Dominic turned with a snarl, staring at his hand as the blisters faded. His eyes jerked to Fatima, and he strode to where she stood. "Tell me what I need to know."

"You will heal from most wounds immediately." She gestured to his hand but then shrugged. "Some take a longer time and others will heal, but scar. It depends on how the wounds are inflicted. "She made a face. "Like the one you gave my lady. That blade was laced with a spell to mark any flesh it cut. The mistress

used it to mark her followers. We didn't know it would also work on undead flesh, but now —" She shrugged again.

"Undead?"

She nodded. "It is what you are now, Templar. A member of the undead. Immortal. For a Christian like you, it means you live outside God's grace. On the wrong side of the grave. Your body defied death, so therefore you live outside the reward of paradise. It's much the same for those who follow the teachings of Allah. If you follow such beliefs."

"Outside God's grace?" he repeated. "Surely if God created whatever I am, whatever Sahira is, then we are His creation as well."

She shrugged for the third time. "I live in the now, Templar. My world is infinitely better since Sahira found me. I serve only her. My opinion of God and his works is tainted by the suffering he allows, but if you want my opinion, it is thus. You live outside God's grace because you must consume living blood to survive.

"You kill that which was created in God's image. Immortals kill at will. They grant immortality on a whim. The gift of glamour can even trick humans into believing they choose to be blooded. Or even choose to serve. The undead can make anyone do anything. You can probe minds and rule your world without conscience or remorse. You are free from the bonds that hold humanity shackled.

"You feel ego and lust, even now. Those are the emotions in which you were created. Fear and anger, too. You will feel those most keenly. You'll find the other emotions that led your human life will be dim recollections. Love, honor, courage, compassion." She eyed him with her head at a curious angle. "Or maybe not. Sahira chose you well. You are strong. Perhaps you will be lucky

and hold onto the shreds of your humanity. That's if the mistress doesn't beat it out of you first."

Anger and shock suffused his body, and his mind raged with despair and thirst. With a snarl, he lunged, ripping Fatima's throat open and burying his face in her warm, thick blood. He tasted Sahira in the coppery flow and moaned at the taste just as Fatima said. Even now, his cock thickened, especially as the older woman's heart slowed. He felt her blood grow sluggish in her veins and with a final pull, he took her last heartbeat. The taste was exquisite, and now he knew. He was a demon on earth. Sahira had made it so.

He flung Fatima's body to the corner of the tent, surprised at how light her empty husk felt in his grip. The sun had set. He knew from the infused strength flowing through his body.

Without a moment's pause, he grabbed a set of fresh clothes, his tunic and his sword, and left the tent, wiping the last of the woman's blood on his sleeve. He had only one thought. Get home to Céleste and pray to God she could love a demon.

***

Dominic stood on the deck of the merchant ship as it slowly pulled into the dock at Marseilles. The journey had been hard. He'd glamoured the captain into granting his passage, working when he could to earn his keep. He could easily have made the man believe he'd paid full fare, but he worked to assuage his own guilt.

His thirst overwhelmed at times. He lived off the blood of rats in the hold, but even their abundance wasn't enough to quench the raging parched thirst. He feigned exhaustion and sometimes sickness during the day and to keep the crew at bay. It was for their sake. He refused to take innocent life, let alone risk damning some other poor soul to his purgatory.

Marianne Morea

After months at sea, finding relief was his only thought. He rationalized his ethics and took to the streets at every port, succumbing to his hunger. He probed minds for the truly criminal, feeding from their polluted veins and polluted minds.

Fatima was wrong. He fed but didn't have to kill. The realization gave him hope. Perhaps he wasn't living without grace after all.

"You're finally home, eh?" the captain said, clapping Dominic on the shoulder. "You're a strange one, that's for sure. I've never met anyone as much a night owl. But you're good company. I'll give you that." He chuckled out a wheezy laugh.

Dominic met the man's kind smile and matched it. "I'm sorry I wasn't much of a sailor, but I appreciate the kind words."

"Ach, I've seen worse than you in my day. Greener than seaweed and just as slimy. You didn't eat much, but maybe that helped keep your innards intact." He laughed.

"Maybe," Dominic replied. If the man only knew, he'd have had him staked to the mast to char in the sun.

"Well, I hope your sea legs will be under you better on your next voyage." The man waved goodbye, shoving a pipe in his teeth before shouting orders to his men to be careful with his cargo or he'd have their guts for garters.

The gangplank cleared enough for Dominic to disembark. The crew continued to unload, but their thoughts were on women and rum and not the captain's cargo.

He stepped onto French soil for the first time in a year and exhaled. Not that he needed the calming breath, but he was barely gone from his human life to give up old comforts. He'd used his time alone onboard thinking about what Fatima said about his human emotions. Reciting the commandments helped, but it was remembering the emotions on the faces of the people he knew and

loved that solidified the feelings in his breast. For months, it had been his daily mantra. Remember and repeat. Remember and repeat. Assigning the mental image with the emotion, he willed himself to feel until his feelings came as easily as humans breathe.

Glancing at the high peak to the west, Dominic drew in another breath and his fangs tingled.

Mont Majeure.

Another revelation from his time onboard ship. He had no real heartbeat to race in his chest, at least not the kind an average human could discern, but his fangs tingled in much the same way when anticipation called.

"I'm here, my love," he muttered, issuing a quick prayer. Céleste was but a few hundred yards from him at last.

The sun was well below the horizon when he made his way through the abbey gates. Slipping inside the cold stone building, he inhaled, searching for Céleste's remembered scent.

Nothing. Had her father had her moved?

Anger bloomed, and he had to calm himself or someone would die needlessly. He followed the winding stone passages until he found himself outside the abbey chapel.

He reached out with his senses and found Frère Michel's thoughts inside. He was deep in prayer. Fear and sorrow etched his mind, and then Dominic saw the reason clearly.

Céleste was dead.

Rage erupted in his chest, and he splintered the door with his fist. Kicking it open, he stood in the ruined entry, his eyes burning.

She was there. Wrapped in rough linen in a plain wood box in front of the altar. Candles burning at her head and feet.

Cowering, Michel turned frightened eyes toward the door. "Dominic! Thank God, you're alive! We heard you died in the

Battle of the Field of Blood, that the Saracens buried you in the sand without absolution."

The old monk straightened from his prie-dieu as Dominic approached the altar. "I'm so sorry, my son. Céleste suffered much this past year, but nothing like what happened to cause her untimely death."

"When?"

"Two days ago. I waited to bury the poor girl, hoping her father would change his mind and come to offer prayers for the repose of his daughter's soul, but he refuses."

Dominic reached for the wrappings covering Céleste's face.

"No! For the love of God, Dominic, I beg you. Don't. The sight will haunt you for the rest of your days." The monk's breath caught in a quiet sniff. "There was nothing we could do for her."

Dominic pushed the old man's hand from his arm and unwrapped the linens from Céleste's face and chest. A sob rose at the horror still etched on her pretty features.

Céleste's throat was torn out and her heart ripped from her chest. There was only one person who would do something like this to her.

Sahira.

She had seen Céleste in his thoughts, felt his love for her even as his body writhed, dying to this condemned existence. His eyes burned, but this time with grief as well as anger.

A cry ripped from his throat as he sank to his knees. "That evil bitch! She did this. I know it." His fingers curling over the edge of the plain pine, cracking the wood. "I'll kill her, I swear. I'll rip her black heart out with my hands."

"Dominic, please. Whoever you think responsible will meet their punishment at God's hand, not yours. Your anger won't bring Céleste back."

Condemned

Dominic's head dropped, and he pressed his forehead to the side of the rough wood. Blood tears ran down his cheeks, dripping from the end of his chin to the chapel's stone floor.

"Weep for Céleste's soul, and for your own." The monk paused when he saw the red splatters on the stone at Dominic's knees. "You're bleeding. Let me help you."

Dominic turned his head, and Michel recoiled back in horror at the blood smearing the young man's cheeks.

"Demon! Be gone from this holy place!" The small man tried to shove Dominic from Céleste's coffin. "Unclean! Like the succubus who killed that poor girl. Ruination. Damnation!"

Dominic stood, his body uncoiling with deadly care. "Where is my child?"

Michel's eyes went wide, but he mashed his lips together, shaking his head.

"Michel! Where is my child? Tell me, or I'll rip it from your mind."

The old monk cowered at his words. "He died!"

Dominic shook his head slowly, letting his eyes narrow. He slipped into Michel's mind again, but this time he focused on Céleste's life, at the hardships she'd endured at the hand of the abbess.

Probing further, he watched her give birth. His heart ached for the pain she suffered but filled again with the love he saw in her eyes as the midwife handed her their son.

Son.

He had a son.

The priest's mind showed Leandres taking the baby, promising to keep him safe until they could be reunited.

Marianne Morea

Dominic released the old man's mind and exhaled. At least some good would come of this. The world thought him dead, and that's the way he needed to let it be.

"Whatever befell you, Dominic Favreau, you are now a vessel of evil. I'm glad Céleste cannot see you for what you've become. You broke her heart enough. The day you set eyes on her, you ruined her life!"

He grabbed the old man by the nape of his neck and bent him over the coffin. "Look on her face, Michel. See her wounds? I may be a vessel of evil, but there is evil even worse than the vile creature responsible for Céleste's death. You and your hate and prejudice! This is your doing. You and your hypocritical lot. Céleste and I could have been happy, if not for you!"

He threw the man to the stones, leaving him sobbing in the corner by the altar stairs. He turned on his heel, but Michel called after him.

"Promise you'll leave that sweet babe alone." The monk struggled to his feet. "I know you saw him in my mind. Promise me, Dominic. On what you once were. Promise you'll leave that child to grow into the man he should be and not be tainted by whatever ills you sent to curse his mother."

Dominic glanced at the man's face across his shoulder. "On the soul of the man I once was, I give you my word."

"And the abbess and Èmile Colbert?" he pushed.

Dominic turned his back and walked out without reply. Would he kill them for making Céleste suffer? His mind was in a whirl, and he wandered out the back of the abbey to find himself in a grotto filled with celestial silver light.

He sank to his knees. Céleste had died because he loved her, and now guilt and shame warred in his breast with anger and grief. What would taking two more lives do other than damn him

Condemned

further to hell? His jaw stiffened. His revenge would find the one who made his suffering irrevocable. If he was truly an immortal, then time was something he had in abundance. Time and patience. He would wait and strike when the time was right, but only when no one else would suffer because of him.

He lifted his face to the sky, letting the wind muffle his agonized prayer. "On what's left of my soul, I will find grace in my new existence, but as God as my judge, I will rid this world of Sahira, someday." His fangs descended and tore his wrist, squeezing dark blood to the cold earth, sealing his oath.

Marianne Morea

Chapter 8

Belinda couldn't sleep. She tossed and turned, punching the pillow, but nothing helped. She sat up with a huff and snapped on the light beside the bed.

Nothing was the same since she'd left Rome four days ago. She knew she must have fainted or something because she had no memory of how she got to the guest room at La Corsicana. Dominic must have carried her up the stairs.

She was still naked from their sexcapade the night before, but she was under the covers, her freshly washed and folded clothes on the trunk at the end of the bed. She didn't know how she knew, but that's where the story left off. He hadn't crawled into bed with her or tried any funny business.

Rubbing her palms over her face, Belinda scrubbed her eyes. As if that would rid her of the images or the questions whirling through her mind since she'd found his note on the night table next to her bed.

The letter was written in beautiful, old-world-style cursive. The kind of looping script you see on historic documents like the Constitution or the Magna Carta. She snorted to herself. According to Dominic, he was only old enough to witness both of those events.

She exhaled, shaking her head. "This is absurd, and I'm insane to even entertain a shred of validity about any of this," she muttered, digging for the note in her diary on the hotel nightstand.

Condemned

She'd read Dominic's letter at least a hundred times since arriving in Cairo. Crazy vampire fetishist or not, at least the man was true to his word about booking her a first-class flight. He'd even left her enough money to fund a decent hotel for the two nights before her internship started, and she moved into a field barracks at the dig.

She exhaled again and unfolded the letter, scanning the words she knew by heart.

Belinda,

By now you've probably dismissed me as certifiable, though I'm hoping the compassion I sensed in you will paint me more as wealthy and eccentric. The truth is, I'm wealthy, but I'm not crazy, and the only eccentric thing I've done these past centuries is collect artifacts cataloging my long existence. I know. That sentence alone makes me sound like I dropped my basket. I'm not insane. I'm vampire.

You're probably shaking your head or running a nervous hand through your gorgeous red hair as you did that fateful night. It's understandable. This situation is about as far from the norm as any human can get. Yes, I used the term human. That's what you are, Belinda, and that's what I once was, a very long time ago. Humans are skeptical creatures by nature. They repudiate what doesn't fit the box marked rational, even when empirical truth is staring them in the face.

Everything I told you is true. I am vampire. Not some fringe-loving freak that imagines himself fanged and fabulous. I am vampire, and have been since I was turned in the summer of 1119 AD. My kind does exist. Like mankind, some are good, and some are evil. Our world exists in parallel with yours. We overlap, and sometimes even interact. I wish I could explain everything. Introduce you to my loved ones so you could see we're not that different from you and yours. With your passion and fascination for history, I believe you would understand and appreciate my story. There is much you need to know, especially now you've come into

Marianne Morea

contact with the undead. We aren't the monsters you've read about in horror books, but neither are we lovesick voyeurs climbing through windows at night. We are individuals, as separately unique as human beings, each with different experiences shaping us to who we are. You are a unique woman, Belinda. A woman I could love if such things were allowed. If you ever wish to find me, I will come. No creep factor, I promise. ;)

Always,

Dominic

She couldn't help a soft chuckle. "The man ended his letter with a wink emoji." She didn't know if that punctuated his insanity or made him really, really likeable.

She folded the letter and placed it on the nightstand again. "If you ever wish to find me, I will come," she murmured. "How, Dominic? Vampire GPS?"

Shaking her head, she snapped off the light. If she ever did get the chance to see him again, she wouldn't run naked and screaming for the door. She'd pack holy water and Mace to cover all bases, and then pepper him with questions.

"No creep factor." She flopped over onto her side.

Problem was, Dominic wasn't creepy, even when he was in vamp mode or whatever. He was sexy. The make my panties wet still thinking about him kind of sexy. She closed her eyes. If she was lucky, maybe he'd visit her in her dreams. That's if she ever got to sleep. "His claim is *vampire*, stupid. Not *incubus*. Vampires don't hunt dreams. Some antiquities scholar you are."

Yawning, she pictured his dark eyes and the gorgeous curve of his mouth when he smiled. "Mmmm, and that sexy French lilt." She closed her eyes and snuggled into her pillow.

Belindachka, he haunts your thoughts for a reason.

Bubbie, please. Let me sleep.

Condemned

You study the past, my darling. All that book learning, and you still can't see what's in front of you.

Belinda's eyes opened.

They repudiate what doesn't fit the box marked rational, even when empirical truth is staring them in the face.

Shows such intelligence, no?

Bubbie. There's a fine line between genius and insanity, and Dominic may have crossed the border into Crazytown long before I let him in my pants.

Belindachka! Be a lady.

She smiled to herself, picturing her grandmother's feigned shock.

There are things in this world that defy explanation, but that doesn't make them any less real.

Maybe, Bubbie, but you need to shut up so I can sleep. Tomorrow is a big day.

Her grandmother's laughter floated across, and a soft kiss brushed her mind. *Good night, moya solnishka…*

Belinda drifted off, letting images of Dominic and his Old-Hollywood sex appeal play in rerun behind her lids.

***

"Hello?" Belinda fumbled for her cell phone on the night table, still half-asleep.

A night of erotic dreams left her more exhausted than she was when she snapped out the light. She groaned, almost letting the call go to voice mail, but she was to hear about her interview today and didn't want to take the chance.

"Ms. Force?" a male voice on the other end asked.

"Yeah, this is she." She yawned, slapping a hand over her mouth to camouflage the betraying inhale. Holy crap. Could she sound any more like a loser stoner?

This was it. The yes or no on the one assignment she really wanted. The subterranean excavation beneath the port of Akko, about two hours from Jerusalem. She shivered just thinking about the possibilities. The port was one of the richest archeological sites in a country full of them, and she wanted in on the historic discoveries, pronto.

"Ms. Force, I'm Kir Aziz, from the Archeological Society, calling to schedule your official meeting with the council."

"Okay, great. I'm eager to get started."

"Yes, but first, Dr. Khalid wants to know when you are set to arrive in Cairo."

"Cairo. But I thought—" Belinda stopped herself. Damn. She was back to square one. Still, she was here, and that's all that mattered.

"Yes. She wants to meet with you personally before the assignments are decided, but between you and me, it appears Dr. Adams's recommendation put you at the top of the list for the Israeli project."

"Akko? Really?" The excitement in her voice was palpable, and she nearly bounced to the edge of the bed.

"Please don't tell anyone I let the cat out of the bag, but you sounded disappointed, so I figured it wouldn't break protocol too much to tell you now."

"Please don't misunderstand. Cairo is amazing. I spent three months working there last summer, though, and was hoping for something different," she replied, wanting to kick herself for being so goddamned transparent.

"I understand. You probably don't remember me, but I was one of Dr. Khalid's teaching assistants last summer."

"Kir, right. Of course, I remember you. I ran into Ari in New York right before I found out I was chosen for the internship program. He was with Dr. Khalid. The woman is one cool customer. She didn't let on one iota she had handpicked me for the project."

"Dr. Khalid's coolness notwithstanding, if nothing goes wrong, Ari will most likely be assigned to Akko as well. He's been training with Dr. Khalid personally for this, so if this is your dream assignment, take my advice. Don't be late for your interview, come prepared, and for God's sake, don't pull what you did in class last summer. Dr. Khalid likes to sit back with a bag of popcorn and watch the cage-match debates between students, but *she* doesn't like to be questioned. This is her gig. Understand?"

"Got it."

"So, when are you getting into town?"

Belinda hugged her middle with her free hand. "I'm already here. I'm at the Nile Ritz Carlton."

He whistled low. "Posh digs. How are you affording that on a postgrad stipend?"

"I sold bone marrow before I left New York."

"Shut the front door!"

She stifled a laugh at his accented American slang. It was like listening to Adam Sandler in *Don't Mess with the Zohan*, but she was not about to tell him the truth. Yeah, this ultra-sexy vampire left cash on my nightstand for services rendered, with a little extra thrown in for post-traumatic stress. Not.

"Anyway," Kir continued, "the first available appointment with Dr. Khalid is Monday morning at ten. Why don't you let me show you Cairo this weekend? Last summer, you had your nose

buried in textbooks or in the dirt, digging. You didn't get to see much outside the Valley of the Kings. Not that *that's* not every antiquities student's dream, but there's more to the city than artifacts and ruins."

She laughed. "Yeah, I don't usually get out much. If you're serious, then I'd love to see the sights."

"Good. Maybe you'll get a chance to meet the crew. Khalid's crew." He laughed. "At least that's what we call ourselves, though some people think we're more acolyte than postgrad."

Belinda winced. That was the exact snarky remark running through her head. Ugh, was she projecting over FiOS now? Or maybe the dude was psychic.

She forced a chuckle. "So, when do you want to meet up? I could cab it over to the Cairo Museum."

"How about I pick you up at your hotel instead? That way we can take my car. Eight p.m. Saturday sound good?"

"Sounds fun."

"Listen, wear something casual, but nice. If you're anything like the rest of the crew, you probably packed dig clothes and not much else."

She laughed. "Not much else is an understatement. Are we going someplace special I should know about?"

He paused. "Not exactly, but I want the option to show off more than the sights. I'm sure you clean up good. See you then."

Pressing end, she put her phone on the night table and rolled over, taking the covers with her. Clean up good. It seemed some of Dominic's post-traumatic guilt money was going toward new clothes.

"Khalid's crew." Kir Aziz was in for a big fat disappointment if that's who he wanted her to impress. Not after the mega dose of

creepy she got outside the Arts and Sciences Building when she ran into Ari and the good doctor. "Not on your life, buster."

She exhaled, punching her pillow one more time. Ari's tattoo popped into her head as she settled. She blinked, giving the image a moment's hesitation. Ari was cool, and she'd work well with him, but that was about it. She yawned and hiked the covers higher, dismissing the thought. No thanks.

***

"So, where are we headed?" Belinda asked as she walked with Kir through the hotel parking lot. She promised herself she'd be on her best behavior and not embarrass Kir or herself if she ended up the main attraction for his crew.

She'd gone shopping at the main *souk* instead of the mall, for a taste of old Egypt. The bazaar was as magical as the images in her head. Why she didn't get around to shopping last summer was beyond her. Vibrant and alive with people, the souk was an exercise in color and noise. Dyed fabrics and silks, hookahs and oil lanterns, and every kind of knickknack you could want were there for the having.

"I was right." He winked. "You do clean up good. In fact, you look beautiful," Kir said, inclining his head.

Belinda glanced down at the flowy emerald skirt, watching it shift and move as it skimmed her ankles. The dyed fabric graduated in color, and she topped the light green at her hips with a coordinating top that skimmed her waist without being offensive in the conservative city.

Kir was being polite. There was no untoward vibe, and she was grateful they were just colleagues with nothing brewing on his end. Not that he wasn't attractive. He reminded her of Ari in that they were both on the small side, with thick, dark hair and even

darker eyes, but with fine features like 80s pretty boy, Rob Lowe. They were handsome, but way too delicate. To be honest, she still had Dominic's old-Hollywood good looks and muscular body on the brain. Crazy or not, the man had rocked her world.

"I thought we'd go to Al Azhar Park. There are fireworks over the lake on Saturday evenings, even during Ramadan. Families come out after their fast to eat and enjoy the fine weather." He glanced at his watch. "The pyrotechnics will be over about ten. After that, maybe we could meet my friends at 1897."

She chuckled. "1897? Sounds like we need Dr. Who and his Tardis."

Kir's answering grin had sci-fi fantasy geek written all over it. "Oh man, I wish. 1897 is a cigar bar at the Royal Maxim Palace Kempinski Hotel. The cocktails and food are the best in the city. It will give you a flavor of both old and new Cairo, plus the mistress is a regular, so the crew gets the royal treatment at the Royal Maxim."

A chill went up Belinda's spine at the word. It was just a coincidence, right?

"Oh man. The expression on your face is priceless. Dr. Khalid doesn't carry ball gags in her purse. Though, with the way she rides us sometimes, it's not a stretch." An amused smirk tugged at Kir's mouth. "She's exacting, so we call her the mistress, as a joke."

"Funny." Belinda forced a chuckle.

"Come meet the gang and see for yourself. They all know about you. When Zahra Khalid singles someone out as special, the news makes the rounds."

Warning bells went off in her head. Why was he pushing so hard for her to meet this crew of elites?

"I'd love to meet your friends, but I should tell you I'm not interested in joining some postgrad secret society. No offense."

He shrugged. "We're exclusive. I'll admit that much, but we're not exactly a secret. We're like-minded students with similar purpose. Zahra thought you'd be a perfect fit."

So, she was Zahra now. Way familiar compared to Dr. Adams, but maybe that's the way they played it here.

With a quick smile, he clicked the button on his key fob, unlocking the doors. The telltale chirp was followed by the lock release, and he opened the passenger door, holding it for her to slide in.

"Thanks," she mumbled as she slipped onto the cool leather seat and closed the car door. He went around the other side and got in as well, dropping the key fob into the front cupholder.

Belinda took a breath and let it out quickly. Maybe she was overreacting.

"Something wrong?" he asked with his hand poised on the ignition button.

Surprised he was that perceptive, she lifted a hand in a preemptive apology. "What I said before," she paused, "it came out wrong. I don't want you to get the wrong idea. I'm not a snotty American trying to glom all the published glory for myself. I don't do politics, and because extreme group-think has puts its thumb on campus life, I don't join groups, either. I'm too independent. To be honest, I stay away like the idea carries plague."

He laughed. "We're not like that at all, but I get it." He glanced at her from the driver's seat. "Why don't you come meet them anyway? No pressure."

He started the car and signaled to pull into traffic. Belinda noticed his hands on the steering wheel. Kir had a blended Lilith sigil tattooed on his right hand, same as Ari.

Not like that at all, huh?

Yeah, right.

Chapter 9

Kir steered his car across town. Traffic was crazy. Not just the volume of cars. Crazy Egyptian drivers made the cabbies in Rome seem like little old ladies as they zipped past, cutting in and out as if traffic rules were mere suggestions rather than law.

They pulled into the parking lot, and Kir cut the engine. Belinda got out from the passenger side, watching as he went around to pop the trunk. He pulled a blanket from the back and gestured to it with a sheepish shrug. "I thought it would be nice to sit on the grass rather than stand with the crowd."

Cairo was a sprawling metropolis, but it was still the desert, and the temperature dropped significantly. She'd brought a jacket, but the heat of the day radiated from the sandstone architecture in the park, making the cooler air comfortable.

She took in the expanse and the unparalleled view of the city at night as Kir paused for her to experience the big picture.

"And I thought Central Park was a big deal." She chuckled, scanning everything. "This place makes my hometown park seem like a suburban backyard."

Kir beamed his approval. "The park is reflective of so much that is beautiful from our past yet married to the contemporary. The park's architecture is traditional, from its terraced gardens and fountains to the geometry of the multicolored stonework and the specific greenery. The ponds and lake are fed by the Nile, which you know is the very symbol of Egypt."

"Wow, if archeology doesn't work out for you there's always the Travel Channel." She smirked, giving his shoulder a bump.

"Ha, ha." He rolled his eyes. "Hey, I'm proud of my country."

"And you should be. I wouldn't keep coming back if I didn't think it was pretty amazing." She followed him down the steps toward the main mall. "If you really want to show off your mad know-it-all skills, tell me about the excavations going on with the *Ayyubid* walls and towers. Is the site still active?"

He shook his head. "The excavations were completed in the mid-2000s, but restoration is an ongoing thing. The walls stretch for a kilometer and a half around Al Azhar. With their various gates, towers, interior chambers, and galleries, it's turned out to be one of the most significant finds of the late twentieth century."

"Was it really discovered under piles of rubbish?"

Kir nodded. "When they broke ground for the park, they found treasure beneath 500 years of desert dust and rubble. I was lucky. Zahra was involved in the first excavations, so I read her field journals. It was pretty cool. The walls and surrounds were constructed in the twelfth century by Saladin. His aim was to connect the Ancient Fatimid city of *Al-Qahir* with the Citadel and its aqueduct."

She squinted into the distance. If Saladin constructed the Ayyubid in the twelfth century, was Dominic there to see it built? She mentally squashed the thought. Even if he was a Templar Knight as his artifacts suggested, it didn't mean he was stationed in the Holy Land at the same time. She should've asked him when she had the chance. If the world of the supernatural wasn't just folklore and fiction—

Belinda turned her head at her own absurdity. Dominic's letter was eloquent and sincere, but no way. She was an academic. A scholar. Not some starry-eyed teen with an Edward Cullen fancy.

She smirked to herself. Not that the fictional character could hold a candle to Dominic's style and sex appeal. Her sexy Templar would wipe the floor with sparkle boy.

Ugh. Obsessed much? Get a grip.

Really. And what is it you spend your dissertation studying? Ancient blood sects of the Middle East?

"You okay?" Kir asked, angling his head her way.

"Yeah, just preoccupied about my interview."

"It's in the bag, trust me. Everyone needs a release now and then, so relax and enjoy yourself." He held out an elbow, but the moment she slipped her hand into the crook of his arm, vertigo hit and her vision swam.

Stunned, breath locked in her throat, and she froze. Images flashed fast and furious. Him, Zahra, and Ari. Their bodies locked and sweat sheened. Carnal, almost primitive.

"Belinda?"

Squeezing her eyes shut, she gasped, pitching forward. Kir gripped her arm harder, but the concerned touch sent visions blurring one into another. Zahra. Her body stretched and tense as she writhed in pleasure. Kir in a rough ménage with her and Ari, the two men tied as Zahra performed all manner of debauched acts.

Belinda's knees buckled, and she jerked her arm from his hold to stop the onslaught. She squeezed her middle but shook him off when he tried to help. "Just give me a minute."

"What can I do?" he asked as people around them gawked. "Do you need a doctor?"

"I h-had an accident in Rome a few days ago," she stuttered, blurting any feasible excuse. "I guess I hit my head a little harder than I thought." She didn't have to feign the shiver.

"Car accident?"

Her vision steadied, and she dragged in a breath. "No. Roller bag."

He blinked, but then burst out laughing. "You had a fender bender with a suitcase?"

"More like a moving violation. It's a long story. Don't ask. I'm fine, but maybe I overdid it too soon."

"You think?" he replied with a laugh. "Why didn't you say something?"

She swallowed, still trying to regroup. What could she say? She had a head-on collision with a living, breathing vampire?

Living vampire.

Now that was a contradiction in terms. Did vampires actually breathe?

Ugh. Focus.

She never got vertigo. And the visions? What the fuck?

Breathe, my Belindachka.

I'm trying. What the hell was that?

Something has ripened the vĕdma's blood in your veins.

Seriously, Bubbie. Not again. I don't need this now.

Need or not, you have no choice but to believe. You will need your gift to help keep you safe.

"Are you okay? Can you stand?" He held his hand, but she waved him off. The last thing she needed was to end up on the ground again.

She gave her head a quiet shake to clear what was left of her whirls, offering him half a smile. "Some fun date, huh?" Climbing to her feet, she shrugged, hoping he bought the concussion story.

It was partly true, partly lie of omission. Then again, Kir had way more skeletons in the cupboard compared to her vampire. He also had way more than just Zahra Khalid's ear.

Had.

As in Triple X.

Kir slid another quizzical glance her way, so she plastered a smile on her face, ignoring the doubts and questions buzzing in her head.

Awkward silence fell between them as Kir picked a spot on a grassy patch away from the crowds. He spread the blanket, and she took another steadying breath and settled toward one side, leaving plenty of room for him to sit.

So, her gut feelings were more than just intuition on steroids. Okay, fine. Now what? Was she now some weirdo tactile voyeur? Was she headed for a face full of people's deepest darks every time she shook someone's hand? If she was truly clairvoyant, what did that mean going forward?

"You look like you could use one of these." He reached into his pocket and pulled out two bags of M&Ms.

A genuine smile curled on her lips. "How did you know?" She took the offering, careful not to touch his fingers. Seeing him lick chocolate off Zahra's body would definitely ruin M&Ms for her forever.

He shrugged. "I remembered from last year. You always had a bag on your desk at lecture."

"There were three hundred students in that class," she replied, tearing open the top of the packet with her teeth.

"Yes, but only one redheaded American with rapid-fire questions."

In one sentence, Kir moved the chess piece from friend zone into something else. She exhaled, keeping her face placid. She needed this right now like a hole in the head. Even if she was interested, she'd never get past him porking her internship sponsor.

She lifted the bag of candy in as benign a gesture as she could muster. "Chocolate is always a good idea. You're a pal, Kir."

The fireworks started at that point. They were better than she expected, and so loud there was no way for them to talk. He'd get the not-interested vibe soon enough.

The display lasted about forty-five minutes before the finale lit up the sky. Tension ebbed from her body, and she took an easy breath. If her visions weren't some freaky one-off, then there had to be a way for her to control the deluge. The thought of never touching another person was ridiculous. And forget sex. Visions with that kind of skin on skin would definitely kill the mood. An up-close-and-personal sexual catalogue in 3D Technicolor featuring everyone your partner ever bonked.

As the last of the pyrotechnics faded into the night, she gave Kir a reticent smile. "This was terrific, Kir, but I think maybe I should call it a night, considering. Would you mind dropping me back?"

He blinked. "It's only ten fifteen. The crew is already waiting at 1897. They're expecting us."

She opened her mouth to argue, but his face told her he wasn't taking no for an answer, so she simply shrugged her acquiescence. She'd use her departmental holiday party move. Do a single circuit, talk to whoever she needed to speak with most, and then leave.

All without touching a single soul. Ugh.

"Shall we?" he asked. Getting up, he offered her his hand, but she waved him off.

It took them longer to get out of the Al Azhar parking lot and onto the street than it did to drive to the Royal Maxim to meet his friends. Kir valet parked and then led the way into the hotel and up to the bar.

As they passed, people nodded to him as if he owned the place. But the bar manager's grin broadened most when he saw them approach.

"This must be the newest recruit," he said tapping the edge of the cocktail menus in his hand. He gestured toward the inside bar. "They're in their usual place."

A hint of cigar smoke and leather danced on the air as Belinda followed Kir toward a plush back alcove. The place was intimate. More private library than a bar. Buttery leather couches and soft club chairs. She scanned the place, easily picturing Dominic's old-Hollywood style fitting the vibe perfectly.

"Kir!" a girl sitting on the arm of a chair called, raising a hand. She got up from her seat as they approached. "You must be Belinda," she said with a grin.

There had to be fifteen people gathered in the comfortable space, though some chose to sit on the floor. "Guilty," Belinda replied with a polite smile.

"Quick." The girl chuckled. "You are definitely a welcome change around here. I'm Rachel." She held out her hand.

Belinda inclined her head but didn't take her hand. "It's nice to meet you. I'm a little sticky, so you'll have to forgive me." She shrugged again. "M&Ms. They're my kryptonite."

"Mine is Starburst. I have a stateside friend send me my fix." She winked.

Rachel turned and scooped up an empty beer from the table, using her class ring to tap on the glass. "Everyone, this is Belinda. The gal Zahra personally chose to join us this summer."

All conversation came to a halt, and fifteen sets of eyes turned her way. "Wow, talk about a tough crowd," Belinda mumbled, and Rachel's eyes flashed with humor.

Condemned

A sandy-haired guy got up from the couch, picking his way over sprawled legs. He gave a quick chin pop to Kir but kept his eyes on Belinda. As he approached, he snagged a half-empty beer from a friend and tipped it to his lips.

Right there on his hand was the same sigil tattoo as Ari and Kir. Belinda did a quick scan of the others trying not to be too conspicuous.

"Since you're too polite to ask, but obviously curious, the answer is yes, we all have one," he said with a sight German accent, holding up his hand.

"Why? Is it a prerequisite?" The Skull and Bones Society at Yale popped into her head, but even that cloak-and-dagger organization didn't require ink.

His eyes traveled her length, giving her a scrutinizing once-over. "Zahra likes to acquire pretty things. Jewelry, artifacts. Even men and women. I can see why she wanted to collect you."

"Wow. I suppose I should be flattered. Except for the fact it's completely offensive." She met his blue-eyed stare without flinching. "I'm not an acquisition, dude. I'm an academic, like everyone else here, or so I assume."

He lifted one shoulder almost in dismissal. "Zahra doesn't do stupid. The IQ in this room is stratospheric. Present company included. I read your dissertation, or at least what you've written to date. Impressive."

"What?" Puzzled, she glanced at Kir who conveniently moved to stand beside Rachel. "What the hell is he talking about, Kir? You arranged my interview with Dr. Khalid, so don't tell me you don't know. What's going on?"

Kir exhaled, shooting Fredric a dirty look. "What my tactless friend meant was Zahra appointed a committee." He gestured to himself, Rachel, some random guy sitting on the couch across from

them, and finally the blue-eyed bastard still smirking at her. "We are her elites of the elite. When Zahra finds someone she wants to collect, she makes up her mind but gives her original members a preview." He shrugged. "Ari is part of the team as well, though he's not here tonight. Zahra has him tied up."

She snorted. "I'll bet."

Fredric raised an eyebrow at that, but she stared him down. It was clear no one was going to give her real answers. Not complete ones, anyway. Well, two could play at that. She had her own weapon for getting at the truth. Hopefully, she wouldn't end up on the floor when she pulled the trigger.

She straightened her shoulders and plastered another faux smile on her face. "Since I didn't apply for this internship myself, I can only assume Dr. Adams is responsible for letting my dissertation out of the proverbial bag. It's a safe bet he was under the impression my unpublished work would be for Dr. Khalid's eyes only. Imagine his annoyance when he finds she breached protocol."

"Dr. Adams doesn't dictate to the mistress," Fredric replied.

Belinda burst out laughing. "Dude. You really need to lighten up there, chuckles."

Forewarned is forearmed, and this time she knew what to expect. She would control the visions, not the other way around. She put a hand on the back of the couch, hoping the physical grounding would help her if vertigo hit again. Steeling her mind, she put her hand on his arm, keeping the gesture light and fun.

Her vision blurred, and she squeezed the sofa's hard leather-covered back. Images formed, but no vertigo. This time they were clear snippets. She saw the five elites. They were around a table. Scattered between them was her work. Even the handwritten

pages. Annoyance bit at her belly, but she pushed it aside. There was time for formal complaints later.

From her hazy vantage point she watched Fredric slide a photo from the edge of a folder on the table. She caught a glimpse of red hair in the picture as he stared it for a moment before shaking his head. So the blue-eyed bastard didn't want her for their stupid club.

She almost laughed out loud. She could see his kind coming a mile away. Misogyny cloaked in an overeducated wrapper. Rachel was the only female member of the fabulous five elites, and with the way the girl batted her eyes at Freddie Boy, it wasn't hard to see why he wanted things status quo. Rachel could be manipulated. Belinda was an unknown quantity.

A black tray with five glasses and five white pills flashed, but she couldn't quite make out the details. She squinted to see, but Fredric pushed her hand from his arm. The visions cut the moment he broke contact. No residual dizziness. No nausea.

Okay. This was good. Belinda let out the breath she'd been holding. She could handle this. A secret smile tugged. Bubbie would be so proud.

Fredric eyed her, his head angled as if trying to figure her out. "You're certainly odd enough for our group, but in the future, I don't like to be touched."

"No touchy, future. Got it. Does that mean you like to be touched in the present, instead? Any specific way?" Belinda smirked, giving it right back.

Kir nearly choked on his beer, but Rachel laughed out loud. Maybe the girl wasn't as malleable as she'd first thought.

"Didn't I say she was quick?" she said, still chuckling. "Anyway, your work is impeccable. I can't wait to read the final

published paper—" She paused with a blink. "Shoot, I almost forgot."

Rachel dug in her purse, producing a letter with Belinda's name scrawled across the front. "Sorry. I was supposed to give this to you. It's your assignment. Dr. Khalid isn't available to meet Monday morning, so she rubberstamped your placement in Akko." The girl handed the letter to Belinda. "Congratulations. I heard it was your first pick."

Belinda's fingers closed over the envelope, but she wasn't about to open it with fifteen sets of eyes watching. "Thanks. It was my only pick, really."

Fredric opened his mouth to fire off a retort but was shut down when a server passed with an array of crystal flutes filled with pink effervescent liquid.

Strawberry Prosecco? Wishful thinking.

Everyone reached for a glass, and Kir snagged two. One for him and one for her. "For our guest of honor," he said, holding the drink out. At Belinda's hesitation, he gestured with the glass again. "Take it, please. It's our tradition."

She took the glass, sniffing the contents. Her nose wrinkled immediately, and she pulled it back from her face. Whatever was in the glass smelled god-awful. Like sulfur and something she couldn't place.

Kir watched her reaction, as did Fredric. They weren't pleased, but she didn't care. She had no intention of drinking something that foul just to be polite.

Other servers made the circuit with the same drink, passing one to everyone in the group. One, though, carried a single glass filled with white pills. The same white pills from her vision.

"Drugs?" Belinda shot Kir a look. "What is this? Some sort of LSD party? Sugar pills dipped in hallucinogenics?"

"No! Of course not! The wine is proprietary to the crew. It's Zahra's personal blend. Unique."

A doubting brow quirked up. "What's with the pills, then?" she asked.

"Willow bark. It dilates the taste buds to help absorb the *uhm*...flavor," Rachel replied.

Belinda's eyebrow shot even higher. "Willow bark is a medieval analgesic. Basically, aspirin. Why the hell are you taking it with wine? Some sort of hangover prevention?" she questioned.

Rachel opened her mouth to answer, but Fredric lifted his glass, in effect, shutting her down. The rest of those in the room followed suit, each lifting their glass in some silent salute.

Belinda held hers out of respect but kept it level with her chest. She blinked, watching as they each dropped a pill into their glass and then drained the lot in one go. Fredric smacked his lips as if downing ambrosia instead of brimstone. Maybe it was an acquired taste.

Yeah, like drinking the Kool-Aid.

"You're not going to try our wine?" Kir gestured to the full glass still in her hand.

"Roller-bag collision. Remember?"

"Of course." He nodded. "Next time, then."

"I appreciate the invitation, Kir—" She placed the untouched glass on the closest table. "But I don't think so. I told you before. I have no interest in joining any kind of affiliation, especially not one where everyone wears a brand."

"It's just a tattoo, Belinda. Lots of serious associations have them."

She swallowed the urge to snort. "You're a group of archeology postgrads, not the Marines. Even then, inking Semper Fidelis is optional."

No sooner did the words leave her mouth, then an eerie feeling crept over her shoulder. Her skin chilled, and the scent of cinnamon and vanilla replaced the hint of cigar in the air. It was the same kind of sweet scent she'd caught that night she ran into Ari in New York.

"Do you smell that?" Belinda asked, curious if it was just her.

He didn't answer. Instead, he angled his head, assessing her again. "I shouldn't have insisted you come tonight. Clearly, you're not ready," he said.

"Ready? For what?"

"For us." He shrugged. "There's time, though. Zahra has never been wrong."

"I came to Cairo for a coveted internship, Kir. I appreciate Dr. Khalid's vote of confidence and her invitation to join her group of elites, but I'm simply not interested." Whatever envy she'd felt last summer was long gone. This was an episode of *The Twilight Zone*.

"I look forward to working with Ari and anyone else who'll be in Akko with me. Maybe even grab a pizza or something, but I'm not into this kind of thing." She shook her head. "It's no reflection on you or your choices, but it's my choice to decline."

Kir put his empty glass on the table beside her untouched drink and then straightened. "Maybe I should take you home, then."

"Thank you," she murmured. "I'm just glad Zahra isn't here tonight. This didn't go exactly as either of us hoped." The sweet scent thickened then, tickling her nose.

"I'm sure Dr. Khalid already knows," Kir replied with an odd smile. "She has a way of sensing things."

Belinda snorted to herself, following him toward the door.

Join the club.

Chapter 10

Belinda stood holding the railing as their small boat bumped over choppy water. Small sailboats and pleasure craft bobbed in their wake like a postcard come to life. The old city was gorgeous in the morning sun. A perfect amalgam of modern world meets antiquity.

A soft wind teased her hair as they left the protected port for the breakwater, a half-submerged ruin referred to as the Tower of Flies. In its heyday, the structure had doubled as a Crusader lighthouse and guard station, used to protect the Christian stronghold from raiders and attacks from the sea.

She had been in Akko for two weeks. The place was magical, and it didn't take much to set her fancy soaring. Everywhere she looked was the twelfth century, so of course there were reminders of Dominic.

His letter and his face at their last encounter played in her mind like someone possessed.

"Okay, I'll buy. For shits and giggles, when were you born?"

"In the year of our Lord, 1097. I was twenty-two years old when I was turned to what you see before you now..."

As they passed the historic ruin, she did the math. He was twenty-two. Five years younger than she was now. If what Dominic said was true, then his life met its human end and its new vampiric beginning in 1119. One year after the Templar Order was

formed. If he was already here and fighting, then he was one of the first Knights sent to the Holy Land.

She was beyond chastising herself for even entertaining the idea of his immortality. Not here. Not in this place with such connection to him and his past.

You don't know that.

Why else would he collect Templar relics and artifacts?

For the same reason you would.

Shut up.

So, you think he's telling the truth?

I'm seeing people's thoughts and memories. So why not?

You going to call the thousand-year-old hottie, then?

Inner monologue or not, she blinked at the possibility. She didn't have his number, but she did have his address. Even if she did show up unannounced, what could she say? Hey, remember me? The crazy scimitar-wielding redhead who fucked you and then freaked before passing out naked in your doorway?

Putting it that way, she sounded more like the crazy one. Since her clairvoyant revelation, she was attuned to the inexplicable. Subtle vibrations and energy in the air. Knowing the shadows watched and listened. Dominic was right. It was dangerous to play in the dark, and she knew that now more than ever. So why not give the man a chance to show her his empirical truth?

The boat's horn sounded, pulling her back to the here and now. They were headed for open water and the main dive boat, Galatea. A floating field camp permanently moored in the deeper water off the coast, the Galatea kept vigil over the archeological site against treasure hunters searching for a quick buck.

Her skin was already freckled from the sun and her hair in a permanent ponytail against windblown frizz. Weather this time of year was perfect. High seventies during the day and mid-sixties at

Condemned

night, with hardly any rain. Of course, it was only May, and that wouldn't be the case as the summer progressed.

The Mediterranean was so blue you'd imagine it warm and inviting, but nope. Sea temps were in the low-sixty-degree range, and she shivered thinking about that first plunge of the day. Locals hired to do the heavy lifting dove in wearing bathing suits and snorkel masks. Forget that. Sometimes her wet suit wasn't even enough.

"What's the matter?" She nudged Ari's arm when he joined her on the bow. "You've not said two words since we left the dock."

"I'm starving."

She laughed. "Then eat something." She pulled her canvas backpack around and opened the top flap. "I've got a couple of granola bars in here you can have."

"Thanks, but I can't," Ari replied with a shrug. "Ramadan started yesterday. I can't eat or drink until after sundown."

"Oh man. I forgot, Ari. I'm sorry." She gave him an apologetic smile. "Are you going to be okay diving all day?"

"Yeah, I'll be fine. I would've been better if I hadn't slept through my alarm. I had it set to wake me thirty minutes before daybreak so I could eat." He shrugged again. "Just don't drown me if I'm a cranky bastard, okay?"

She laughed. "Dude, I'm the queen of hangry. I get it."

"Hangry?" He grinned, raising an eyebrow.

"The worst that PMS has to offer. Hungry and angry at the same time."

He snorted out loud. "*That* alone is funny enough to get me through the day, but tonight it's pizza. My treat."

"You're on." She pushed flyaway strays. The heavy spray whipped at her face, and she turned her back to the bow, facing the coast instead.

The Templar tunnels ran along the edge of the walled city, and she smiled to herself. If she ever got the chance, she'd have Dominic explore each with her, recounting every detail.

The boat slowed, and the spray dissipated enough for her to turn as they approached the Galatea. The floating field camp was impressive. A professional live-on dive boat tricked out with every amenity. This was her dream dig, and she'd take the frizz and the freckles any day and twice on Sunday.

One hundred feet long, the Galatea had two main decks with a wide hull-side dive platform on the port side. The lower deck housed the galley and the living quarters for project leaders and the boat's professional crew, while the upper was for socializing. A storage room off the bridge held their dive equipment, air compressors, and emergency oxygen for easy access.

"What kept you two, or don't I want to know?" Ben Yuri, the team's dive master joked from the Galatea's main deck.

The transport pulled alongside and cut its engine, and Ari tossed him the tie lines to raft the two boats together. "My fault. I overslept."

Ben waited for the smaller boat to bob on the next swell and held his hand out to Belinda. They locked palms, and he helped her onto the ladder.

"You ready for another exciting day?" he asked.

His weather-wrinkled eyes glistened, and she met his good humor smirk with a smile. "Always."

He gave her shoulder a squeeze before turning to help Ari aboard. She slid her backpack from her shoulder and walked toward the upper cabin to stow her bag. Glancing back, a self-

satisfied pride bloomed. She had gripped the man's hand, and even when he rested his palm on her shoulder there wasn't a whirl or a dizzy hiccup in sight.

"Guess practice does make perfect," she mumbled, squatting to open her bag for her sunscreen.

Experimenting with turning her gift on and off at will, she read people constantly since she and Ari arrived in Akko. She'd even read him once while he slept, but only to see if it made any difference from reading people awake.

She grinned, thinking about it. It's not like she snuck into his bedroom or anything. He fell asleep on the couch, and the boy snored so loud it was either shove a pillow under his head or smother him.

Curiosity and opportunity got the better of her, and she slipped her hand onto his chest as it rose and fell. Images flashed quickly, but they were distorted and choppy.

The boy was preoccupied with food. All different kinds, in huge quantities. She had to laugh. This was a complete REM cycle backstage pass to his dreams, and with Ramadan starting, it was no wonder he was obsessed with food. Still, not a single X-rated interlude or private fantasy screening. Ari had his interludes. She'd seen them a little too up-close and personal. Still, the food thing made her like him a little more, despite his group affiliations.

Ben gathered the divers and pointed out their assigned sections on a whiteboard. "We're covering a different quadrant today," he said. "We've just completed mapping the perimeter, so the grid markers are in place. This is new territory. We're not expecting much on the first go, but who knows? The other quadrants have been archeologically bountiful, so I and our antiquities host are hopeful. The pieces we've found are small, but

important. Be precise in your work, and don't stray from the gridded areas. We're watching the currents."

He dismissed them, but then whistled, calling everyone back. "Oh, and to sweeten the pot, Dr. Khalid has made this a contest. Whichever one of you finds the most significant piece will get to see their find and their name on display at the Israeli Museum in Jerusalem." With a nod, he winked. "Gear up, good luck, and no cheating."

Together with her and Ari, there were four other interns from Israeli Antiquities. Enthusiasm was high now that Ben had raised the stakes, but so was the level of cutthroat competition. Scholars spent their time in libraries and labs, but when it came to academic accolades, it was every man for himself.

The found pieces Ben mentioned were from a previous internship. No one from their team had found anything so far, and they were already two weeks into their rotation. Two more weeks was all they had before they were knee-deep in subterranean dust, hauling buckets of unsifted dirt on another dig.

"Did you hear they located another wreck off the Bay of Haifa? It's supposedly a Crusader ship sunk during the Siege of Acre," Ari said, squatting to check his air levels and test his full-face mask regulator. "Radiocarbon dating puts the ship between 1062 and 1250."

Belinda's brow knotted. That's a two-hundred-year spread," she replied, wriggling her wet suit over her shoulders and pulling the back-zipper cord. "How can they be sure of the battle responsible for the wreck if they can't determine more accurate dating?"

"Wow, and I thought I was going to be the cranky one today." He looked up, teasing.

Pfft. "It's not cranky to expect science to be as accurate as possible. There are enough half-baked hypotheses floating around in our world. Historic fact, backed by science, is how we keep credibility and grant money."

"What half-baked hypothesis?"

She stared at him over the edge of her regulator. "*Ancient Aliens*?"

Ari laughed out loud. "The dude with crazy-hair? I love that show."

"*Show* is the operative word."

He chucked one of the dive pencils at her. "Snob. Anyway, the article went on to say they found a stash of gold florins minted in Florence during the last half of the thirteenth century. Hence the reason for the wider timeline."

"Hmmm."

"C'mon, Belinda. It's a Crusader ship. Right up your alley," he cajoled. Unless one of us hits the antiquities motherlode, we're basically done here. I can send Zahra an email tonight. With a little persuasion, I bet she'd sponsor us for that wreck dig.

"You mean you'd rather do real exploration instead of playing Jack and Jill with pails of dirt and rock?" She smirked, wondering what persuasion Ari meant and if it involved pink fuzzy handcuffs.

Belinda turned so he could help her secure her tanks. "Well, it's worth asking, I guess. Nothing ventured, nothing gained."

He lifted the tank straps over her shoulders, letting his hands linger. "She was disappointed you turned down her invitation to join the crew. Kir and Rachel, too."

She turned to eye him over her shoulder. "But not Fredric. That boy wanted me on his team like he wanted a case of the clap."

"You picked up on that, huh."

She shrugged, hedging. "Fredric's as deep as a puddle and as transparent as plastic wrap. His bigheaded superiority made my jaw hurt, but it also made my decision very easy. I don't do drama."

"Unless you cause it, right?"

"What's that supposed to mean?" She jerked around, brows knotted. "Because I left the party or because I wouldn't drink that foul-smelling wine? You weren't there, Ari. I know they're your crew, and that's fine, but I was being seriously corralled. You know me well enough by now to know I don't play that."

He lifted a shoulder. "It doesn't matter, now. Although, you should know you're only the second person in history to turn down Zahra's offer. Ironic considering the first."

She arched a brow. "Who was it?"

"Dr. Adams."

"Wait. *My* Dr. Adams."

He nodded.

"Dr. *Theo* Adams. Head of Antiquities and Archeological Studies at Columbia University."

"One and the same."

Ben called for attention. It was time to go. She stared after Ari as he walked hull side. He didn't wait for her, but she didn't care. She was too busy wrapping her head around what he said.

It didn't make sense. Adams was in his early fifties while Zahra had to be forty-something at least, considering her degrees. Ari was worse than Giles Newcomb when it came to gossip in academia. He must have gotten it wrong.

"Are you joining us today, Ms. Force?" Ben asked, waiting on the platform. Everyone else had already taken the plunge.

She hurried over to put on her flippers, letting him help adjust her full-face mask. Settled and ready, she held Ben's hand and

stepped down to the platform. Giving him a quick salute, she jumped feet first into the depths.

She bobbed for a moment, waiting for the splash to clear before giving Ben the thumbs-down signal for descent. A stream of bubbles rose as she released her buoyancy compensator to start sinking.

The others had already paired off, but Ari was nowhere to be seen. She scanned the grid sight and beyond.

"Ari, where are you?" she said, grinning at the Darth Vader sound of her voice over the communicator.

"Sorry, Belinda, but I'm going solo on this. I've been digging a lot longer than you, and I need a big fish if I want to stay in Zahra's crew."

"Ari!" She spotted him in the distance and waved him back, but he turned and went in the opposite direction. "Damn it, Ari! I hope your big fish has really big teeth and takes a huge bite out of your ass!

"Fucking hot dog," she mumbled, sparing a glance for the others who'd clearly heard him being a dick.

The other interns were their own clique, so she knew none of them would step up. Ari was no different. Like everyone else, he wanted to win this competition, even if it meant leaving her in his wake.

She swam along the bottom, fifty feet or so from the surface, watching the sea grass to assess the strength of the current before joining the others. The sea floor seemed so tranquil, she felt almost guilty for disturbing its peace.

The dig's underwater grids were set up much the same way they were on land. Small segments cordoned off inside a bigger square, all measured and labeled for accurate location.

From her vantage point, there wasn't much she could do alone. Ari had the waterproof slate and graphite pencils for their field notes, but at least she had the camera.

With Ari off being a jerk, it meant double the work with one less pair of eyes and one less pair of hands. Sight and touch were all the senses any of them had this far underwater.

She stared at the soft silt bottom and the treasures it concealed. Sight and touch. Not exactly separate senses, as far as she was concerned.

She hovered just outside the grid area and dragged a hand through the sand, to see. Her fingers tingled.

So far, so good.

The feeling wasn't painful, and she had no vertigo. She moved closer to the grid area, letting her fingertips probe the newest quadrant. The tingle faded almost completely.

Okay, now what?

She kicked her fins and circled, trying not to disturb the bottom too much. She swam to where she'd first tested her senses and tunneled her fingers a little deeper. Her hand practically vibrated.

Hot damn.

She grinned to herself about her secret game of hot and cold.

Dragging her fingers along the bottom, she kicked her fins again. Considering the currents, she tried to stay in a straight line. The vibrations turned into an itch, and that itch became a thousand little bee stings.

Holy crud. What if her tingle wasn't something extrasensory, but some creepy sand bug enjoying her fingers as a hot lunch? She jerked her hand from the silt, but there was nothing. No welts. No marks.

Condemned

"Beleenda, what are you doing? You're supposed to be wiz za group. Are you all right?" A heavily accented voice crackled through her headset.

She lifted her head, not bothering to answer with anything other than the hand signal for okay.

The Israeli lead diver lifted a hand, but when she waved him off, he shrugged and went back to work. The others glanced back, curious, but no one said a word.

Trying her luck again, she dug her hand palm deep. This time, the bee stings went all the way up her arm.

She closed her eyes and concentrated. Letting her body absorb the signs, she maneuvered almost on autopilot until the prickling reached a painful crest.

She went to yank her hand from the sand, but a sea of images crashed, leaving her paralyzed. Windswept flames and cannon fire. Men jumping from flaming hulls to the depths.

Her fingers grazed something hard and curved, and the visions released. Metal.

The word rang in her head, and she opened her eyes, wiggling her hand along the edge. The item wasn't very long, but its center felt like a knobby pipe.

Heart racing, she slowly unclipped her trowel from her belt. Hovering, she probed the spot with both her hand and the plastic tool. The disturbed silt clouded the water, obscuring her vision, so she closed her eyes again.

A single image formed in her mind. A shallow bowl with a heavy, squat base. Whatever this was, it wasn't garbage metal or a piece off a boat.

Keeping her eyes closed, she worked slowly. She moved on instinct and touch, keeping the image clear in her head. Chanting

and the smell of incense filled her mind, and one word rang above all others. *Chalice.*

Holy fuck! Holy Fuck! Holy Fuckety Fuck!

Adrenaline coursed through her veins as she pulled the item free. At first glance, it looked like a coral-hardened rock, until she turned it over. Preserved in a thousand years of muck, was the undeniable curve of a religious vessel. Dirty, but pristine.

She brushed the side of the chalice, clearing away the dirt. Her heart jumped to her throat, and tears pricked her eyes. At the center of the blemished gold was a Templar cross.

"Bubbie. I did it," she whispered, holding the ancient cup. "You were right...about everything."

I'm always with you, my darling girl. Remember, your journey has just begun...

Yup. She was going to Jerusalem.

Without Ari.

Chapter 11

"Dumb luck, Bels." Giles's voice laughed through her cell phone. "You were born under a four-leaf clover. There's no other explanation for how you always come out on top."

"Yeah, you wish. And I suppose hard work and diligence have nothing to do with it, right?"

"Exactly. I'm so glad you finally see that." He chuckled again.

"Ha. Ha. How are my plants doing? Or have they upped and committed suicide." She listened to the tinny echo on delay. God, did her voice really sound like that?

"Plants? How can you think about your sad experiments in horticulture when you are about to see your first big find unveiled? If I were you, I'd streak naked across the ramparts with a bottle of Cristal in both fists."

A gush of nostalgia hit her, and her chest tightened. "I wish you were here, G...and Dr. Adams, too. Believe it or not, I miss you and your goofy grin."

"Like I said. You want me and my pasty bod."

She rolled her eyes, but her grin stayed put. "Give it a rest, rich boy. If you've got so much money, jump on a flight. I've got the ramparts covered, you bring the champagne."

"I would, if I could," he exhaled a soft chuckle. "But I'm in charge around here. At least for the next few weeks. Adams is out on sabbatical."

Belinda's hand went to her mouth. "Why? Is he sick?"

"No, Belinda. He was attacked. Just like the two from the paper before you left. He survived, but just." He paused.

"What? You're not telling me everything, G. You only call me by my full name when it's something serious."

He didn't reply.

"Giles Newcomb, you tell me right now!"

He exhaled into the phone. "After you left, the murders stopped. The police thought the killer moved on or went underground. The moment we heard about your find, they started up again. Three more. All postgrad archeology students, past and present. Each one was an Adams favorite. It's got us all spooked. I've never been so happy to be considered a fuckup, but you need to watch your back. It's almost like you finding a Templar chalice has pissed someone way off, and they took it out on Theo Adams."

She swallowed. It was just coincidence, right? Why would someone be disgruntled about her find? Had someone else been turned down for a position and blamed Adams?

"It can't be connected, G. It doesn't make sense. Adams has taught hundreds of students, more if you count undergrads and master's degrees." She puffed out a breath. "Talk about sucking the wind out of everything."

"Ding. Ding. Ding. Just the reaction I had hoped to avoid. Now, do you understand why I didn't want to tell you?"

She chewed on the side of her pursed lips. "I don't blame you, G. I wouldn't have told you, either, if the situation was reversed. This isn't about me, anymore. It's about Dr. A."

"Oh, no you don't. This is about you and your find. Adams was practically walking on air when he got the news. He couldn't wait to speak with you. In fact, he had his secretary hunt for flights on ELAL to surprise you."

"Great, make me feel worse, why don't you?" she grumbled.

"Listen to me, baby cakes. Columbia is ranked for everything else but archeology. We don't even make the top ten. You just put us on the map, and that big red push pin has Adams's face on it. He's your mentor. Let him have his moment in the sun, even if it's vicariously through you."

She blinked, a little stunned. "Giles, I don't say this to you often, but you rock."

"Bels, you don't say that to me at all. Ever." He laughed.

Her heart squeezed. "Where is Adams, now?"

"Columbia Presbyterian, where else?"

She grinned through her tears. "Give him a hug for me when you see him. Zahra Khalid is in town and wants to see me before the big reveal at the Israeli Museum. I think she's going to try and coerce me into giving her and her crew credit, but it was her student who left me high and dry for his own fame and glory or he'd be sharing this with me now.

"If she thinks I'm giving her credit, she's got another think coming. All accolades belong to me, my Bubbie, Dr. Adams, and Columbia University. They trained me, formed me. Encouraged me. She didn't know me from a hole in the wall until she read my dissertation, which she then gave out to her students."

"Wait, what?"

"Yup. That tidbit came out in the wash. Adams submitted my unfinished paper with the understanding it would be for Dr. Khalid's eyes only, to review and decide on the internship spot. She gave it to her minions." She snorted. "Strange, selfish, butt-sucking units with the same Lilith sigil tattoo."

Giles sucked in a breath on the other side of the phone.

"What? Did I say something wrong? This is not a PC moment, G."

"No, just...Belinda, can you describe the tattoo to me."

She heard paper rustling. "G, you used my full name again. What's going on?"

"Just describe the tattoo, will you?"

"Okay, *Jeez.* Two perpendicular lines with serif crosses at each end, and the snakes from Hecate's trident entwined. Why?"

"That's exactly the description of the tattoo Adams gave the police."

Her breath locked for a moment. "Giles, was the tattoo on the attacker's right hand?"

"Yeah, how did you know?"

She paused, chewing on her lip. "Like you said. Lucky guess." Her head spun. Was Zahra Khalid a killer, or were her elites acting alone?

She needed to think, but her grandmother's warning was loud and clear in her head.

You will need your gift to help keep you safe.

***

"I'm so glad you decided to come, tonight," Zahra said, stepping onto the terrace, holding two glasses. She held one out to Belinda with a smile. "This hotel is my favorite place to stay in the Old City. I thought you would appreciate the magnificent views from the rooftop.

Belinda took the glass, happy to see it looked and smelled like ordinary champagne. "How could I say no?"

"Far too easily, my dear. As you've already proven." She arched a brow. "Still, I'm happy you accepted tonight, even if my *tyros* couldn't persuade you."

"Tyros?"

She smiled. "Latin. Loosely translated, it means fledgling or in terms of the Roman army, young soldier."

"Interesting," Belinda replied, though knowing what she did, the word made her cringe inside.

"I think what you wanted to say is my nickname for my special students is unusual. I can hear the American vernacular *'What the fuck?'* galloping through your mind."

Belinda nearly choked on her champagne.

Zahra's unhurried reach snagged a bar napkin from the table. She handed it to Belinda, her eyes narrowing slightly. "You know, since we first met, you haven't ceased to surprise me. You have no idea how that appeals." She angled her head. "My crew is talented and intelligent, but they tend to be slightly—"

"Sycophantic?" Belinda interjected.

A wide smile curled the woman's lips. "Precisely." Her eyes skimmed Belinda's face. "Again, you prove my point. I may not like your decision to decline my offer, but I respect it."

Oh God. Would it be rude to crawl under the closest table? "You're right about the hotel. The architecture alone is worth the price of admission," Belinda said, changing the subject. "Not just the view, but the gardens."

"I stay here every time I come to the Holy City. The structure is 425 years old. It was originally a pensione with stables for pilgrims' horses. Of course, they've been renovated, and now that part of the guesthouse is used for luncheons. Still, the history attached reminds me of my early life. The marble and mosaic touches are artistically rich in our cultural history. It is an experience for the psyche."

"No wonder they welcome you back so often. They should cut you a check for unsolicited appreciation," Belinda replied, not knowing what else to say.

Zahra had asked her here out of protocol, or so she assumed. If the woman knew she used extrasensory talents instead of straight

science to find that chalice, would she be as welcoming, or would she dismiss her as a crackpot? Still, every tool in the toolbox, right? Isn't that what they were taught? To follow hunches and go slowly through the process. Be meticulous so no possibility went unexamined.

"Something tells me, you had more than luck on your side when you made that find. A little help from your intuition, perhaps?" Zahra eyed her over her champagne.

Belinda nearly choked again. "If you're asking me if I cheated or took someone else's notes and used them to my advantage, you're wrong."

The woman laughed out loud. "I don't think that at all. Although, I would have put odds on Ari being the first to make a find, either that or steal it before you could claim it. You managed to prevent both." She raised her glass. "Brava."

Between the obsequious minions, and now the creeping feeling Zahra knew more about her than she let on, Belinda shivered.

Thankfully, the night was cooler than usual to cover the involuntary reaction. A deep-purple sweater with a pair of skinny jeans and peep-toe ankle boots she'd picked up at the local souk was her dress-for-success outfit. At least for tonight. She still had shopping to do since field boots weren't going to cut it for the gala or for her meeting at the museum tomorrow.

Field boots and lace panties.

She glanced down at the champagne in her hand. Dominic's face in that moment was something she'd always remember. Humor and desire wrapped together in thick want. She'd never felt more beautiful. With a distracted sigh, she sipped her champagne. It didn't pay to think about it too long, especially since she'd probably never see him again.

Condemned

You mean after you threatened to slice off the protruding parts of his body?

Yeah, something like that.

"So, I hear the lab is finished readying the chalice. Exciting, no?" Zahra asked.

"Yes. The director left a message with my hotel manager this evening. The processing is complete, and he invited me to preview the finished piece ahead of the exhibition. To be honest, I squeaked like a giddy teenager when I read his note."

Private time to examine the piece, awestruck and proud, meant more to her than the unveiling. She was a scientist. An academic. Regardless of fame and recognition, she was happiest in the field, but this rocked.

"I have something for you, to celebrate." Zahra moved to a small table by a potted plant. She reached for a small box and turned with a soft smile. "It's a reproduction of something I have in my personal collection. The real one is a thousand years old and made of pure silver. This one is platinum. More valuable, and it won't tarnish."

Belinda took the box from her hand. A breeze picked up, and the scent of cinnamon and vanilla wafted on the air. She sniffed, knotting her brows at the unusual timing.

"Is something wrong, dear?"

"No, I'm sure it's just a coincidence, but every time you're around, and even when someone's just mentioned your name, I smell coffeecake."

She burst out laughing. "It's my body lotion. It's actually called *Coffeecake*." Amused, Zahra angled her head, her gaze increasing. "I think you might be more perceptive than you think, and that's what led you to the chalice. You listen to things outside the box. It's one of the things I find so intriguing about you."

Ugh. The woman was still trying to collect her, even though she'd made it clear she wasn't buying. Belinda smiled graciously but couldn't help a quick glance for the exit.

"Why don't you open your gift, hmmm?"

Belinda lifted the velvet lid. Inside was a beautiful cross. It seemed almost Celtic in design until she looked closer and saw it was actually medieval Gallic.

"Is the original a reliquary cross?" she asked.

Zahra arched a brow, impressed. "Yes. Twelfth-century nobility, especially in central France, prided themselves on their devotion to the sacred sites of the Holy Land. Hence, the Crusades. Relics from Jerusalem and other Christian strongholds were coveted goods, especially when their claim to fame was wood from the True Cross. Crosses like the original in my collection had a wood core dipped in silver. Their selling point? Spiritual superiority. Selling relics to the gullible and the guilt-ridden made for thriving commerce, even if it was a load of bunk."

The woman's lip curled, punctuating her disgust, and Belinda was a little taken aback. Then again, academics were notorious for dissing people of faith as stupid.

"Enough fairy tales. Let's see how this looks on you." Zahra took the necklace from its box, and Belinda gathered her hair in one hand, lifting it from her neck. After weeks on the water, she'd finally gotten her curls to stop frizzing, so she'd left it down. It was the first time she'd felt completely put together since the night of the fireworks.

Zahra reached to clasp the chain around her throat, but then froze. She pulled her hands back, letting the cross dangle pendulum-like between them. Her nostrils flared, and her eyes narrowed as she lifted her gaze to Belinda's face.

Condemned

Puzzled, Belinda let go of her hair and took an involuntary step back. "Is something wrong? You're eyeing me as if I've suddenly sprouted horns. I promise, I showered today."

"Not at all, dear," Zahra replied, clearing her throat. "For a moment, I thought the chain was too short, and I was trying to remember the instructions I gave the jeweler."

Something about her response screamed tap dance. But why? None of this added up, but when she put it together with what had happened in Cairo and what Giles told her on the phone, it had to be connected.

"You had this piece made?" Belinda asked, doing a tap dance of her own.

Zahra put the necklace back in the box and closed the lid, holding it out to Belinda. "Yes," she replied a little tightly. "I hope that wasn't too presumptuous. It was part reward, part bribe. I had hoped it might entice you to join my crew, but I see now, that's impossible."

Her nostrils flared again, and she angled her head as if examining and discarding options. "Did you fly straight to Cairo from New York, dear?"

"No, I stopped to visit my old college roommate in Rome. I hadn't seen Roxy in almost three years. Not since she married an international med student doing his residency in New York. She went to the emergency room for stomach pains and came home with a new boyfriend. They were married soon afterward and moved to Italy. Why do you ask?"

"No reason." She inhaled one last time, and as she placed the velvet box in Belinda's hand, she let her fingers linger.

Stunned, Belinda's head jerked up immediately. Her eyes widened at the feel of the unexpected mental probe. Every muscle

Marianne Morea

tensed as she stared the woman down, shutting her out of her head like a steel trap.

Eyes narrowed, Zahra yanked her hand back. She didn't say a word.

If Zahra Khalid wanted a true example of American *what the fuck*, she just got a face full, along with a free side of *don't fuck with me.*

"Thank you for an illuminating evening, Dr. Khalid," Belinda said, as the woman watched her gather her purse from the table. "I guess we both have more than *luck* on our side," she added quietly.

She opened the top clasp to her bag and slipped the velvet box inside. Glancing up, she met the woman's stiff gaze, surprised at how white the faded scar on her cheek seemed.

"I was hoping Dr. Adams would attend the museum gala, but that's not going to happen. I heard from a friend, Dr. Adams was attacked on campus a few days ago. He survived, thank God. Luckily, he was able to give the police an accurate description of his assailant, including one important identifying element."

"Identifying element," Zahra repeated.

Belinda nodded. "A tattoo."

Her inner warning bells blared like a five-alarm fire as she headed for the terrace doors and the hotel exit beyond. She poked a sleeping tiger, but there was no way she would blink first. A sliver of fear penetrated her bravado, but she squashed it. Zahra Khalid had trespassed in her mind first.

Good, Belindachka. Do not allow that dark witch to bend your will, or she will own you as she does the others. This is not over, my darling. Your battle has just begun. Remember the power that flows through your veins.

184

Condemned

Bubbie was right. Zahra Khalid had similar psychic abilities. Big deal. That didn't give the woman leave to manipulate or frighten her or anyone else. Zahra probably wasn't Adams's attacker, but from the cold look on her face, she knew damn well who was, and why.

Now what?

You wait and you watch, my darling. There's light coming through the darkness. Be brave enough to let it fill you.

Chapter 12

Belinda stifled a giddy squeal but kept the ear-to-ear grin of anticipation as the museum director opened the door to the artifact lab.

They strolled past hundreds if not thousands of years represented in the artifacts currently being cleaned and catalogued. She slowed, her head swiveling to catch a better glimpse of a simple piece of jewelry on a cleaning mat.

"Ah, I see you have an eye for the twelfth century, as Dr. Khalid said." He came to stand beside her as Belinda stood in front of the work table. "This is from the good lady's personal collection. She bequeathed it to the museum in perpetuity. It is a permanent part of our Crusades exhibit, but she asked that we include it with a sampling of other artifacts to highlight your find. Like satellite moons around the newest planet in the galaxy."

"She gave me an exact replica as a laudatory gift, but I haven't worn it yet."

The director grinned, bobbing his head. "You should wear it. Not just because it represents your accomplishment, but because this original is said to have protected its owner during one of the worst battles in Crusader history, the Battle of *Ager Sanguinis*, also known as the Battle of the Field of Blood. Your mentor came across this piece on her very first dig, much like you have with this amazing chalice. It helped propel her to archeological stardom and academic fame, as I hope your find does for you."

Condemned

The man inhaled and then did a little hop before turning on his heel, beckoning her toward the back of the lab.

"And here is the pièce de résistance. The find of the year. I hope you realize what you've done for this museum, my dear. That underwater site is now fully funded with a round-the-clock marine archeological team assigned to its waters. The Mediterranean conceals so much. It's a veritable treasure trove of artifacts."

Belinda met his bouncing enthusiasm with a smile. "I'm happy for you and for the museum. I only wish I could sign on for another tour."

"Oh, my dear. One phone call and you are on the next plane whenever you wish, and *that* came from the Minister of Antiquities himself!"

"I appreciate that, director." She gestured to the medieval chalice still on the table. "May I? The last time I held the piece, it was covered in rigid coral."

He nodded emphatically, lifting a hand. "By all means. Please."

The director turned for white gloves, but Belinda picked up the chalice barehanded before he could protest. She wanted the history ingrained in the polished gold. The images it would reveal for her eyes only.

"Ms. Force, please—" He waggled the gloves.

She ignored him, closing her eyes instead and opening her mind.

Visions came fierce and fast. The army advanced. Red Templar crosses emblazoned on dusty tunics as they marched. Tensions were clear in the ranks, and whispers feathered across her mind, filled with the fear of death at their leader's arrogance.

"We'll camp here," a voice bellowed.

A lone rider stayed his horse, shaking his head. His face was obscured from Belinda's eyes by a desert scarf. All she could catch was the annoyed flash in his dark eyes.

The man was a knight, of that she was sure despite his Bedouin clothes. He turned to the man on the horse bedecked in noble regalia and lifted his hand to remove the scarf protecting his face from the dust.

Belinda's throat tightened.

Dominic.

She'd know him anywhere. His skin was tanned and smudged with dirt from his ride, but he was just as handsome as when she saw him in Rome. Just more rugged and fiercer.

"Sir, this isn't the place for us to make camp. Observe. We're in a wooded valley with steep sides and few avenues for escape if ambushed. Saladin and his men blend into the landscape, and we cannot hide seven-hundred knights and three-thousand foot soldiers, let alone decamp at the first sign of attack."

The commander's mouth was a slash. "Fine. Fill the canteens, then. We march. We'll meet the heretics on the flat sand and leave them there to bleed."

Dominic opened his mouth to argue, but the man reared his horse and took the head of the line.

A smell of death nearly choked her, and her throat was parched as if gasping for release. Her lips felt cracked and bleeding, and her knees buckled. They would die. All of them. And the chalice they carried to protect them was all that was left.

Her knees buckled, and the director shot forward, catching the relic before it fell from her hands. She hit the floor in a wave of vertigo, overwhelming despair from thousands dying because of one man's arrogance squeezing her chest until she couldn't breathe.

Condemned

The moment the cup left her hands, her chest cleared, and she blinked. She was on the floor with the director and the lab staff standing over her as if she was some sort of freak.

"I...I'm sorry," she stuttered, taking an offered hand and climbing to her feet. "I have low blood sugar and didn't eat this morning. I should know better, especially considering the excitement of seeing my find so beautifully preserved."

"It's understandable, my dear. No harm, no foul. We'll give the cup another polish and put it in its place of honor for Sunday's exhibition. Tomorrow is Shabbat, so all plans need to be finalized by noon."

"Of course. Thank you for allowing me to see the piece before the crowds." She eyed the chalice in his possessive hands. "You have no idea what it means to me."

Every lingering misgiving she had about Dominic faded. She stepped out of the museum into the bright sun and gazed at the people going about their lives without a care, most believing the world to be exactly as they could see, hear, and feel.

For the first time, she closed her eyes and let her body listen to things outside the box, as Dr. Khalid said. Her throat tingled, and she lifted a hand to the spot. Something was out there, waiting.

***

Dominic sat in the Muslim quarter, watching the crowds move through the market. Thick, aromatic coffee sat in his cup, untouched. It was late in the afternoon, yet the sun was still strong. Sunset was in barely two hours, still the rays' draining power weighed heavy.

Sahira had been in the city. The bitch made sure his body knew it the moment she set foot inside the walled ramparts.

It was after nightfall last night as he sat on the roof of the Holy Sepulcher in the Christian quarter. His skin prickled at her proximity, and loathing flooded his body to near choking.

Bitter anger rose like bile, and he jumped from the ancient stones, tracking her through the Old City and then out into the outskirts on the opposite side of the wall. Like vapor, she evaded his reach, yet again.

Disappointment took him again that Sahira eluded him once more. The bitch could find him any day or night, but not the other way around. She was his maker. He had to bide his time once again.

Still, age had its benefits. Just as the threat of daylight faded over time, so did Sahira's hold. Why would she come to Jerusalem then flee if not to taunt him?

Over the years, every time he struck, someone he loved died. It was still a capital offense to bring final death to one's maker, but he didn't care. He had lived far longer than he'd ever expected. Had seen the best and worst this world offered. Besides, who would sentence him? Carlos? Rémy? If there were undead older than him, he'd yet to meet even one.

Sahira was nearly twice his age. Over the centuries, there were those who speculated she was Lilith.

He shook his head.

Sahira was ancient, but not that ancient. Though how she'd survived and adapted over all these eons was still a mystery. He had yet to reach a full millennium in his undead life, and that was hard enough.

He was here in the mid-twelfth century when the Templar brotherhood sweated through the renovations on this ageless land. On the temples and mosques, and on the Holy Sepulcher, itself,

refurnishing the church in Romanesque style and adding a bell tower.

Dominic smirked to himself. They'd even tried their hand at archeology before it was an actual discipline, investigating the Eastern ruins while hunting for a viable cistern. They'd discovered the remnants of a Roman temple hidden under piles of rubble.

Half his men wanted to destroy the pagan site, but he refused to give the order. Roman gods and their mythology fascinated him even then.

Belinda would've loved the history behind that story.

He signaled for the waiter.

"Yes, sir?"

"Bring a bottle of local red and a plate of cheese and bread," he said with a smile, peeling off money for the man's eager hand since it was close to closing time.

"Right away." He bobbed his head and turned on his sandaled feet. The *scuff-scuff* of his soles on the smooth tiles echoed in his wake as he went to get Dominic's order.

The sun hung lower in the sky. Soon the streets of the four quarters of the Old City would roll up for the night. He could hit the bars and stop in for live music.

Or hunt.

His thirst tugged. The pull didn't surprise him. Not when he hadn't fed properly since before Charmaine died.

Just look at you. A sadder case I never I saw. And don't think I didn't hear you order that food. You'll be sick later, mark my words...

A soft grin curled his lips. Charmaine's tutting and fuss were indelibly etched in his brain.

The food came, along with the wine. The waiter poured him a glass and then left with a nod.

Spearing an aromatic chunk, he took a mouthful. The sharp tang and salty bite of the aged cheese filled his taste buds and his memories. It was his mother's kitchen in Provence, before his father left him with the monks to be educated and trained. It was the picnics he took with Céleste. The warmth of the sun and her ripe body in the tall summer grass.

He sipped the local red, letting the taste roll on his tongue. The wine was heady and sweet. Belinda flashed into his mind. The image of her wanton and stretched wide, her veins filling his mouth with her heady and sweet blood. The tips of his fangs pierced his gums as his cock hardened at the memory. The unsated need behind his zipper had his fingers gripping the edge of the small table. He needed release, but the only one who could satisfy his hunger had run from him.

With a guttural rush, he drained his wine, nearly scaring the poor waiter out of his shoes. He paid the bill, leaving twice as much in a tip, and stepped out onto the cobbled stones.

He'd head to the sultan's pool. There was a free concert tonight, and the ancient water basin was always jumping with activity. If there was ever a place where he could lose himself and not think, it was there.

Belinda was somewhere close. Maybe not in the city, but in the region. Cairo wasn't that far, and from there he knew she went to Akko, but that's as far as he let himself go.

He'd fed from her, so she wore his mark. With that, she was protected from lesser vampires. It would fade, as he was sure her memory of him would as well. Humans were a fickle bunch. So quick to chase the next best thing.

It was a product of such a fleeting lifespan. Like the lyrics to that Five for Fighting song. *"There's never a wish better than this. When you only got a hundred years to live."*

Condemned

Why was letting Belinda go so hard? The fiery redhead invaded his dreams still, and he'd had to self-satisfy more times than he wanted to admit, even to himself.

The city was alive around him, with all its diverse scents wafting in a symphony of promise. He could have anyone he wanted. Man or woman. Their blood. Their bodies. But none of it interested him.

Belinda's taste had tainted him like a drug, and nothing else would suffice. The temptation to find her through his mark nearly suffocated him.

He picked up his pace and moved quickly through the twilight streets. He needed a diversion now, or he'd trace her and let the chips fall where they may. With his thoughts whirling, he turned into an arched passage and stopped short.

Belinda.

Raging hard-on and a raging thirst. No wonder. She was right there. An arm's reach from where he stood in the shadowed archway.

She bristled, lifting a hand to the side of her throat. He watched her rub the spot where he'd fed from her and pull her fingers back, puzzled. Her skin prickled, and his vampiric eyes saw the glowing mark on her throat.

If she only knew.

She would run from you again.

Perhaps.

He reached out, probing her mind with a feather's touch, but her mind slammed shut with whiplash speed. Stunned, he jerked back, but before she severed the link, she sent a vicious mental slap.

Back off, Zahra. I mean it!

Zahra?

"Ow. Jesus that hurt." Lifting fingers to the bridge of his nose, he winced. More than simple curiosity piqued, and he couldn't help a silly proud smirk despite the sore nose.

Obviously, Belinda had found her gifts, and someone was trying to take advantage, but the fiery redhead who threatened to cut off his manhood was too strong to allow that to happen.

The sweet witch had come into her own in the weeks since he saw her last. His gaze drank her in as the last of the sun cast a coppery glow around her hair.

Belinda was even more beautiful than he remembered. She had obviously taken advantage of the souk and its treasures. He watched her body stretch and bend as she moved around the wares. Her eyes sparkling as she talked to the vendor, haggling over price.

A soft midriff top and matching ankle-length skirt showed just enough skin to be sexy but covered enough to be classy, and strappy gladiator sandals finished the gypsy-boho style.

He chuckled to himself. Gladiator sandals were ancient combat boots. A faraway smile took him as he remembered her catwalk turn showing off her field boots and lacy underwear.

His cock jumped, thick with unspent need at the intimate image. It wasn't just the sex that made the memory intimate. It was their connection. The humor and wit and the comfort of her. He craved that as much as he craved her blood and her body.

Belinda smiled at the vendor, shoving her wallet into her bag before gathering her purchases. She turned and walked toward the archway. His archway.

Her head was down as she jostled her bags, and he couldn't resist. He stepped out from where he stood just in time for her to smack right into him.

She bounced off his chest again, but this time he was fast enough to catch her before she hit the ground.

Bags dropped, and she stumbled sideways before getting her footing, and when she finally steadied enough to glance up, her mouth dropped.

"Dominic?"

Her eyes widened, but instead of fear there was genuine surprise.

"How? I mean, did…did you know—" she stuttered, giving her head a shake. "What are you doing here?"

He smirked. "Airplane. No. Unfinished business."

She blinked and then burst out laughing. "That was for my pyramid joke, right?"

"Yup." He took in her scent and let it soak into his very being.

"And could that unfinished business be me?" Her eyes found his and held.

Was that a hint of hope in her voice? "Do you want it to be? You got my note, yes?"

She glanced down at her hands. "I got it, and I read it about a hundred times."

"And?" He slipped his fingers beneath her chin, lifting her face so he could see her eyes.

"I want to know more, Dominic. I want to know everything. I believe you. So much has happened in the last month since I last saw you." She glanced past her shoulder as if someone listened. "I don't want to talk here. I'm at the Imperial for the next few days. Where are you staying?"

He grinned, giving her a sheepish shrug. "Great minds think alike. I'm at the Imperial, too."

She took his hand and scooped up her bags. "I don't know where to start or who's going to talk first, but we'd better get some

food and a couple of bottles of wine, because you're in for a long night."

He laughed out loud. "The night has been my domain for hundreds of years, Belinda. And tonight, is all yours."

Chapter 13

The hotel elevator closed behind them, and Belinda stood in awkward silence. She'd been dreaming of this man for weeks, and now he was here, and she had no words.

"Whose floor? Yours or mine?" Dominic asked.

"Mine. That way, if you creep me out too much, I can uninvite you in, or is that all Hollywood?"

"Holy water? Hollywood. Stake through the heart? Well, who wouldn't that kill?" He chuckled, pressing the button for the tenth floor. "Crucifixes, garlic, sanctified ground? All Hollywood. Rescinding an invitation, though? That is very real. As real as our aversion to silver and sunlight. The sunlight thing fades with age, but silver is always a bad thing for the undead."

"I wonder why. I read somewhere that silver was anathema to vampires because Judas Iscariot was the first to be made undead, and he betrayed Christ with thirty pieces of silver."

The elevator dinged, and Dominic extended an arm, letting Belinda step out first. "That is the most Hollywood thing I've ever heard. Judas Iscariot was a weak man who hung himself in his grief and regret."

"Wasn't that way before your time?"

Dominic rolled his eyes. "Funny. First you threaten to castrate me with my own sword, and now it's old man jokes. My son, Carlos, would find you good company. Especially since he's fond of calling me Old Monk."

Marianne Morea

She stopped in front of her door and turned, confused. "Wait. You have a son?" Pain shadowed Dominic's eyes for a moment, and Belinda immediately regretted her incredulous tone. "I didn't mean it like that," she tried.

"I know, *chéri*. I did have a son. A very long time ago, before I was turned. His descendants still exist, so my human bloodline endures. But, Carlos..." He shrugged. "Carlos is not my progeny, but he is every bit my son, as if I was the one woke him to this existence."

Belinda swept her keycard through the digital eye, and the door snicked open. She pushed the handle and stepped inside, snapping on the light.

"So, Carlos is also a vampire, then?" she asked, dropping her shopping bags on the floor by the desk, before kicking her shoes off and leaving them under the chair.

"Yes, as are his mate and the rest of his family. They were once human, and Carlos saved them from death or worse than death."

She turned after pulling the curtains wide so the lights of the city could be seen from her terrace. "Have you ever..." She hesitated. "Saved someone?"

"No." He moved in front of her, lifting his hand to her cheek. "I would never curse someone to this life the way I was cursed."

Her hand went to her throat again, and she lifted her chin, trying to ignore the strange prickly feeling. "I must have gotten bitten by a mutant mosquito or something. The side of my throat is tingling like it's on fire."

"A mutant mosquito?" He burst out laughing. "I hate to disappoint your Darwinian hypothesis, but that would be me."

She quirked up a brow. "You?"

"My proximity, actually. A vampire's mark will prickle his lover's flesh whenever he is close."

Her eyebrow went even higher. "Define close."

"Leave it to a science and arts geek to ask what no one in the history of the undead has ever thought to ask." His brows knotted in amusement."

"Hey, I earned the title geek, and I wear it proudly. Like I wear your mark, I guess. Though I'm a little weirded out, considering I refused to join an elite group at the university in Cairo because they all have the same tattoo. Still, I'm serious. The side of my neck has been tingling all day. Has anyone charted the radius of a vampiric prickle? Is it like a restaurant beeper that only buzzes around the eatery's perimeter, or is it long range? I've been all over the city. First the museum then I hit the bazaars to shop."

"I can tell." He glanced at the bags and then gave her sexy new outfit a once-over. "What happened to lace panties and field boots? Not that I don't like your new look. Especially the tease of skin."

He slid his arm around her bare midriff, dipping his head for a kiss.

"Wait." She pulled back, eyeing him. "So, this mark. Since I can't see it, but you say it's there, and I can certainly feel it, does that mean other vampires can see it, too? I'm assuming you're not the only one of your kind."

He laughed out loud, tightening his grip on her waist. "When the wheels turn inside that beautiful head, I know my kiss will have to wait. You, *chéri*, are too smart. Yes, the mark shows you are under another's protection. It basically tells them you are off-limits. They cannot feed from you or sample your body, no matter how tempted they might be."

"A vampiric hickey." She laughed. "Did you have to suck my blood to make the mark?"

"That is such a Bella Lugosi thing to say. *I vant to suck your blood,*" he mimicked the old Hollywood vampire. "We don't *drink* blood, either, although warmed in a mug when you first wake isn't bad."

"Eew! Stop!" She shoved at his chest, and he laughed out loud.

"We prefer *took your blood,* but yes. I tasted you. Took some of your blood. For my kind, it's not just about thirst. It's arousal. Sex and blood are linked."

She snickered a little. "Are you telling me your fangs descend at the same time other parts of you *ascend*?"

His gorgeous mouth split in an ear-to-ear smile, and his eyes glinted with genuine laughter. "Basically, yes, though I never thought of it that way."

Dominic lifted her left hand to her throat. "Use these two fingers to feel the full extent of your mark," he said isolating her middle finger and ring finger. "There's a reason the third finger on your left hand is called the heart finger, and it's not because of marriage."

Belinda pressed just those fingers to the prickling spot and gasped at the flood of warm desire. Her breasts ached, and her nipples hardened, though he hadn't touched her.

Dark, unfathomable eyes met her stunned gaze, and she licked her lips. He dipped his lips to hers for a gentle kiss. "I can feel your pulse and your arousal, Belinda, and you can feel my—"

A seductive grin spread on his lips, and she gasped again. Thick and corded and invisible, she felt every ridged inch of his phantom cock.

"Oh my God." She sucked a breath between her teeth as he nibbled the underside of her jaw. "So, no mutant mosquito, then."

"Nope. Just me. With much sharper teeth and a cock so hard it could cut diamonds."

She gasped at the raw talk and puddled in his arms. He kissed his way over her jaw and took her mouth, his kiss demanding and hungry.

Letting her defenses down, she opened to every sense, every image and emotion. She wanted Dominic totally and utterly.

He broke their kiss to whisper her name, but when his mouth crushed to hers again, she jerked back, panting. She blinked, squeezing her eyes shut.

"Holy shit!" She put her hands on his chest and pushed him back. Zahra Khalid's face, fanged and grotesque, lingered in her mind.

"What is it? What happened?" he asked.

She paced in a circle, raking a hand through her hair.

"Belinda. I know you have a gift, love. I sensed it in Rome. I saw you at the souk vendors before we collided. I'm the one who tried to probe your mind." He nodded when her eyes flashed to his, and he lifted a hand to his nose. "You pack a pretty hefty mental wallop."

"That was you?" she asked, dumbfounded.

He nodded again. "Vampires have certain gifts as well. It depends on their maker and what gets passed on through the blood during transition. I inherited a sort of telepathy. I can probe minds."

She exhaled a tense chuckle. "Funny you should say that, because I have the same gift. Although, for me to see images and thoughts involves touch." She shrugged. "I'm a tactile clairvoyant."

"I knew you had latent power the moment I tasted you. Your blood is laced with magic and light. Not to trivialize your heritage, but you, *chéri*, are a white witch."

He moved to the couch and patted the cushion beside him. "Sit. Let's talk. I've waited lifetimes to be with you. I can wait a little longer to satisfy that amazing mind of yours. I just have one question. Who is Zahra, and why would she trespass in your head enough to warrant a right hook?"

"You don't know?"

Dominic's brows knotted. "Why would I know this woman? Is she a colleague of yours?"

"Because I saw her face in your head, only she didn't look like she does now. Her face was grotesque. Gargoyle-like. And her fangs—" She lifted both palms to her face, repulsed.

"Don't, love." Dominic got up from the sofa and was at her side in a heartbeat. He slid both arms around her, pulling her close. "What you described is a feeding face. It's how most vampires appear when they take blood from a human."

She let her palms drop to his chest and lifted her eyes. "You didn't look like that. Not that I saw much."

"You saw enough." He chuckled, but then his face softened at the doubt in her eyes.

"In my letter, I said vampires were like mankind, some good and some evil. Except, in my world, it's easier to distinguish between the two. Our true nature manifests on our faces when we feed. Vampires who live a cruel existence with no regard for human life will be the most grotesque. Those who hold tight to the shreds of their humanity won't.

"Vampire-kind is intrinsically selfish. The natural pull toward inborn superiority and impolitic cruelty is constant. It's hard to keep the full spectrum of human emotion, especially when a transition was committed in vice. I have been a vampire for almost a millennium. I never speak of how I was turned, but perhaps I should share it with you. That is, if you're willing to hear."

"I want to hear everything, but I think I need some liquid courage, first." Belinda moved to the minibar and opened the small refrigerator for a half bottle of wine. Unscrewing the cap, she poured a glass and downed it in one shot.

"Would you like a glass of wine?" she asked, and then hesitated. "Wait, you drank wine in Rome. Vampires are okay with *drinking* wine, but they *take* blood?"

He smirked. "Semantics. Take sounds more civilized, and yes, we can drink wine. Most naturally fermented spirits are fine since they are basically water. Blood is mostly water, so I suppose that's the science behind the fact it doesn't make us ill. It also doesn't make us drunk. Food will make us ill at times. It depends."

"So, yes to the wine, then?"

"Sure, why not?"

Her room was a suite, paid for by the museum in honor of her find and the gala fundraiser they'd parlayed into the event. "How about we break open the good stuff?" Without waiting for him to reply, she went to the bar across the living room area and pulled a bottle of merlot from the wine rack. Grabbing two glasses and a corkscrew, she walked back to the sofa and handed the tool to Dominic to do the honors.

"If you saw this woman Zahra in my mind, and you're sure it wasn't a projection from your head, then I must know her," he said, wiggling the cork loose.

He poured two glasses, sliding one to Belinda.

"I don't know if it was a projection or not. My gut says not."

"Then it's not. If there's one thing I've learned, it's that a witch's intuition is almost never wrong. My maker was a witch in every evil sense of the word, but she had powers. Powers that didn't diminish with her undead status."

"What was her name?" Belinda asked.

He took the wine glass from her and placed it on the coffee table next to his. Taking her hand in his, he leaned in and kissed her softly. "Why don't I show you who she is instead?"

"How? Are you going to introduce us?"

"In a way, yes. I'm going to show you what happened. I'm going to let you into my memories."

Dominic slipped his fingers around the back of her head and then leaned in, pressing their foreheads together. He laced his free hand with hers and lowered his shoulders, relaxing his guard.

Belinda held tight and closed her eyes. She sent her senses out, slipping tentatively into Dominic's head. A soft buzzing formed, and the feel was different than when she read Ari or even Kir. Was it because Dominic was undead? She dismissed the thought. She needed focus, not hypothesis.

Scenes opened, and she saw him clearly as a Templar Knight. Gorgeous. Strong. He was mounted on a horse in full armor with his white tunic and red Templar emblem. He rode at the front of a line of men hundreds strong. A smile slipped across her lips.

"You were so fucking hot," she giggled.

"Were?"

"You know what I mean."

"I could dress up for you, you know. I still have my tunic and sword."

"What, no armor? What kind of knight doesn't have armor?"

He paused. "The kind who was left to die by a jealous commander and then made vampire before he could find his legion."

Belinda squeezed her eyes tighter as those images flooded her mind. She saw everything that happened and gasped when she saw his commander's face through Dominic's memories.

She hadn't told Dominic about the chalice or her find, but she would. For now, her heart squeezed, as she watched him suffer.

"No one came for you?" she asked, her breath hitching.

He exhaled a rough breath. "No, someone came. Keep watching."

It was weird to chat while surfing his memories like images in a Google search. Weird and freeing. Kind of like watching a movie together.

The images flew past at blurred speed until her body tensed, and fear and anger coalesced into a choking burn in her throat.

"Zahra," she whispered.

She watched her enter the tent, the woman's eyes intense as flame as she saw through Dominic's mind. Belinda pulled back, breaking contact. Hand shaking, she lifted her wine, draining the second glass just as quickly as the first.

"Why did you pull away? I thought you wanted to see how I was turned. See the witch who tore my life from me."

Belinda shifted on the cushion to face him. Their hands were still linked, but she had shut down the images. She didn't need to see the particulars. The grotesque image in his mind earlier was enough of a hint.

"Was your maker the dark-haired woman dressed in that see-through gold outfit?" she asked.

He nodded slowly. "Yes, but there is nothing about her that's appealing, Belinda. You don't have to be jealous."

"Jealous." She snorted. "That's funny." She looked at him, pointed and serious. "I've spent years of my academic life aspiring to be that woman. You see, I know her. In fact, she's the reason I went to Cairo. Why I'm in Jerusalem right now."

He pulled his hand from hers and stood from the couch. "I don't understand," he said, pacing. "Did you know her when I met you in Rome?"

She nodded. "I was awarded an internship co-sponsored by the University of Cairo and Egyptian Antiquities, headed by Zahra Khalid." She gestured to him. "The same woman I saw in your head earlier and just now. Although, she has a scar on her face that wasn't in the image I saw in your head."

"That's because I hadn't tried to kill her yet." He blew out a breath. "The last image you saw was my final night as a human. She seduced me and then ravaged my body, my blood. I died at her hand, and her foul blood prevented me from entering paradise. She cursed me to this life." He exhaled again. "But her turning me vampire isn't why I long to rip her heart out with my teeth. It's because of everything she's taken from me, beginning with my first love."

He paced back and forth in the dining room area. He passed the small table with Belinda's room key and her purse. On the white marble surface was the velvet box Zahra had given her the night before.

It was half-open, and Dominic stopped mid-pace and turned. He lifted the lid on the small jewelry box, and he jerked around toward Belinda.

"Where did you get this?" he demanded, motioning with the box.

"From Zahra. She gave it to me last night to congratulate me on my find."

"Your find? What find?"

She shrugged. "Seeing you again threw it out of my mind. I've spent the last month with you invading my thoughts so much, everything I did and everywhere I went somehow circled back to

you and our time in Rome. To your letter. I regretted not listening to you. Talking to you when I had the chance.

"I told you, I was awarded this internship. Part of it was an assignment on an underwater dig outside the port of Akko. I uncovered a pretty significant find at that dig." She gave him a soft smile. "It was a gold chalice. With a Templar cross embossed on the bowl. The cup was sent to the museum here in Jerusalem, and I accompanied it. I held it, Dominic. And when I did, I saw you. It was when I knew for sure you were telling me the truth about your life…your existence."

"You didn't believe me before."

"No. But I fantasized about you, and that made me want to believe you. My gut is never wrong, and I knew you wouldn't harm me. I hear my dead grandmother's voice in my head sometimes, and she's totally Team Dominic."

He chuckled at that. "Tell her I said thank you." His soft laugh faded, though, as he looked to the city lights spread out beyond the hotel terrace. "Zahra Khalid. So that's the name that black witch has made for herself in the human world."

"She's made a name, all right. In my world, she's an archeological superstar. She's even got a group of rabid disciples to do her bidding. They tried to coerce me to join." She gestured to the velvet box still in Dominic's hand.

"Zahra knows my fascination with all things twelfth century, so she had that medieval carrot made specially to dangle on her stick. The original is part of her private collection."

Dominic's eyes flashed. "What?"

"It's on permanent load to the Israeli Museum. "I saw it today. The reliquary cross is amazing, considering its age. They plan to showcase the piece at Sunday night's celebration gala, alongside my chalice." She eyed at him. "Why are you so interested?"

He lifted his gaze from the velvet box. "Because that cross was once mine."

Belinda's mouth fell open. "The museum director told me Zahra found it on her first dig."

"Zahra Khalid found nothing. She took. In fact, she ripped it from my throat the night she stole my life. She is not human, Belinda. Not even a facsimile. She shed whatever was left of her humanity like a snake sheds its skin. Her real name is Sahira. She is an ancient sorceress who has been undead for nearly twice as long as me. I've never met an older or more powerful vampire."

Her hand went to her stomach, and Belinda felt the blood drain from her face. "It all makes sense, now." She lifted her eyes to his. "I thought Zahra was trying to collect me for her elites because of my intellect and talent in the field. Now I know she wanted me because she and I have the same blood."

"No." Dominic stalked from the terrace doorway to sink onto the couch beside her. "Never say those words. You share nothing with that creature except me because she's my maker. There is no real bond between Sahira and I. Not anymore. My advanced age has withered her control to almost nothing. She's tried to compel me, but I've ignored her for years. Having a strong-blooded maker is often a good thing. Your talents ripen quicker, and you benefit from their strength, but your maker's hold stays longer. I've outlived it all.

"You said Sahira wanted to collect you. That's chillingly parallel to what she wanted with me. She wanted me to rule the desert at her side, but also at her feet. She never dreamed I would refuse, let alone try and kill her for it."

"Maybe she's gotten better at rejection. To be honest, she seemed to take my demur with grace. That is, until she went to

fasten that necklace around my neck." Belinda's eyes flew wide. "Holy fangdom! She saw your mark."

Her eyes found his, and she nodded. "That's why she got all weird and cold. She tried to probe my mind, but I felt her immediately and slapped her down. Shutting her out of my head was easy, though I know it pissed her the hell off."

"Tell me about these elites. Sahira had an entourage of women following her when we first met."

Belinda shrugged. "Equal opportunity minionism must be the name of the game, now. She's got men and women alike as adherents. They all wear a strange Lilith sigil on their right hand. In fact, one of her sycophants attacked my mentor. He's the head of Archeology and Antiquities at Columbia University."

"How do you know the assault was connected to Sahira?"

"Because the attack failed, and Dr. Adams survived. He identified the sigil tattoo. If that isn't proof enough the two are connected, then it's an inexplicable coincidence."

Dominic took her hand and held it tight to his chest. "You must leave this place and go back to New York. Carlos is there. I'll call him. He can keep you safe until I settle this with Sahira one way or the other."

"No. I refuse to run scared. I've had to fight for everything I have in this world, and I'll be damned if I turn tail now."

"This fight is not an academic debate or a street brawl. It's a supernatural power struggle. It has been for centuries. Sahira is the queen of stealth and patience. She strikes and then disappears, leaving grief and fury in her wake. It's her favorite game, and I am her favorite game piece. She moves me around the board, stirring both wrath and impotent frustration. My hands have been tied for centuries. A vampire cannot kill their maker or progeny. It's our

most absolute law. Each time I strike back, someone I love dies. It's her favorite way to tighten my noose. So, I chose to be alone."

She clutched his shirt in empathy.

"It's exhausting. She lulls me into a false sense of security, disappearing for a century or more and then bam, she strikes, just to remind me I am never alone and never free. So, the game begins anew. I've had no real peace in almost a thousand years.

"I will end this game of cat-and-mouse with her once and for all, but I refuse to let you get caught in this final round. I've already put you in grave danger because you captivate me body, mind, and soul." He lifted her fingers to his lips. "I can't help myself."

Belinda slipped into Dominic's mind unannounced and saw his plan. His rage at Sahira's most recent strike buffeted her mind. Resolve hardened in its place as he cradled the woman's dead body. She saw him visualize final death. For him and for Sahira. Felt him open and resign himself to it as a means to an end.

"No!" She shoved at his chest, releasing his mind. "You tell me I captivate your soul and then plan this? Are you insane or just the most selfish creature on the planet? You opened me to this amazing, surreal life and even more amazing, surreal love, and then what? Hit me with *c'est la vie*? That's all, folks? No." She shook her head. "You should've left me to my fantasies."

"I have to do this, Belinda. What you saw are possibilities. I'm tired of living with this blackness over my head, over my life. I told you I could love you if such things were allowed. They *are* allowed in my world. Carlos's mate was human. She chose to join our ranks. It's the same with other members of our family. Well, damn the blackness to hell and me with it. You have my heart, or whatever is left of it." His eyes searched hers. "I don't want to be alone anymore."

Condemned

Belinda touched his cheek. "You don't have to be. You have me, and I'm not afraid. Not of you and not of Sahira/Zahra or whatever she calls herself. We will fight her together. Now, show me everything I need to know."

She moved to press her forehead to his, but he shook his head, cupping her cheeks. "Later. Right now, all I want is you, you amazing, fierce little seer."

Chapter 14

Dominic took her by the hand and led her out to the terrace. "I want you in the cool night air where I can watch you shiver as desire licks your body along with my tongue."

He lifted the midriff top from her shoulders, and she stood back and unclipped her bra. The lace fluttered to the ground.

She reached behind and unzipped her skirt, letting it fall to her ankles. Stepping out of the cotton puddle, she stood with her shoulders back in nothing but a lace thong.

A teasing grin tweaked her lips. "Something about this rings a bell. Should I go and find my field boots?"

With a playful growl, he scooped her into his arms and laid her on one of the plush chaises. His hand trailed from her shoulder over her breasts to the thin lace band at her hips.

His eyes darkened with desire. They were almost black in the shadowed light on the terrace. Centuries upon centuries had formed this man. This extraordinary, supernatural man. She'd seen what happened to him at the hands of his Templar brothers, yet he revered the order still, keeping the treasures from his human life.

She couldn't bear to see more of the images in his head of what Zahra did to him, but she'd glimpsed enough to know it was depraved and agonizing. Yet, through all that, despite the unquenchable thirst and uncertainty, Dominic had kept his soul.

The Templar she saw through his shared memories, and the one she viewed unsolicited from the chalice, painted enough of a

picture for her to see Dominic's true nature. Honor. Reverence. Nobility of spirit... Love.

Belinda knew he had evolved over his long life, but the man he had been was still there in the one standing on the terrace tonight. There were two things about which she was certain—one...Sahira's curse had changed Dominic's body, but it hadn't changed the man, and two, she had fallen for him head over boots.

The romanticized image she built in her head this past month was nothing compared to the real thing. Dominic was truly the knight of her dreams. Right here. Right now. In the flesh. It didn't matter that flesh was undead.

Hollywood had it wrong. His flesh wasn't grave cold. Nor was it marble hard. He was cool to the touch, but no more than average, and when she rested against his chest in Rome, he'd had a faint heartbeat. Weak and slow, it seemed almost negligible, but there, nonetheless. Something she wanted to ask about...but not now.

Dominic wrapped a finger through the lacy elastic and snapped the delicate thong with a single twist. "I'll buy you more," he said, kneeling at her hip to press a kiss to her belly just above the red fluff between her legs. "Two for every day of the week. One to keep and one for me to tear off your luscious hips."

Kissing his way up her body, he stopped to circle one nipple with his tongue. One hand trailed through her red fluff, gently stroking her soft folds.

She lifted his head from her breast to meet his eyes. "Kiss me," she murmured.

His lips took hers, and she drove her hands into his thick brushed-back hair, crushing his mouth to hers. His tongue plunged, tasting her, teasing her until she gasped. She kissed him

back with such hunger he moaned, and when her teeth grazed his tongue, he growled.

Breaking their kiss, he pulled back and stripped out of his clothes. Belinda sat up, letting her legs fall to either side of the lounge. Dominic was impressive fully dressed, but when he straddled the chaise, naked and aroused, his massive erection made her blink twice. Corded and swollen, the sight of his full length was just as delicious and daunting as it had been in Rome.

She licked her lips and leaned in, cupping his balls in one hand while wrapping her other around his shaft. Tantalizing with tongue and teeth, she trailed a line of kisses and nibbles down through his nest of black curls to his thick member.

His cock jerked as she circled her tongue under his ridged head. A small smile tugged, and she nipped the smooth velvet. Strong thighs tensed as she teased his bulging head.

Belinda stroked and sucked, and Dominic's body hardened. His muscled stomach clenched when she licked his hard length from base to head, letting the flat of her tongue rasp along the ribbed underside vein.

He fisted her red hair, lifting it from her neck to watch his cock slid in and out of her mouth. He growled low, tightening his hold.

"More," he rumbled, urging her to take him, deeper, faster. The growl in his chest changed to something primal and raw, and when she looked up, she saw his face had changed.

Nothing like Sahira's grotesque gargoyle-like monster she'd seen in his mind, but enough that she knew he was close to the point of no return.

"Woman, any more and you'll have to swallow what I give," he ground out.

She reached up and scraped her nails over his broad chest before pulling her mouth from his member.

He hissed in protest but knelt on the end of the chaise between her splayed legs. Crawling forward, he couldn't be more predatory. She drew both knees in, letting them fall wide in invitation.

"Such a tease." He smirked. "Two can play at that." Leaning forward, he flicked his tongue over her soft slit, his breath feathering across her red fluff. The combined sensations made her lower belly throb, sending prickles straight to the mark on her throat.

Fingers brushed sensitive folds, caressing her swollen bud in light, languorous strokes. Heat exploded down to her core. Her breath came short and fast. Belinda strained, reaching to urge his fingers deeper.

"You want something more, love?" he asked, as he continued.

"Damn it, Dominic! You! Deep and hard," she panted.

Dominic slipped his fingers deeper into her slick sex, curling them into her G-spot. "You're so beautiful, Belinda. Beautiful and so very wet."

He circled her taut nub with his thumb, and she gasped. Raising her hips, she bucked against his hand. Her stomach tightened as she rose toward climax.

Every muscle tensed until her body exploded in spasms. Pleasure rocked her core, and her breath locked as her sex clenched in waves of release.

Fingers dug into Dominic's shoulders, and she arched her back for the next rush. Her head fell back as her climax faded, and Dominic pulled his hand from her cleft.

"Your scent is driving me crazy, love. Your slick sex and your desire-laced blood." He fisted his cock, spreading her slippery wetness over his shaft. "You're intoxicating, Belinda. The simplest taste, and I'm drunk on you."

Her body still hummed with aftershocks, but she wrapped her legs around his hips, his bulging head pressed against her slick entrance. "Now it's my turn to ask. Do you want something more, Dominic?"

Belinda's voice was throaty and breathless, and when she lifted her hips, Dominic drove his cock between her swollen folds with one furious thrust. His hips pumped wild and rough, as he buried himself balls deep.

Heat skittered across her flesh as he filled her, stretching her wide and full. Sweat trickled between her breasts, and her legs shook.

Oh my *God*!

Her mind spun, every sense alive and on fire.

He took her mouth, devouring her lips, kissing her wild and hungry. His tongue sought hers, demanding. She kissed him back as eagerly, grazing the edge of his fangs.

Trace blood trickled from the scrape, and Dominic groaned. He sucked her tongue deep, his body rigid and strained.

He ripped his mouth from hers and turned his head. The muscles in his jaw clenched, and self-restraint warred on his face. Even in profile, Belinda saw his dark struggle, and she knew. If she wanted him, it was all or nothing. And she wanted him. Bad.

"Take, Dominic." The breathless words left her mouth in a rush.

He turned back to her, his eyes fathomless and questioning.

She kept her eyes on his as she lifted her chin. Lifting her chin, she let her hair tumble back from her neck. "Take," she repeated, shivering with the forbidden.

His cock jerked deep in her tight channel as his eyes searched hers for the truth. "Are you sure?"

Dominic's voice was a low, sexy rasp, and the raw sound made her breath hitch.

Her body quivered with the thought of the unknown, but she nodded anyway. "Just don't kill me, okay?" She turned her head again, but this time she closed her eyes.

Dominic's fangs descended. He pressed a kiss to her throat, circling his mark with his tongue. Each rasp sent tiny electric jolts through her body, and she gasped, not knowing what to expect. The tips of his fangs grazed her skin, and she tensed.

He pulled his hips back, letting his cock slip from her body. "You said take, but you didn't say what," he whispered, kissing her throat again. "Did you mean this?"

Dominic plunged his cock instead of his fangs, his full length filling her once more.

"Or maybe this is more to your liking, *hmmm*?" He slid his cock back again, feeding her inches slowly in and slowly out, before thrusting hard, all to bring her to another peak. "I crave the squeeze of your tight shaft on my cock and the taste of your sweet blood on my tongue."

Anticipation flooded her body, and her breath came rapid and short. The unknown both frightened and intoxicated, and her pulse quickened with the thrill as much as it did from his rock-hard cock.

Dominic had tasted her blood before, but not with her fully aware and fully involved. She trembled in suspense and arched, dropping her head back. In that moment, he sank his fangs deep into her throat.

Her eyes flew wide at the surge of pleasure and pain. A carnal rush unlike anything she ever felt flooded her body, and the wave swirled in a vivid flash, sending colors exploding. She crested hard and fast, her body rocketing into climax.

Dominic groaned, taking deep pulls of sweet, adrenaline-soaked blood. The heady taste mingled with the residual tang of her sex on his tongue, the visceral combination almost too much to bear.

The scent of her heady release filled his nose, and he drove his cock even deeper, his fangs buried. She met his hips thrust for thrust until his tension reached its apex. His head bulged, ready to burst. He released her throat, and with a guttural snarl, exploded hot and deep within her. He held himself taut, letting every last pulse fade before dipping his head to lick the line of blood trickling from her throat to the valley between her breasts. A swipe of his tongue healed the marks on her throat, and he let his body slip from hers before sliding in beside her on the wide chaise.

"You okay?" he asked, brushing damp hair from the side of her face.

She nodded. "Can I ask you something?"

His lips spread in a small smile against her skin and he kissed her shoulder. "Of course."

"Do you have a heartbeat? Or did I just imagine it?"

Stunned, he lifted on one elbow. "You heard my heartbeat?"

"Very faintly, but yeah."

Baffled, he shook his head slowly. "For as long as I have existed, only other vampires can hear an undead heart. I'm...amazed."

"You're amazed?" She snickered. "I just had mind-blowing sex with a vampire who drank my blood as he climaxed. I am a walking, talking paranormal-romance novel!"

"*Took* your blood, love. Don't say drank. It's too slurp-sounding."

"Did you just say slurp?" She burst out laughing. "You just ripped the sexy right out of this whole experience, you know that, right?"

His eyes darkened and he pressed a kiss to her glowing mark, circling it with his tongue. Her breath hitched at the phantom feel of him inside her again.

"Still unsexy?" he murmured.

She licked her lips, giving her head a shake. "Nope."

He kissed her mark once more and then pecked her cheek. "Good. I was afraid I had lost my touch."

"Trust me. You have all the touch I will ever need and then some. I don't think I could stand, let alone walk."

He chuckled, slipping his arm under her shoulders, squeezing her in close. "So, we sleep right here. The sun rises over that ridge to the east of the city, and it's truly a sight to see. I remember the first time I could withstand the heat of the early sun. I cried blood tears. It was like being reborn.

"Of course, it took centuries before I could survive more than a few minutes at dawn. Now, I can withstand the entire day. Not often, because death-sleep still calls, and the sun weakens me as it does all my kind, but I can endure enough. Especially when my incentive is you."

"Death-sleep? That sounds a little creepy. Like I'm going to wake up next to a corpse whenever I get up to pee."

He laughed. "Not quite, but close. You won't be able to wake me, not unless I feel your fear." He shrugged. "On a positive note, you'll never have to worry about earplugs."

"Earplugs?"

"Vampires don't snore."

With a grin, she wiggled from his arms and swiveled off the chaise. "C'mon, Vampy. Let's do something wild."

Marianne Morea

He chuckled. "I don't know what's funnier, that you called me Vampy or that you think there's anything wilder than what we just did." He waggled his eyebrows.

"Humor me. I want to see the city the way you see it. I want to live the history surrounding us through your eyes, your memories."

"That's going to be hard to do. It has changed a little since then." He smirked, swinging his long legs over the end of the wide lounge.

She held her hand out. "Then let's go celebrate my find. Celebrate us..." She giggled. "We really are *us*, right?"

Dominic was on his feet, and in one fluid move had her in his arms. "Us," he whispered, brushing her lips. "We...ours. All of the above."

"Then why don't *we* go to the ramparts." She grinned. "A colleague of mine said, he'd streak naked across the city walls two-fisting bottles of Cristal if he were me. Well, there just happens to be a bottle of that very champagne chilling in the bar refrigerator."

"Why the ramparts? Why not the Holy Sepulcher or the Dome of the Rock? Or even Temple Mount? They're way older."

"Because, those are all ancient sacred sites, and my thoughts are impious when it comes to you."

He smirked. "Impious?"

"X-rated, then. I was trying to be genteel." She blew out a teasing breath. "Since I can't jump your bones in the twelfth century, let's go where it's the closest I'll get. C'mon, knight o' mine. I promise. I'll make it worth your while."

She went up on tiptoe and nipped his lip.

"Ow," he chuckled. "No biting allowed."

She snorted. "Says the vampire."

Condemned

***

"How did you get the sphincter police to let us slip through? I was hoping my credentials from the museum would buy us a pass, but that guard wasn't budging," Belinda asked, glancing over her shoulder as they climbed the stone stairs to the wall walk.

Dominic held his hand out for Belinda and helped her from the last few steep steps. "The Force can have a strong influence on the weak minded."

"You mean like, *these aren't the droids you're looking for* kind of influence?" She grinned.

He smirked, letting a sheepish grin spread.

"So, Mr. Millennium is a Jedi wannabe." She hugged his arm. "So much to love about you, Vampy."

"Can't you come up with a better nickname for me? Mr. Millennium and Vampy?"

"Since Obi-wan is taken, maybe I'd better stick with Dominic." She smirked. "Either that or sexy-fangs."

"Nope."

"Titillating Templar?"

He growled, and she laughed

"You know this was originally called a *chemin de ronde* or patrol path. An allure or *sèduire*. The sight of men patrolling the parapets seduced people inside the city walls. It made them feel safe, he said, changing the subject from nicknames.

He slipped his arm around her shoulders. "I would never harm you, Belinda. I am your *chemin de ronde*."

"So, you're planning to seduce me to come inside?" She grinned.

He pressed a kiss to her temple. "*Chéri*, my seduction is all about getting you to come. Any way you want, as many times as you can handle."

High color stained her cheeks, and he inhaled, turning her in his arms. "I love your scent when your blood is high. It's like perfume."

"I love the view from up here. I can't help but wonder what this was like in its historic heyday. This whole city and its surroundings. It's a storybook come to life." She exhaled a little laugh. "At least to a geek like me."

He kissed the top of her head as she gazed out at the expanse and the few twinkling stars. "Secrets yet to be discovered."

"Exactly."

They walked arm in arm farther down the stone ramparts. "I have something I'd like to show you. It's about a three-hour drive from here, and after that we're on foot so it'll take most of the day," he said.

"What it is?"

"It's a place called *Galgal Refa'im* or—"

"Wheel of Ghosts," she interjected.

An impressed smile played on Dominic's mouth. "I forgot you're so learned in these matters." He nodded. "In Arabic. It translates to *stone heap of the wild cats.*"

"I know the site's name and reputation, but to be honest, not much more. It's not far from Akko, but it was off-limits because of the fighting." She made a face. "Two countries squabbling over a strip of land no one really wants. Worse than children squabbling over a broken toy."

"I can get us there, no problem. No one will touch us or even see us. Especially if I use my Obi-Wan powers again."

She giggled a snort. "My very own sexy geek."

"Now there's a nickname Vampy can sink his teeth into."

"Oh, really."

He kissed her hair again. "Maybe we should get going."

She quirked a brow, confused. "Why the one-eighty turn? Did I say something wrong?"

"Of course not, but it's late, and I want to be rested enough for tomorrow. I may be able to withstand the sun, but it is not my friend." He scanned her disappointed face. "What's wrong?"

"I don't want the night to end."

He inhaled, lifting his face to the sky. "It will whether we want it to or not. After so many centuries, my body knows dawn is approaching."

"Is that the only thing your body is telling you?" She let her fingers tiptoe over his belly toward the top button of his jeans. "I still have a twelfth-century fantasy that needs your help."

Dominic's eyes darkened. "You are turning out to be an insatiable white witch."

She turned in his arms and wound her hands into his hair. "Well, like the song says, only the good die young, so what are we waiting for?"

Her sexy smirk turned panicked yelp as he threw her over his shoulders and stepped up onto the parapet.

"Dominic! What are you doing?" She squeezed her eyes shut. "Only the good die young was a joke! We're gonna fall!"

No sooner did the words leave her mouth than he leapt for the ground. She screamed, but the shriek clipped short in her throat as they landed without a sound on the grass below. He let her down, making sure her body slid over every hard plane.

"That was a dirty trick," she said, straightening her clothes.

He smirked. "Just another geeky power courtesy of my undead status. Maybe tomorrow we won't drive to the Golan. Maybe we'll fly."

"I'm guessing you don't mean in a helicopter or a prop-job Cessna."

He shook his head. "Piggyback style."

"Not liking this part of vampy geekdom much. Just do me a favor. Give me a heads-up next time. You really don't want to need an extra set of clothes because vertigo empties my stomach down your shirt." She glanced up at the tall ancient wall. "So, Sherlock. How are we supposed to get back up? Or is vertical leap another hidden talent?"

He laughed.

"Hey, I don't doubt your mad skills. I just want to brace myself."

"Maybe you should brace yourself for what we've got for you, honey," a sneering voice said from the shadows. "The moon is full and we've got a pack full of hard inches just waiting for a little human fun. Don't count on your vampire, either, cuz he's outnumbered."

Her eyes flashed to Dominic, as he stepped ahead of her and pushed her behind his back.

"Who are they?" she whispered. "They know who you are."

"No. They know what I am. They have no idea who I am." His face changed, and his fangs descended fully. "They're about to find out."

Their thoughts buffeted her mind unsolicited. Her on her hands and knees in the dirt as they each took their turn with her. Dominic with his throat ripped out while they howled to the sky. A fire. Their faces smeared with his blood as they drank their fill from his undead veins.

"I heard them!" She gripped his arm. "They're planning to kill you and gang rape me. They want your blood."

"Addicts." He snarled low, crouching. "Just stay close and don't let them get behind you." He didn't take his eyes off the pack. "Can you fight?"

She nodded. "A little. I used to take karate when I was younger."

"Good. Just stun and run, got it? A good shot in the balls will do nicely. Keep a decent distance, Belinda. Can you still do a jump front kick?"

"Field boots. Not just a fashion statement."

His lips twitched. "God, I love you."

Belinda heard the words and blinked. The man told her he loved her, now?

Five scrubby youths stepped from the shadows. They reeked of body odor and beer, and their stench assailed her nose. Unwashed clothes were caked in dirt and she didn't want to know what else. What the hell were these creatures?

Dominic said they were addicts. Addicted to what? The images assailing her mind showed them reveling in blood. Was vampire blood addictive?

"Leave now while you can, boys. I have no quarrel with you or your kind. Go menace someone else tonight."

The loudmouthed leader snorted, grabbing his crotch. "What are you going to do, vampire? There's five of us and only one of you." He snapped his fingers and his compatriots fell into fighting formation at his flank. "We're not boys, you undead piece of shit. We hunt with the moon, and tonight we hunt blood. Sound familiar?"

The others sniggered, but he shut them up. "We're not interested in your late-night snack, but she won't go to waste. We'll use her good, but it's your blood we want." He rubbed his thumb and two fingers together. "Worth a lot of coin to the right people, and a quick fix for us."

Belinda cringed. There was her answer. *Gross.*

The five moved forward, and Belinda flinched, but Dominic didn't move. A single snarl was the only warning he gave, and he blurred like something out of a movie. Blood sprayed the ancient stones as he ripped their heads from their shoulders.

They toppled in a heap where they stood, like so much dead cordwood. Their heads were nowhere to be found.

Dominic bent, panting and bloodied. Belinda moved toward him, but he held out one hand, stopping her in her tracks.

"Don't, Belinda. I will never hurt you but give me a minute. I don't want to take the chance."

He stripped his T-shirt from his shoulders and used it to wipe their blood from his face and arms. He tossed it to the ground and then held out his hand, whispering words in a strange tongue. Fire sparked in his palm, and he tossed the flame to the ground, burning his shirt. Waving a hand over the bodies, he did the same and his blood crisped, but their corpses stayed untouched.

With a steadying breath, he turned to face her. "I'm sorry, Belinda."

She walked straight into his arms, not caring if Dominic still smelled like dead whatever. "Sorry? You saved my life and your own. It was total self-defense."

His chest vibrated beneath her cheek. "I was hoping you'd see it that way and not be repulsed."

"What were they? They mentioned pack and the full moon. Were they some sort of werewolves?"

His hand came up to smooth her hair. "Yes. Addicted Were scum, but Were nonetheless. Weres and shifters are another supernatural race. We have a tender truce with them, and like vampires and humans, some are evil, and some are good. The alpha of the Brethren of Weres leads the Weres in North America. He and his mate and those at their compound in Maine are friends

and allies of ours." He turned his head toward the stinking carcasses. "These scumbags were rogues. That they banded together was more for rape and pillage than for pack purposes. Packs don't attack innocents."

He kissed her head once more and then stepped back. "C'mon. We should get back to the hotel. I'm a bloody, half-naked mess, and the police will be here as soon as someone notices the bodies."

She climbed on his back and tucked her head, knowing she needed to hold tight. He blurred through the streets of Jerusalem and then through the hotel lobby, taking the stairs to the tenth floor. They stopped in front of her door, and she slid from his back, wobbling as if getting off the world's dizziest rollercoaster.

"I need to shower and change," he said turning to head for the stairs. "I'll be back."

She held his arm. "No, please. Shower here. You can get your clothes in the morning." She went up on tiptoe to kiss his mouth. "Trust me. You won't need them tonight."

He smiled against her lips but shook his head. "Death-sleep, remember? I don't think you're up for that. Not after what you witnessed."

"After what I witnessed, you'll be lucky if I let you out of my sight." He angled his head and she exhaled, finally. "Go. But you've got two minutes, speed demon. If you're not back in that time with your toiletries and your clothes, I'm coming for you."

Chapter 15

Dominic stirred in his sleep. His body lay as still as death, but his restless mind tossed and turned with dreams and voices.

Awareness never left him, even as his body sank into its death-like state. He waited for the blackness of vampiric rest, but it never came.

Belinda breathed soft and sweet beside him. Her warmth flooded their bed. A comfort that should have lulled him. Instead, uneasiness poisoned his peace once again. Sahira would come for her. It was only a matter of time. The dark witch waited as long as she had with Charmaine because she wasn't deemed a threat. But Belinda?

He had used the words. He loved her. More than Céleste or anyone else since. Her life gave his hope. Sahira would crush that, given the opportunity, and that was what he had to prevent.

Perhaps Belinda's stubbornness was a blessing. Putting her into Carlos's care would free him to hunt, but it also put Carlos and his family in danger. Sahira wouldn't bat an eye at slaughtering an entire coven to serve her own purpose. She'd bleed his family dry and then laugh about it as the grief drove him to the shores of final death. She had to be stopped.

Templar, you are mine. I tasted your little Corsican's blood. Sahira's cruel voice tsked. *Poor thing. You used her body and her blood like I taught you, but you never loved her. Perhaps I was too hasty in ridding you of your plaything."* She laughed, but the sound faded, and a cold chill

replaced the sarcasm in his mind. "Your newest ginger is another story. I feel your attachment growing. I will take her heart and eat it with a knife and fork. Mark my words.

Images formed unbidden. Sahira's cold eyes. Charmaine's terrified ones. A man stood with a blade at her throat as Sahira watched from a plush leather chair. Her icy laughter sent pain reverberating through Dominic's head as the image progressed.

A Caesar-like thumbs down. Sahira templing her fingers and a fanged grin spreading across her face as her minion pulled his blade across the woman's throat. Only it wasn't Charmaine. It was Belinda who crumpled to the ground in a puddle of blood.

A sharp breath sucked through Dominic's teeth, and he woke, bolting up. He blinked for a moment before slumping back on his pillow. All was in peace.

The moon hung on the night horizon as thin sheers billowed in a gentle breeze from the terrace. Belinda stirred, opening her eyes. "What is it?" she asked, her voice groggy.

You think you can find me? Think again. I will shred your little whore before your eyes, and you will weep blood tears once again.

"Dominic?"

"Nothing, love. Go back to sleep."

The last image before blackness found him was a lone tent, billowing in the desert, and a pool of blood staining the sand. He strained for the location but couldn't see. Sahira had moved her chess piece. The next move was his.

***

"Good morning," he said, putting the paper down on the table. "I took the liberty of ordering a full American breakfast. Eggs, bacon, pancakes, waffles, sausage, and muffins. I know you drink coffee, but I ordered orange juice as well."

Belinda blinked at the amount of food on the terrace table. "Dominic, I'm one human girl. I can't possibly eat all of this. There's enough here for ten people."

He shrugged. "I know, but we'll pack it up and bring it to a shelter I know before we head to the Golan Heights. It's Saturday. Most of Jerusalem is shut down for Shabbat. The shelter will be happy for the food."

He slid a folder full of printed pages toward her along with a cup of hot coffee.

"What's all this? It looks like research notes." She picked up the top sheet and scanned the first paragraph.

"I figured with your background, you'd want a synopsis of where we're going and what we'll see when we get there. The excavation was completed years ago, but this is not your typical tourist destination. I'm not sure why it doesn't get the kind of press it deserves, but I think it's because of IEDs so close to the Syrian border."

"IEDs?"

He turned the newspaper around, and on the cover was a picture of a destroyed jeep. "Improvised explosive devices. The darling of this godforsaken war."

"Are you taking me to a war zone?"

"Of course not. The site is only open on weekends and holidays, and today is Saturday. I won't even have to dip into my geeky powers. So, eat up. A car is coming for us in an hour."

She sat down at the table as Dominic handed her the cream for her coffee. "Take a look at the printout. It's pretty interesting if I do say so myself. This predates everything else in the whole region."

"Even you?" she teased, giving him a wink.

"Ha ha. But yes. Even me."

He piled food on a plate and put it beside the folder. Belinda was already in academic mode, and he smirked at the tiny wrinkle between her brows as she concentrated. She chewed absently, ripping off pieces of her pancake one by one and plopping them into her mouth.

"You are too damn cute, you know that?" he said with a wink, pouring her a glass of juice.

She glanced up as he held out the tall glass. "I can feed myself, you know. Been doing it for years." She took the drink but put it down next to her plate.

"Juice is good for you, especially since I took your blood last night." He scooped a handful of supplements into his palm and held those out as well. "Wash these down, while you're at it."

"Wow, it's like waking up to the Red Cross." She smirked but did as he asked.

He lifted the newspaper again. "If memory serves, there was a giant red cross on my tunic, so—"

She burst out laughing at that. "Touché." Picking up her fork, she dug into her food, watching him while she chewed. "Your accent. It's French, right?"

He nodded.

"And you didn't lose it after all this time?"

He shrugged. "I never really thought about it. After Sahira changed me, I escaped her and traveled back to Marseilles to search for Céleste, but what I found there—" He shook his head. "Anyway, I traveled the world after that. Latin was the international language until about the sixteenth century. Then it was French until quite recently. I suppose whatever I did lose, came back at that point and stayed put."

"You never got around to telling me," she said blowing steam across her coffee cup."

"Telling you what?"

She gestured with one hand as she took a sip. "About your past."

"You didn't want to watch, remember?"

"I meant about your past loves. What happened with them?"

His face hardened. "Sahira happened to them. It's why I still want you to go to New York. Especially after what happened outside the ramparts last night. There's no way to know if Sahira or one of her cult members put them up to it or not."

"I'm not going anywhere, Dominic. I have my gala tomorrow night, and *you're* coming with me. We are going to confront Sahira together. She'll be there. He ego would never allow her to miss a moment in the spotlight, but she's got plenty more reason to show. My gut is churning, so I know she's going to be on the prowl looking for you as well. I'll be ready. I'm as much a witch as she, and you are strong. Together, we can bitchslap that she-devil back to hell."

He laughed, leaning up to kiss her across the table. "My son would laugh at that."

She raised an eyebrow.

"Not because you think you can fight a vampire, though the very thought is ridiculous, but because your fiery temperament matches your hair. Carlos says I have a weakness for hot redheads."

"Sahira isn't a ginger."

"No," he frowned. "She's as dark as her soul. But Céleste was a ginger, as you put it, and so was Charmaine."

"Charmaine? Is she the woman I saw in your mind? Not Sahira. The other one. The friend who died recently, right?"

"Yes."

"Who was she? Was she your lover, too?"

He lifted his hand to cover hers on the table, caressing her fingers. "A long, long time ago."

"How long is long, long?" she asked in part curiosity, part jealousy.

"Over a hundred years ago, love. There's been no one since but you."

She blinked. "A hundred years?" She pressed her lips together, skeptical. "Wow, she was better preserved than some of the artifacts I found."

"Vampire blood has healing properties, and in tiny doses, droplets really, it can preserve you and extend your lifespan. Not indefinitely, but for a while. Charmaine was my friend and companion. She wasn't vampire. I didn't love her in that way. In the beginning, I shared her body and her blood, but the attraction faded along with my interest. Sahira had more to do with that than Charmaine. It was just easier to be solo. She stayed with me, though, and I thought her safe because I never gave her the dark gift or my heart." He glanced away, and a shadow crossed his face. "I was wrong."

"What about Céleste?"

"She was a long time ago, too."

"How long?"

He shrugged. "Your favorite century. I last laid eyes on Céleste in 1118 A.D."

Jesus. She laced her fingers with his. "Tell me about her."

"The story doesn't have a happy ending, Belinda. In fact, it plays more like a twisted Shakespearean tragedy."

"I still want to know. It's part of you. Part of what shaped you and what led you to me."

He smiled. "How about I show you, instead."

She moved to sit beside him instead of across the table.

"I mean it when I say it's not a happy story," he reiterated.

She shrugged. "I'm ready. If seeing what this bitch did steels me even a little more, then it's a good thing."

"Okay, but we have a long drive, remember, and we can't continue this conversation in the car. I don't want to risk an accident by glamouring the driver into deafness."

"We have plenty of time. You even said the city is practically on lockdown. I have nowhere else to be today, so I'm all yours."

"Woman, you don't know how much I wish that were true."

She held his gaze. "Even with our gifts, neither of us knows what the future holds. We see past actions and can read future intentions, but like you said last night, it's just possibilities. Right now, in this moment, my possibilities involve you and only you. In my life. In my heart." She hesitated. "I heard you last night."

"Heard what?" he hedged.

"You said you loved me. Of course, your timing sucked as we were about to be killed or worse, but I heard you just the same."

He kissed her fiercely, his body hardening for hers even as his heart squeezed in his chest. "You warm even the coldest darkness for me, Belinda. My sun in what has been an endless night. Every precious beat of your fragile heart means more to me than a thousand lifetimes."

He looked at her again, this time his face serious. "I know you're fierce, Belinda, but you are in more danger now than you realize. Sahira may have wanted to collect you or frighten you into joining her elite blood cult, but it's deeper now. You're a threat."

"Frighten me into joining her cult? What do you mean?"

"I didn't want to say anything, but the whispers from the shadows that night in Rome? I killed the one responsible. He was Sahira's puppet."

She blinked, struggling to sit up. "Wait, did he have a Lilith brand on his hand?"

"No."

"Then maybe he was just what we originally thought, Dominic. A creeper."

"No, love. He threatened me with a blade that carried Charmaine's blood scent. He killed her for Sahira. To prove his loyalty and earn his brand. Taunting me was part of his plan. You happened to cross my path as I tracked him, and he put two and two together. What the dumb fuck didn't consider was he was no match for an elder vampire, regardless of who sent him. And toying with you? Even if he managed to escape me, the moment Sahira read his mind or his blood and saw his mind games, she would have ripped out his throat. He messed with her latest treasure."

"How many others has Sahira taken from you?"

His eyes softened. "Too many, love. But the first one was Céleste. She was the woman I loved before I was sent to join the Templars."

"Show me. In fact, show me everything. I don't care if the car has to wait. I'm in this for the long haul, you sexy geek. I need to know."

She pressed her forehead to his and held tight while he wrapped his hand around the nape of her neck, as he had the last time they shared memories.

The images came fast, and she watched, awestruck and speechless. Tears formed, dripping down her cheeks at how much he'd endured. The love and the injustices. The betrayal and deceit, and finally Sahira and what she did.

Belinda sucked in a breath at the force of his raging thirst and the daily struggle to stay as human as possible. How he nearly lost

that battle when he saw Céleste's body in the plain pine box, yet how he let those who'd wronged them live instead of seeking revenge.

The visions fast-forwarded to Carlos and Trina and Charmaine. To finding Charmaine's body and the new rage that formed and faded into a resolve to find and end Sahira once and for all.

She saw herself in his eyes the first time he beheld her. The instant desire. The pull of her blood, yet how it went deeper than that. How he fumed with himself for frightening her but let her go for her own good. How he dreamed of her. Wondered about her every day until the moment he saw her in the souk.

Dominic broke their connection at that point. He kept his hand on the back of her neck and inhaled, trying to gauge her reaction.

"Wow. It's a wonder you didn't walk into the dawn and fry yourself to a crisp," she said taking a ragged breath.

He chuckled, pressing a kiss to her forehead before letting her go. Sitting back in his chair, he lifted his coffee to his lips and took a sip. "I've wondered that myself, but looking at you sitting across from me this morning, it was worth the wait."

"I want to rip her heart out and feed it to you," she said with a grimace, and he froze. "What?"

He shook his head.

"No, seriously. What?"

He exhaled. "She invaded my dreams last night, and that's what she said she wanted to do with your heart, except she said she'd eat it herself."

Belinda belly-laughed. "Oh man. Ain't that a kick in the pants? She and I thinking along the same lines. Kind of scary."

"You think?" he said.

"I'm starting to think she and I are two sides of the same coin. Light and dark. So, it's no wonder we have the same kind of reaction. But, on the flipside, I like to think my vengeful thoughts are justified."

"Good way to think." He pushed his coffee cup away. "So, now that your private tour through my head is over, it's time to make some new memories." He got up from his chair and held out his hand. "Go get cleaned up, and let's—"

"Blow this pop stand," she said, cutting him off with a giggle.

"Not quite what I was going to say, but you got the picture."

"I sure did. In 3D Technicolor."

***

"You sure this place is only accessible on foot?" Belinda asked, wiping her brow. "Jerusalem was at least twenty degrees cooler. This is bordering on hellish. Forget IEDs. *This* is the real reason no tourists come here. You need to be a mountain goat."

"It's Israeli Stonehenge, Belinda," he replied. "The sun is sapping my energy by the second. At least you sweat water. I sweat blood. I may replenish myself with one of those pretty Israeli army gals we saw a while back."

"You do, and the *Force* won't be with you, it'll be with me and my field boot up your butt."

He laughed out loud and then stopped to shield his eyes. "I think we're here." He pointed to a rocky spot in the middle of a green flatland. "That's it. See how the outer rings shape the inner cairns. They say it's a contemporary of Stonehenge in England. Maybe even made by the same people."

"Basalt stone cairns from 3000 and 2000 BCE. Holy rock salt!"

"You know, this place is still waiting for its own Indiana Jones moment to make it famous. Maybe that'll be you, now that you've got clout in the archeological world."

Pfft. "I don't have clout. I got lucky. At least that's what I hear through the grapevine Sahira/Zahra whatever is saying. She's not only out to eat my heart physically. She's out to do it in every way possible. She wants to obliterate me."

He didn't reply. What could he say? Belinda was absolutely right. And his gut told him Sahira was gearing up for something at the gala.

"What time tomorrow night does the gala begin?" he asked.

"Seven p.m. Why?"

"I have a few tricks up my sleeve. If I've learned anything in the last hundred years, it's that people like headlines and headliners. We are going to give them a show like they've never seen. I'm a collector. Believe it or not, that collection you saw in Rome was only a tenth of what I have. It's been photographed and catalogued. Both Oxford and The Metropolitan Museum in New York have been dying to get their hands on some of my pieces. I took it upon myself to call home for my staff to ship over a few choice twelfth-century pieces. I am donating them to the Israeli Museum in your name, to honor your Templar find. You, my love, are going to make a splash, and the way I've got the night planned, it will be one we'll never forget."

"Let's hope that spectacle includes ending that dark bitch."

His face took on a cautionary air. "We will deal with her, for certain. But guard your heart, Belinda. Don't let hate in. It will take root and fester there. Justice, yes. Revenge?" He shook his head. "We will blur the lines, if necessary, but justice will be enough."

Condemned

She threw her arms around his neck and kissed him. "Enough about the Wicked Witch of the East. I refuse to let that walking corpse ruin my day. Not when history surrounds us like this."

"Mmmm."

"Can't you feel the vibrations? They residual emotion? This place was as much a holy site as any in Jerusalem, except here they held sacrifices." She eyed him. "Blood sacrifices."

"Really."

"So, sexy geek. You made me take my blood-building supplements this morning. How about we explore one of those underground prehistory cairns and see if we can warm them up with a little hot and heavy? Give them a taste of our kind of blood sacrifice. There's no one around for miles. Let's roll around in the Stone Age and leave a little modern DNA just to screw up the carbon dating." She winked.

He grinned. "Dirty insatiable white witch."

"Hey, I'm committing archeological blasphemy by even suggesting you bend me over the basalt, but c'mon! Tell me your fangs aren't tingling at the thought of an illicit adventure?"

"My fangs are tingling, love, but not from the fear of getting caught. I can cure that with a wave of my hand. It's you that makes my fangs tingle and my mouth water for your taste. You that makes my body ache for your touch."

She shivered.

He pulled her into his arms. "Tell me, professor. What kind of blooding do you think would hit the mark?" The hard bar of his erection pressed against her stomach, and he bent to swirl his tongue over his mark on her throat.

"I think you know." She shivered again.

"What I know is you are everything to me, now. So, if you want a little forbidden love in the afternoon? I am all yours."

"You mean afternoon delight."

"There's a song in there somewhere," he chuckled, and threw her over his shoulder, to her squeals and laughter.

Chapter 16

The limousine pulled up in front of the Israeli Museum, and the driver opened the door. She and Dominic got out of the elegant car to camera flashes and a red carpet. Reporters from all over the world covered the event, and she spied the museum director near the entrance, looking a little green from the stress.

"You pulled all of this together in one day?" she whispered, taking his arm. She kept a beaming smile on her face as photographers snapped away, their flash nearly blinding her.

"Money can do anything in this world, Belinda. The museum director was more than happy to have me take over the cost for the night. I took care of the publicity and the fanfare, and he arranged the inside exhibition. The guest list was already a who's who from the academic and scientific world. I simply peppered the existing list with A-list celebrities. All expenses paid certainly gets people to turn on a dime."

"Ms. Force! Ms. Force!" A roly-poly reporter huffed his way through the crowd. "What do you have to say to Dr. Zahra Khalid's claim that you took the credit for something another student found? Ari Weiss?"

Belinda glimpsed down at the man's cell phone, and on his hand was a Lilith sigil. She gave a small chin pop to Dominic, gesturing toward the tattoo with her eyes.

"I see you belong to Dr. Khalid's elite cult of sycophants," Dominic replied with a chuckle. "She tried to get me to join them

years ago as a collector. I refused. She tried the same smear campaign with me, back then. Ms. Force found the twelfth-century chalice using her knowledge of the time period to recognize even the faintest clues covered in coral and a millennium of muck. Ari Weiss has yet to make a find or publish his dissertation. Zahra Khalid is a force in the academic world. How Ari is still a member of her elite group is beyond me, unless of course there's something untoward going on between teacher and student.

"You might want to check into that. As to the claims? Sour grapes. Ms. Force not only found the piece but published her dissertation on the twelfth century and its seminal contributions to the dawn of the Renaissance centuries later, proving her knowledge and expertise."

Whether or not Dominic planned it that way or not, other reporters smelled blood in the water. Any hint of scandal would sell papers.

"What cult, Mr. De'Lessep?" another reporter asked. "Are you saying Zahra Khalid has done something inappropriate?"

Dominic grabbed the chubby reporter's hand and lifted it for the others to see. "She has a private group of elites. They all wear the same tattoo. In fact, Ms. Force's mentor, Dr. Theo Adams, Head of Archeology and Antiquities at Columbia University, was recently attacked on campus, and his assailant?" He nodded for effect. "Had the exact same sigil tattoo on his right hand. I should also note that Dr. Adams is not affiliated with Khalid's Crew, as they like to be called. He, like me and Ms. Force, declined her offer to join."

It was like catnip to cats. The chubby reporter slunk away as the others shouted questions after him, snapping pictures of his tattoo. The poor guy was lucky to get to the street.

"This could backfire, you know. They could find out about us and turn the tables," Belinda said as they made their way into the gala.

"Don't worry about that. Sexy geeks are not as soft a target as the popular kids like to think. There are more of us than you know. You pick on one, and you pick on all of us. The press will pick up on the story and run with it as we hoped. The only collateral damage will be Ari, but if you get in bed with a snake, be prepared to get bitten."

She snorted a chuckle. "I've been in his head. Trust me. Biting is child's play compared to what I saw. Between him and Kir, they like it rough, and Sahira delivers."

"I remember." He made a face.

She winced inside. "I'm sorry, Dominic. I didn't mean to be glib."

"It is what it is, love. Blood in the sand. It evaporates or gets blown away in the next storm. Either way, it doesn't last unless you let it."

"Did you somehow manage to get my dissertation published without my knowing? Or was that a ruse?" she prompted.

He laughed. "That was the easiest part. Your work sold itself, love. I simply had a friend from Oxford call your university and beg for the rights. Worked like a charm." He snapped his fingers.

"Yeah, right. What artifact did you have to promise Oxford in return?"

"Not a thing."

She eyed him skeptically as they entered the large courtyard. Belinda's mouth dropped. The museum was lit like a wonderland for the night's event. At the center, a laser-light show flashed frenetic blue-and-red beams into the night sky.

Photographers meandered around, grabbing photo ops of international jet setters. It was a proper mix of academic elites, society wannabes and celebrities, politicos and philanthropists mingling in the marble courtyard. Celebs wanting to seem more intellectual, and academics still looking to be accepted by the cool kids in school.

The museum was majestic. Banners with twelfth-century images and pictures of the chalice and other artifacts draped the walls in color and fantasy. Glass cases with precious artifacts surrounded the narrow koi pond that ran the center length of the room, and guests were clearly impressed.

Belinda was about to reply with something snarky when the director ran over, one hand wiping his brow while the other sloshed a glass of champagne on his tux. "Monsieur De'Lessep!" he called, rushing to shake Dominic's hand. "Oh, monsieur! How can I ever thank you? This is the most exciting night. All this press! All these celebrities! American A-listers at our museum event! And in two days' time!" He waved the same sweaty hand in front of him, seeming as though he might cry. "I can't even imagine the cost, and then to have the pieces you sent for permanent loan! Sir, I am *verklempt*."

Dominic inclined his head, gently extricating his hand from the man's sweaty palm. "It was my pleasure. Ms. Force and her find deserve the recognition." He raised an eyebrow and looked the man in the eye. "I hope you will put an end to the vicious rumors started by certain academics whose horse came in second place, if you know what I mean."

"Of course." He bobbed his head. "I know exactly what to do about that. To be honest, the woman in question has a lot of clout, but she's always given me the willies."

Condemned

He walked away with a steadying breath, like a general ready to give his staff a proverbial boot up the bum if they didn't snap to it tonight.

Belinda laughed. "Well, at least the director isn't green around the gills anymore. How did you get him to stop licking Sahira's shoes?"

"Money, love. A big fat yearly endowment in your name."

"I still can't believe you did this all for me," she said, blowing out a breath as she took Dominic's arm.

"All for the cause, my love. Battle lines have been drawn, and we took first blood with that reporter. Gird your loins. The next wave is coming."

"I don't know if I can defend myself without letting on that clairvoyance helped me find that chalice. If I do, they'll label me batshit crazy."

"You won't have to. I will go to battle for us, plus I've got ringers and stringers planted in the mix. You don't get to be my age after dealing with Sahira for almost a millennium without learning how she maneuvers. I was a military strategist for the Order of the Templar Knights. Just because my immediate commander was an ass doesn't mean I didn't know what I was doing. He didn't take my advice and lost his men. In the end, he met his death at Sahira's hand as well, but not like me. At least he got to see paradise or hell. His fate was decided for him, the same as it was for me, yet, at this moment, I'm pretty grateful I survived."

"At last. The credit I deserve for deciding for you, Templar."

They both turned, and Dominic pushed Belinda slightly behind him, but she wasn't having it. She moved to his side and stared Sahira down.

Marianne Morea

"You have some nerve," Belinda said, squaring her shoulders. "You think you're intimidating, but you're not. You're sad…and alone. You think you have me by the short hairs and that you have Dominic under your thumb. You don't. Together, we are stronger than you will ever be."

Sahira's eyes narrowed. "Your passion was amusing for a while, little girl. Now, it's just bluster. I can smell your fear. You think your puny gift is going to help you? I was a priestess of Isis when your tribe was still learning to master fire."

"Insults and selfish notions about yourself. Wow. Do you do that to make yourself feel better? How sad it must be to be you. After your eons on this earth, what do you have to show for it? Money? Fame?" She shrugged. "All you have are toadies and people that fear or despise you. You, Sahira, have nothing and no one."

The woman's mouth mashed to a thin white line, and her dark almond eyes narrowed to slits.

Instinctively, Dominic tightened his grip on Belinda's arm, but the move wasn't missed on Sahira.

"Your little white witch has a lot to say." She sniffed. "I'll chalk that up to her limited human character and fragile constitution. Easily remedied, eh, Templar? That is, if you recall."

Dominic took a step forward. "You won't touch her, Sahira. She is not for your collection. Not now. Not ever."

"Don't threaten me, progeny. You seem to forget who controls whom in our game of cat-and-mouse."

She flounced away, and Belinda exhaled the breath she held. "I shouldn't have poked the tiger."

"No, but you struck a chord. You might not have seen it, but I certainly felt it. She hates you, now. Not because of me but because you see her for what she really is." He turned her toward him. "A

246

light within you glows with its own luminescence. It comes from deep inside your core. I told you. You are the sun in my darkness. The warmth in the cold night. Vampires may not need to breathe, but you truly take my breath away."

Tears pricked at the corners of her eyes, but Belinda blinked them back. Dominic spent a lot of money for the gorgeous emerald gown that skimmed her curves tonight, as well as the professional hair and makeup. She'd be damned before she ruined the look that made him gaze at her like she was the only woman in the room.

They mingled around, chatting with people, and she found herself giving Dominic a history lesson as they passed the different pieces, including the ones that belonged to him personally. He chuckled indulgently, and she stuck her tongue out at him.

"C'mon, I have to play my part. I'm the studious academic here, and you the fawning collector," she argued with a laugh.

"You might be the studious one, but right now all I can think about is steering you to the nearest dark corner so I can shimmy that satin dress off your luscious curves. I keep picturing you bent over those smooth rocks at the underground cairn. Your body suffused with heat and racing blood."

"Stop," she whispered. "You're making me wet, and I don't need Sahira picking up on that."

Dominic leaned down to her ear and nipped her lobe. "She already knows. She's my maker, Belinda, and if she can sense the air around me, then she'll have no problem sensing the raging hard-on I have for you right now."

She licked her lips, consciously trying not to look at his crotch. "Do you think anyone would mind if we slipped out a little early? The director decided against my giving a talk, instead wanting the exhibition to speak for itself. My guess is he didn't want Sahira's trolls to steal the spotlight."

"That and my endowment more than doubles what he expected to make in donations tonight. He is not going to rock the boat. Me? I'm going to rock your world as soon as I get you in the back of that limo."

She rose on tiptoe to kiss his lips but stopped as the hair on the back of her neck went up. Dominic glanced past her shoulder when her hand went to her nape.

"We're being dogged," she said.

"If you mean we're being tracked? Then yes." He nodded. "Since we got out of the limo." He steered her toward the exit.

"What are you doing? We haven't said our goodbyes, and you haven't seen your reliquary cross yet."

"Don't worry about that." He guided her through the doors and then down the steps to the car. He opened the door, but no sooner did he pull it open then a hand shot out, grabbing Belinda and pulling her inside as the limo screeched from the curb.

"Fuck!"

Dominic hissed, blurring after the car. He leapt on its roof, but the limo swerved, throwing him to the ground. He dive-rolled across the pavement and got to his feet, but the car was gone. He swore again. God help whoever took her if they harmed one hair on her red head. She wore his mark, so he could track her easily enough. This had Sahira written all over it. She wouldn't touch Belinda until he got there. She'd want him to watch. To suffer. After that, it was war. Exactly the way she wanted.

Chapter 17

Dominic cut the engine to the Land Rover he'd stolen from valet parking at the gala. He needed something fast that could handle the desert, and a normal four-wheel drive wasn't going to cut it.

Belinda's fear had buffeted his mind for the last hour. They hadn't touched her. That much he knew. But she was bound and gagged. Her mind raced, trying to keep her wits, and she sent mental images of where they took her.

She was somewhere in the Judean Desert to the east of Jerusalem. Thankfully, the overnight temperatures in the desert this time of year wouldn't be too cold if they had her outside.

He smirked to himself. She kept a running dialogue with him via images and the snarky thoughts she had for each of her captors. Three guys. Two dark and one light. She showed him mental images from her time in Cairo. Ari, Kir, and Fredric. The elites from Sahira's crew.

Typical.

She never did the dirty work herself. She blew in, arriving for the vainglory. Or more like the vein glory.

Not this time.

He switched the Land Rover to manual four-wheel drive and turned the knob to rocky terrain. Where he was headed, the Judean Desert was more rock than sand, gaunt and majestic with

craggy outcrops and escarpments and plateaus giving anyone who wanted them lots of places to hide.

Dominic followed his instincts, and the vampiric GPS Belinda's mark sent out was like a Bat-Signal in the sky. Stars blanketed the heavens, but the desert itself was like pitch. The 4x4's headlights cut a narrow swath of soft yellow light. May was warm, but not quite summer, so scorching temperatures hadn't really taken hold. His vampiric eyes saw through the murk to the patches of green and the flora growing from cracks in the rocks.

He had to be on his toes. Sahira's entourage would kill with the slightest nod from her. Devotees were one thing, but this smacked as much of addiction as those stupid rogues he'd slaughtered outside the Old City walls.

Cutting the engine far enough away to give him an edge, he pulled alongside a curved rock formation shaped from erosion. Concave in shape, it gave him the cover he needed. Not that Sahira wouldn't already sense his presence. Still, she never showed until things got hot. As for her minions, they were clueless.

He moved quickly on foot, keeping a low profile in his approach but also in Belinda's mind. Sahira didn't need more of a heads-up than she already had, plus the idea of him sharing thoughts with Belinda would only infuriate the crazy witch. He wanted Sahira calm and rational. Well, as calm and rational as a two-thousand-year-old sociopath could be.

The rocky expanse opened to a stone fortress carved into a natural ridge. It was a mini citadel, and Belinda was somewhere inside. There was no one around, and the outside of the stone edifice unguarded. Still, he didn't need his vampiric senses to know he was watched. Sahira's human acolytes. Like rats in the cracks and shadows.

Condemned

He stepped through the wide-hewn entrance to what looked to be a rough-carved antechamber. The rock had been cut in large chunks, as if in a hurry. He sent his senses out, surprised there wasn't another undead to be found. The scent in the air told him Sahira's humans were close. From the narrative in Belinda's mind, she knew three of the five. Ari, Kir, and Fredric.

The three ambled into the antechamber from different passages leading out of the rock face. Addicts. Definitely. Sahira had surrounded herself with slaves. Belinda was right. The dark witch was more alone than he.

Belinda was in one of the rooms on the other side of the carved passages, but he wasn't in the mood to play eenie, meenie, miney, moe. The humans would tell him what he needed to know or die. Simple. He was beyond his limit for the high road, and nearly laughed when they stepped through the carved arches.

Clearly, Sahira chose them for brains and not brawn. Still, they were—pretty. There was no other way to describe their handsome, yet delicate features. Not effeminate. Just pretty. A smirk tugged at the corners of Dominic's mouth. Belinda would get a kick out of watching him screw with the pretty boys.

"You're expected," one said with a sniff. "The mistress hasn't arrived yet, but her gift is waiting for you inside."

The young man's stance was almost comical. Legs apart, arms folded at his chest. Like he stood a snowball's chance in hell against a full vampire. Sahira must have convinced them he was more walking wounded than undead. Crying in his cups over his lost humanity. Leave it to her to mistake compassion for weakness.

"My gift?" Dominic flashed them a little fang. "Isn't that you three? Sahira knows my appetites, so I'm always up for new blood." He inhaled, eyeing the one standing center. "Ari, right?"

The boy let a smirk quirk up. "I am, and...?" he replied.

Marianne Morea

"AB Negative, yes?" He inhaled deliberately, letting his fangs descend even more.

The boy's eyes widened, and his throat visibly squeezed in a tight swallow.

Dominic chuckled, nodding. "I thought so. Very distinct flavor, yet not easily found." He gave a chin pop to the other two. "Fear adds a nice kick to average blood types, so I'll drain you first and let them watch."

The blood drained from Ari's face along with his bravado, and the distinct scent of urine hit the air.

Dominic blurred forward, his hand around Ari's throat. "Pissant boys fancying themselves an elite vampire frontline. Is that the line Sahira fed you along with her blood? Sex and blood are her tools, boys. Haven't you figured that out yet? She will never give you the dark gift. She hasn't turned a soul since she turned mine in the twelfth century."

Fredric stepped forward but froze when Dominic snarled, turning blood-red eyes his way.

"She's going to end you tonight," Kir replied for his frightened friend. "You and your blood-whore. Then one of us will be chosen." He motioned to Ari. "He just pissed himself, so he's out. You can have him for your last meal."

"Belinda, a blood-whore? That's the pot calling the kettle black, don't you think?" Dominic shrugged. "While this has been enlightening, boys, I have a lover to save, but in the spirit of goodwill, since I was once human, I'm going to give you a choice. You can leave and take your chances in the desert or stay and die." His hand tightened on Ari's throat. "I wouldn't hedge my bets."

Fredric's gaze darted for the exit, but he didn't move.

Tsk, tsk. "I thought I saw a spark of self-preservation for a moment. I'll tell you what, blue eyes. Tell me which passage leads

to Belinda, and I'll let you leave. No questions asked." Fredric opened his mouth, but Dominic caught a quick flick between him and Kir. "See? Now, that tiny exchange tells me you were going to lie. Know this. Whatever nonsense Sahira told you about me, I have no compunction taking human life."

Ari's eyes bulged when Dominic turned to probe the boy's mind. He found Belinda there, surprised to feel regret mixed with the boy's addicted haze. "Do you want to tell me where Belinda is in this rock maze?"

He nodded, and Dominic released him. Crumpling to the ground, Ari gulping in jagged breaths.

"Well?" Dominic asked.

The boy's hand went to his throat, and he coughed, unable to speak. He pointed to the right-side passage, and Dominic picked him up by his collar, letting him dangle. He bared his fangs Hollywood-vamp style and the boy shit his pants.

"If you lie, I will find you and rip your throat out. I'm giving you a chance to redeem yourself, Ari. Belinda trusted you most, liked you most, yet you tried to screw her over. If you live, you will make amends and retract your false claim to Belinda's find. Do *that*, and I might show benevolence, later." Dominic flung him to the side.

The boy curled in a soiled ball and sobbed, but Dominic had no time for him. He'd made his choices and had to live with the consequences, including the painful withdrawals heading his way.

Fredric and Kir stood motionless, but when Dominic moved, they rushed to block his way. Without breaking his stride, he backhanded them both. They crashed in tandem into the roughhewn walls, the force splintering the rock face. They crumpled to the ground, dead, their necks snapped on impact.

Dominic spared a glance for Ari. "Do not make me regret my compassion, boy. Reclaim your life and remember what I said, or I will come for you. Now go."

The boy's mind showed regret, and that's why he was spared. He truly liked Belinda and had fought Sahira on her plans for sabotage.

Ari scrambled to his knees, his eyes bloodshot and his neck already black-and-blue. The scent of fear and adrenaline covered the stench of his filth as he crawled for the exit.

Dominic didn't wait. He rushed into the stone passage and followed the winding rock deeper into the mountain. Belinda's scent saturated the air. Sahira was toying with him, but her game would soon be over. Another stone archway at the end of the passage was where her scent was strongest. Inhaling quickly, Dominic's mind raced to ascertain life or death.

If Belinda was dead—

He growled low. That was not an option.

Belinda?

He reached out with his mind, but silence answered. He focused on her trace and his entrenched mark. Her heart still beat, and her pulse was strong. Was this some kind of new game?

The air was thick in his nose as he turned into the archway. He tasted black blood on the back of his tongue. Sahira's blood. His body tensed. Was she turning Belinda? The trace was too faint to tell for sure.

Dominic's nostrils flared as he rushed into yet another room. It was empty, and anger tensed every muscle in his back and shoulders. He'd rip Ari's head from his shoulders if he didn't find Belinda in this part of the maze.

Condemned

His head whipped around, and he spied three more passages. What now? Stepping toward the center of the rock room, he lifted his face and inhaled deep. His head jerked up.

He'd caught a flicker from her mind, and he knew. He raced down the center passage stopping short as it opened into a stalagmite cavern. Sharp mineralized pillars rose from the rock floor and dropped from the ceiling like icicles. A murky-green acidic pool at the center gave the cavern an open-jawed, fang-like feel.

An acrid taste burned his tongue as Dominic scanned the dripping grotto.

"How lucky for me you're so predictable." Sahira stepped from behind a large stalagmite on the opposite side of the pool. She pulled Belinda into view, shoving her forward.

Tied and gagged, Belinda fell to her knees. She winced, lifting her eyes to Dominic's fury. Her throat was smeared with blood, but it wasn't hers. He was at a stalemate. By the time he got to her, Sahira would snap Belinda's neck. He had to finesse this so he could get close enough to strike.

"Strong as an ox, as you can see. Still, I couldn't resist feeding her some of my blood just to see how she'd react." Sahira tittered, lifting her wrist as if inspecting the underside. "Not much, though. What good would it do if she turned before you got here to join in the fun? Still, they don't make witches the way they used to. Bloodlines are too diluted."

"Sahira, let Belinda go. I'm here. Isn't that what this is all about? Your control over my life?" he tried.

She angled her head, eyeing him. "Is that what you think? This has nothing to do with control, Dominic, and everything to do with reminding you where you belong."

Sahira moved in a circle around Belinda before yanking her to her feet. "You should be proud of your white witch, though. She put up quite a fight. She broke Kir's nose and gave Fredric quite a kick in the balls. I was impressed. Of course, I wasn't serious when I gave her the option to come to play in the dark"—she shrugged— "as a sister of sorts, but she refused anyway." Sahira tugged her toward one of the columns, but Belinda fought back, nearly yanking Sahira off balance.

"See? Fiery." She slipped a rope over Belinda's shoulders and gave it a brutal yank, tying her arms to her sides. "Much more fun than your other two gingers," she said, wrapping the rope around a stalagmite and securing it tight. "I'll enjoy killing this one the same way I killed your Céleste, only more because this time I'll do it in front of you."

Blind rage flooded Dominic's body. Without thinking, he blurred forward, ready to rip Sahira's heart from her chest. Belinda screamed, despite her gag, and he stopped short as a silver net dropped from the rock above. The deadly trap missed him by a fragment, and Sahira snarled, backhanding Belinda across the face.

Blood streaked red from her nose and mouth, and an evil smile spread on Sahira face. "Waste not, want not."

Dominic's mind worked every possibility, but without knowing where Sahira hid her other booby traps, he was caught. He judged the distance if he leapt across the acidic pool, measuring where he'd have to land to strike first. Fury and frustration warred in his chest. He needed a diversion.

"Do you know the best part of being both witch and undead?" She posed the question to Belinda as if the girl would answer. "It's that I can drain your blood and absorb your gift at the same time. How else do you think I've kept myself so strong after all this time?"

Condemned

She yanked Belinda's head to the side and opened her mouth, but before her fangs descended, her eyes widened, and her hand flew to her throat. An unseen force flung her to the side, and she skidded across the damp ground.

"I warned you, Sahira," a gravelly voice called from somewhere in the darkness. "I told you the girl was not to be touched. That she was not for you."

Sahira moved to get up, only to be knocked to the ground again.

"What am I to do with you?" the voice tsked. "All this time, and you still haven't learned."

Dominic's gaze searched the cavern, checking for scents and signs, but nothing registered.

Belinda's eyes found him across the pond, and she sobbed, her chest rising and falling with panicked breaths.

Sahira hissed, blurring to her feet. She turned with her back to Belinda, scanning the cavern as well. "Stop hiding, Father. I know you're here somewhere." She cocked her head, listening.

Dominic moved around the perimeter, keeping his eyes on Sahira but his ears on everything else.

"No?" Sahira laughed. "I learned this game from you, Father. Such a fuss over a feeble human. Even her witch's trace is weak."

"You did not learn this from me, Sahira. I showed you better. I saved you from death, hoping you would appreciate life. I should have known it was a wasted effort. You are as selfish and greedy as ever. I have waited long enough. It's time to pay the fiddler, my girl. You've danced enough."

For the first time in his existence, Dominic saw fear in Sahira's eyes. She whirled on her feet, sniffing the air. With a growl, she pivoted again, fisting Belinda's hair.

"Greedy? You both want this little bitch so much, you can fight over her bones!" With a vicious wrench, Sahira sank her fangs into Belinda's throat.

"No!"

Every muscle in Dominic's body surged with force as he leapt over the acidic pool to yank Sahira back from Belinda. She snarled, swiping at his chest with razor-sharp nails. He jumped back, circling to put himself between her and Belinda.

"Can you feel her life force fading, Dominic?" she said, twisting again with another swipe. Her voice was slurred through her fangs.

His eyes never left hers, even as he listened for Belinda's heartbeat. It was slower but still strong enough. Whatever blood Sahira gave her earlier may have just saved Belinda's life.

"I can see why both my sire and my progeny are so enamored with the little witch." She licked her lips. "Her blood isn't as weak as I thought." She laughed, wiping her mouth on her sleeve. "You just can't resist a piece of witch ass, huh? Even if it's not as good as mine."

"You have way too high an opinion of yourself, Sahira. Belinda is twice the woman and twice the witch you'll ever be." He snarled, reaching for her.

She blurred from him as she had centuries before, but this time she wasn't fast enough. He wrenched a handful of dark hair, forcing her to her knees.

"Do it! Rip my heart out. Take your revenge. Maybe you and my pathetic father can share the deed and suffer the consequences together."

Dominic pulled a blade from his boot. The same one he used to cut her a millennium ago. "I've suffered lifetimes at your hands,

Sahira. I no longer care about consequences. This isn't revenge. It's justice."

"So predictable, and so weak," she sneered, but her eyes narrowed despite her laugh. "I made you a prince, and you chose to be a hermit living in the shadows. Was your pathetic choice worth every life I took from you? Go ahead. Kill me. I've already won. Your witch dies? I win. You turn her to save her pitiful life? I still win."

"No, my child. It is you who is predictable and weak." An elder of advanced age walked from the shadows. His skin was almost translucent. Blue veins mapped his throat and chest from where his shirt opened at the collar.

Dominic's hand tightened on his blade as the elder blurred to his side. Sahira's eyes went wide, childlike, before filling with blood tears. "Papa, please," she said with a choked plea. Her voice was so sweet, so disarming.

The elder shook his head. A sadness deeper than any ocean reflected in his ancient eyes. "You were such a beautiful child, Sahira. You were once my greatest joy, but you have long since become my greatest sorrow. I only wish I had the strength to end you myself."

Stepping back, he nodded to Dominic, but with a snarl, Sahira gripped the knife's edge before he could strike. She tore the blade from Dominic's hand and twisted on her feet, plunging the knife point into her father's chest.

She whirled to run as always but couldn't resist one last taunt. "This game isn't over, Templar." With a laugh, she took a step only to land on one of her own booby traps.

With a snap, a silver bear claw clamped on her foot, stopping her dead. Her shriek echoed in the cavern and pained eyes darted to Dominic and then to her father's crumpled form.

Dominic lunged. With a roar, he separated Sahira's head from her shoulders, letting her body crumple to the ground. Tossing her head over his shoulder, he heard the dull splash as it landed in the acidic green water. He reached for her lifeless shoulders, plunging his hand through her chest to rip her heart from the open cavity.

The black organ turned to ash in his hand as the rest of her decayed to a sooty, blood-soaked mound. Dominic rushed to Belinda's side, his heart clenching with how pale and lifeless she seemed.

"Can you hear me, love?" He lifted her chin, wincing at the raw wound, grateful it had closed on its own.

"She lives, son. Have no fear." The elder coughed, sliding the sharp blade from his chest. "Sahira was never one for planning things all the way through, and her aim was terrible. Much like your friend Fouquet."

Dominic's eyes widened as he helped the man to his feet. "How did you—?"

"Sahira was my blood child, but she was also my human offspring. I turned her when she was near death as a young woman. Though I had failed her and her mother during my human life, I thought I could make up for those failings in immortality." He glanced at the soot pile and exhaled. "I should have ended her before she caused so much grief and pain." The elder's eyes sought Dominic's gaze. "I'm sorry."

Belinda's eyes fluttered, and she raised her head with a wince. She lifted her lids and blinked.

"Belinda, it's okay. I'm here. You're safe." Dominic cut her bonds, catching her as her knees buckled. He scooped her into his arms, cradling her against his chest. "I'm so sorry, love. I told you I would never hurt you and look what happened."

She smiled weakly. "It wasn't you who tied me up and then bit me, though if done right, it might be fun."

The elder cleared his throat, and she turned, blinking stunned eyes at the man. "Dr. Adams?"

"I'm sorry, Ms. Force. I should never have entrusted you to my daughter. I thought as Zahra Khalid, Sahira had finally turned a corner. She had all the adulation she craved, plus fame and money. I truly believed she would respect my wishes and leave you be." He smiled sadly. "I told you before, you are special, and not just because you have your grandmother's flashing eyes and her witchy ways."

"You knew my bubbie?"

He nodded, glancing over his shoulder. "Well, that's a bit of a long story."

Her grandmother stepped from the shadows, her face no longer ravaged with pain, her body no longer ravaged with cancer. "He knows me well, Belindachka."

"You...you...you're alive?" Belinda's eyes were like saucers, and her mouth went dry.

Her grandmother shrugged. "That's a matter of semantics, my darling. I think the proper term is I'm undead. Just like your wonderful Templar Knight." She smiled at Dominic before moving to stand beside the professor.

"Theo and I met a year or so before I was diagnosed with cancer. We started seeing each other, and when the doctor gave me the long face, Theo told me his secret. He also said he could heal me, but it would involve much sacrifice." Bubbie took Belinda's hand and squeezed her fingers. "The hardest thing I had to do was leave you, my darling girl. I've never been too far, though. Our special blood enabled me to talk to you, even if you thought it was just your imagination."

Belinda glanced between them. "So, you both knew this would happen?"

"I had visions, but nothing concrete." Her grandmother exchanged a look with Adams before glancing back to Belinda. "It's why we came when we did. We arrived just as Dominic got to you." She hesitated. "I'm afraid we underestimated Sahira's level of crazy. It had to happen the way it did for so many reasons, my darling. Dominic needed closure, and you needed to truly trust that he would sacrifice himself for you if necessary. Thank God, you're both all right."

Belinda didn't know how to react. "I'm speechless, Bubbie."

She reached out to stroke her granddaughter's face. "I know, my darling. You have a lot to process, and it's going to take some time. Plus, you're going to need a few *infusions* to help you heal." She winked at Dominic. "That is if your Knight is *up* for it."

Belinda burst out laughing. "Bubbie, I think you just made a thousand-year-old vampire blush."

She met her granddaughter's laugh with a slightly fanged grin. "Vampires can be insatiable, my darling. Sir Knight is *up* for the task, no doubt, but he needs to remember you're still human and need to eat and sleep. Man cannot live by sex alone."

"Bubbie!"

"What?" She winked. "It's an old woman's prerogative, and vampire or not, you are still my granddaughter. You, *Belindachka*, are the light in my undead life."

Dominic dipped his head, kissing Belinda's hair. "Mine too."

Epilogue

"How much longer do we need to do this?" Dominic grumbled, nipping Belinda's lip. "Your photog thinks he's bucking for an Oscar. I may have to go all Obi-Wan on him if he doesn't speed it up."

"You promised, so be quiet and smile."

"C'mon, you two. This is supposed to be the happiest day of your life. Look at each other like you mean it. Last set." The photographer circled them, snapping picture after picture.

"I know I promised, but we're going to miss our flight. Technically, our honeymoon started ten minutes ago."

"Your side of the family had to have an evening wedding, so just chill. Besides, the night shots are going to look amazing."

"Yes, but our guests are gone, and Carlos, Trina, and the rest of my family went to hunt the piazzas, yet this paparazzo is still here."

She kissed his nose. "You made me a famous archeologist. You read the article in Archeology Magazine. I'm the new female Indiana Jones, with my own personal hotter-than-hell collector."

Belinda touched Céleste's reliquary cross at her throat. Dominic had the silver specially coated, so it was safe to handle. "You're not going to tell me how you got the Israeli Museum to let you buy this piece, are you?"

"Nope," he whispered nipping her ear. "Trade secret. I could tell you, but then I'd have to kill you and turn you."

She laughed out loud at his playful smirk. "You wish."

"Wow! You guys are naturals! Spontaneous, funny, sexy. All of the above. I think I've got everything in the can, so that's a wrap. I should have the proofs ready in about two weeks." The man took his camera off his neck, and then held out his hand to them both. "The aerial drone shots of the villa are going to be off the chain. Have you ever thought of listing this place for location shots? You know...movies? It's even got a cool name. La Corsicana."

Dominic took the man's hand. "Like us, La Corsicana is very private. In fact, you're lucky we let you in the door, so if you don't mind, my new wife and I have a honeymoon to get to."

The guy laughed. "Loud and clear, buddy...and I don't blame you. Your wife is a real looker."

The photographer turned to corral his crew, and Dominic stepped back from Belinda, keeping her hands in his. "He's right, you know. You take my breath away."

She giggled, pulling her hands from his. Stepping back, she lifted the hem of her wedding gown.

"Field boots?" He laughed. "Whatever possessed you?"

Shrugging, she turned, giving her butt a little wiggle. "Hey, at least they're white. Do you know how hard that was to find? I've got a lace thong on as well." She waggled her eyebrows. "I figured it would bring this whole thing of ours full circle, and since your scimitar would raise a few eyebrows at airport security..."

He grinned pulling her into his arms. "You are the sun in my endless night, Mrs. De'Lessep," he said dipping his mouth to hers.

"Speaking of sleepless nights, I think we need to get ready for the plunge."

Condemned

Smirking, he angled his head. "Been there, done that, love. I've got our wedding certificate right here in my breast pocket." He tapped the front of his tux. "And I said endless night."

Belinda took his hand and bit his forefinger, letting a little smile tug at her mouth. "Well, they might seem endless, considering midnight feedings and all those diaper changes."

He froze with his finger still between her teeth. "Are you telling me you're—?"

She nodded. "I didn't think I could be happier than I was when I woke up this morning. Until I saw that little blue line on the test. To be honest, considering your history, I didn't think it was possible."

Dominic pulled her into his arms and held her so tight she coughed. "Human wife still needs to breathe."

He loosened his arms but didn't let go. He didn't say anything, either.

After a minute, Belinda wiggled herself back to look at his face. "Dominic, aren't you happy?"

His eyes found hers and they were wet with blood tears. "I had heard this was possible." He shook his head, dumbstruck. "Rare, almost never. I...I...think I'm in shock."

"But you're happy, right?" she asked again, chewing on the side of her lip.

Dominic's flabbergasted face softened, and he exhaled a chuckle. "Happy? Try stunned and thrilled and worried and excited and—" He stopped mid-gush to swing Belinda up into his arms and headed straight for the stairs.

"Where are you going?" she laughed. "We have to change and get to the airport or for real we'll miss our plane."

He kicked open their bedroom door and carried her through the threshold. "Screw the plane. I want to make love to my

beautiful pregnant wife, right now." He put her down and walked her backwards toward the bed.

"Field boots and lace thong?" she asked with a giggle.

"Is there any other way?"

Acknowledgements

When an author publishes a book, whether it's their first or their five hundredth, it's nothing less than a defining moment in their life. This is my seventh novel in the Cursed by Blood Saga, and I still have to pinch myself. So many people have helped and encouraged me, even when the writing dragon had me spewing fire and belching smoke at every turn.

My unbelievably patient husband, for putting up with the insanity and verbal barrages that accompany being glued to my laptop for hours. Our three kids for knowing enough to leave Mom alone when she's writing, despite laundry piling up and pasta for dinner, yet again.

My amazing alpha readers: Kathryn Parson, Tricia Statham, Lisa Errion and Bonnie Jean Aurigemma. Without you guys I would be lost. My editors Kate Richards and Chelly Hoyle Peeler. Whether it's a full line edit, a copy edits, content brainstorm or proofreading, you guys rock!

And last, but certainly not least, I want to thank God for all his blessings. The longer I live, the more I learn to appreciate what could very easily be taken for granted.

God bless. I hope you enjoyed the book.

About the Author

 Marianne Morea was born and raised in New York. Inspired by the dichotomies that define 'the city that never sleeps', she began her career after college as a budding journalist. Later, earning a MFA, from The School of Visual Arts in Manhattan, she moved on to the graphic arts. But it was her lifelong love affair with words, and the fantasies and 'what ifs' they stir, that finally brought her back to writing.

Visit her website: **http://www.mariannemorea.com**

If you enjoyed the story, please feel free to email me.
Reviews are always welcome on Amazon and Goodreads!

BOOKS BY MARIANNE MOREA

THE CURSED BY BLOOD SAGA
Hunter's Blood
Night Play
Twice Cursed
Blood Legacy
Lion's Den
Power Play
Collateral Blood
Condemned

THE RED VEIL DIARIES
Choose Me
Tempt Me
Tease Me
Taste Me

THE LEGEND SERIES (Teen)
Hollow's End
Time Turner
Spook Rock

THE BLESSED SERIES
My Soul to Keep
**Celestial

ROGUE OPERATIVE SERIES
(Suit Romance)
Dangerous Law

TWISTED FAIRYTALES
(Howls Romance)
Her Fairytale Wolf
The Wolf's Dream Mate
Her Winter Wolves